FREEUSE RESORT TOURS COLLECTION

---

5 First-Time Hotwife Getaway Stories

A Freeuse Hall Pass
Her Freeuse Escape
Her Freeuse Break
Her Freeuse Retreat
Her Freeuse Holiday

Lacey Cross

TWISTED ROSE
+ PUBLISHING +

Contents

A Freeuse Hall Pass

Chapter 1   3

Chapter 2   11

Chapter 3   25

Her Freeuse Escape

Chapter 1   41

Chapter 2   49

Chapter 3   59

Chapter 4   69

Chapter 5   77

Chapter 6   87

Her Freeuse Retreat

Chapter 1   93

Chapter 2   99

Chapter 3   105

Chapter 4   109

Chapter 5   119

Chapter 6   131

Chapter 7   143

Her Freeuse Break

Chapter 1   153

Chapter 2   161

Chapter 3   167

Chapter 4   175

Chapter 5   187

Chapter 6   195

Chapter 7   203

Her Freeuse Holiday

Chapter 1   211

Chapter 2   219

Chapter 3   227

Chapter 4   237

Chapter 5   247

Chapter 6   251

Chapter 7   261

About Lacey Cross   267

A Freeuse Hall Pass

A First Time Hotwife Story

CHAPTER 1

"Here's your room key card, Ms. Sinclair."

I bring my attention back to the perky woman checking me into the private Maui resort. She's holding a plastic room key out with a huge smile, and I take it from her. "Thanks."

"Will it be just you with us this weekend?"

"Yep, just me."

My husband, Quentin, booked us a three-night stay at a private resort on Maui. This resort is so private it's not listed in any travel brochures, and you basically need to know someone to get a reservation. Quentin's partner at work told him about it and hooked us up for a weekend getaway...only now I'm here alone because of a stupid work emergency.

The woman slides a printed brochure along the counter and starts talking about the resort's amenities. I've lived in Hawaii my entire life, and I tune her out as two sexy guys walking past catch my eye. They're in their 30s, tan and fit, wearing white button-down linen shirts and shorts. Mmm, maybe this is just what I need to recharge. I've always had an incredibly vivid fantasy life. I can relax and enjoy the eye candy and daydream about what I'd do if I had multiple guys to play with.

I glance at the woman and realize her mouth is still moving. I should be listening, but I just want to escape into a book and drink fruity alcoholic beverages with umbrellas while I think about getting all my holes filled at once.

She finally stops talking and beams at me. "If you have questions or need anything, feel free to ask for me personally. You can reach me via the main number, and I'll do whatever I can to help."

Her name badge says she goes by 'Joy,' which fits her sunny disposition. She seems genuinely excited about my stay despite the fact my husband can't join me, so I smile. "Thank you, Joy."

"You're welcome!" she chirps. "Read over the event details in the packet in your room if you decide to participate."

I have no idea what event she's talking about, but I'm not interested unless it involves me in a lounge chair by the pool admiring a ton of wet, hard bodies. I gather my luggage and give her a final smile before heading to my bungalow.

The resort is gorgeous, and I slow down to enjoy the walk. The landscaping is immaculate, and the entire property brings me a sense of peace. It seems more like a wellness retreat than your standard beachfront hotel.

The bungalow is a single room, but it's huge and luxurious, with a massive king-size bed, a large bathroom, a kitchenette, and a private terrace that faces out toward the ocean. I drop my bag and walk out the back sliding door. I can smell briny ocean salt in the air as I stroll down a winding stone path. There's another smaller building that I'm assuming is a sauna next to an outdoor pool surrounded by lounge chairs, a bar, and a cabana. Hell yeah, that's where I'll be all weekend.

I wander down another path until it leads me to an expansive golden beach. I slip off my sandals, dig my bare feet down into the warm sand, and breathe in the tropical air as I stare out at the blue water. Damn, I wish Quentin was here. This was going to be an epic fuckfest weekend after several busy months. He's been putting long hours in at work, and we haven't had as much headboard banging against the wall as I need.

I sigh. Well...he's promised me a romantic night when I get back with a nice dinner while I tell him all about the trip. I'll work up an appetite by enjoying the...scenery...before I come home. Thinking about the yummy guys I saw at check-in makes my body hum with a low level of desire, and I daydream some more about how this weekend could have gone with Quentin as I spend an hour wandering the beach and then exploring the lush grounds.

When the sun starts to set, I go back to the bungalow, feeling a little lonely. Damn, this just isn't as much fun without Quentin. I really wish I was getting all the sex he's been promising me for weeks. Ugh, there's no sense in dwelling on it. I'm determined to be happy and relax on the trip.

I've always had a higher sex drive than Quentin. Over the years, we've talked about opening our marriage up for me to play with other guys, but I've never really felt the need. My husband and my battery-operated boyfriend, when Quentin is busy, have served me well. Doesn't mean I don't still fantasize about fucking other guys, though.

As I unpack my suitcase, I think about what my crazy husband said last night. He joked that he could make arrangements for me to get some action at the resort because he loves me that much. He's a total goofball. How was he going to make a guy who wants to fuck me magically appear with only one day's notice?

Laughing at the memory of our conversation, I pull my e-reader from my luggage and set it on a packet of information that the resort left on the nightstand. I'll spend the rest of the night curled up reading spicy stories while the sea breeze comes in through the open windows. I even brought a few sex toys if I get in the mood...and I'm definitely feeling in the mood.

As I unpack, I think about my husband's offer—he called it a hall pass to make up for him working. Hmm, I wonder how many women actually fuck other men if their husbands allow it. I've read stories about wives cheating on their husbands while on vacation, but I wouldn't be cheating if I asked permission. But does any of this happen in real life? I mean, I know there are swingers' clubs and stuff, but I've never been interested in anything like that. What guy wants to share his wife without asking for the same treatment to fuck other women?

I kick off my sandals and stretch out on the bed, crossing my ankles and admiring the red polish on my toes next to my golden-brown skin tone. My legs have always been my favorite feature. They're long and slender from years of playing tennis and swimming regularly. My ass is pretty good, too. Since I was expecting a bunch of sex this weekend, I'm waxed and soft in all the right places. I plan on wearing shorts or a bathing suit all weekend. I might be alone, but I'm going to feel damn sexy. If I catch someone checking me out, even better.

My phone lights up, and I can tell by the ringtone that it's my husband.

I smile as my stomach gives a happy flip, and I answer, "Hey babe."

His voice is low and smooth. "Hey beautiful. Are you settled in?"

"Yep, I am..." I give him my best fake pouty voice. "*All alone.*"

I can hear that he's outside, walking as he talks. "Are you in the bunga-low?"

"Yeah, all checked in. Where are you?"

He sighs. "I'm heading to the car to go home."

I frown and pick at the hem of my shirt, wishing he was here. "It's lonely without you. Stupid work. Your partner should feel bad. We could have been having sex right now in this wonderfully soft bed."

"I know," he says with regret in his voice. "I'm really sorry, baby."

I don't want to ruin both our weekends, so I change the subject and tease him. "Well, I'm going to enjoy myself. I'm going to read a lot of books and relax...or maybe I'll just hang at the pool and flirt with a few guys."

Quentin laughs. "There'll be plenty of single men at the resort tomor-row. I wanted to ask you what you thought about the event."

He knew about that? "What's the event about?"

"You should have information on it. They told me all the information would be in the room."

Oh! I sit up in bed and grab the folder on the nightstand. "I haven't read it yet, but what's going on tomorrow?"

"It's a freeuse day at the resort. There's supposedly a wristband in the packet if you want to take part in it."

What the...suddenly I realize this is why he casually mentioned he saw something about freeuse a few weeks ago and explained what freeuse was. My entire body buzzes and my pussy tingles as I think of those sexy men again. I decide to play dumb and see what he says. "Wait...what does 'freeuse' refer to?"

"Remember? I looked it up online. It's where someone makes themselves available for whoever wants to fuck them. In this case, the resort has a day where the women wear a wristband that says any of the guys at the resort can fuck them."

I'm so horny my clit aches, but I need to verify he's really saying what I think he is. "So if I wear the wristband, any of the guys here can approach me and ask to have sex? Like...I'd be freeuse for them?"

"Yeah, though no one is going to ask. If the wristband is on, that means you're open for business and anyone can fuck you...if that's what you want to do," he suddenly sounds unsure, as if he doesn't know how I'm going to respond.

Holy shit! I'm already soaking wet at the idea of fucking a stranger or two...or three. "You'd be okay if I did this?"

"Yeah, I mean, it's totally up to you, but I thought it might be something that you'd be interested in." He chuckles and adds, "And...you know...I'm okay with it. Your hall pass is good for whatever you want to do this weekend."

Holy shit! My mind races with the possibilities, and I'm almost shaking with desire. I'm so aroused my nipples ache, and I squeeze my thighs together to relieve the tension. Oh god, I really am desperate for a cock. It's been several weeks since Quentin and I've had sex. I thought my sex toys would do, but now that I hear about a freeuse offer, I just need to fuck someone.

My voice sounds breathy when I speak again. "What if they run a train on my ass?"

He laughs. "Baby, if it happens, go wild."

"Are you serious?" I ask incredulously. This is a joke. I can't even process this right now.

I can tell he's amused. "Only if you want to, but baby...I want to know every detail. Every. Single. Detail." He pauses and I hear him breathing heavily like he's turned on. "I'm okay with whatever you want to do. I love you, and I trust you completely. You know that."

Wow, he is serious. My entire body is flushed and hot at the prospect of fucking multiple guys in a row with no inhibitions or rules. I can't even wrap my mind around it. It sounds too good to be true, but I'm dying to explore.

He clears his throat. "I have to go now, baby. Keep me posted tomorrow if you decide to go for it. You can call whenever. I'll keep my phone on while I'm working."

I'm speechless, and my pussy is throbbing with need. I can hardly think of what to say, so I give a soft, "Uh huh."

I hear him laughing. "Have fun, baby. Love you." I echo back that I love him, and we disconnect.

Dropping the phone in my lap, I lie back and stare at the ceiling. Oh, my god...did my husband actually give me permission to fuck as many people as I want?

Needing to know the details, I quickly grab the paperwork and search for the section describing the upcoming event.

Welcome to Paradise!

The staff here at Maui's exclusive Freeuse Resort would like to welcome you. If you are reading this, that means you're interested in participating in the event. Tomorrow, our resort will open our doors to all guests for the monthly Freeuse Day event.

Freeuse Day is a special event where our guests can participate in our unique brand of resort hospitality. We offer the opportunity for the enthusiastically consenting women to be used by the men visiting the resort for their enjoyment. Don't worry, the women report high levels of satisfaction in the exit surveys.

If you choose to partake in tomorrow's festivities, slide one of the provided wristbands on to show your willingness.

Please note: the band is optional and is not mandatory for enjoying the resort during the day. No one will touch you if you don't have a band on, but this is a special weekend that most guests book months in advance for, so we encourage people to be open to the possibilities.

If you choose to wear the wristband, you agree to the terms below...

I scan the list of terms, and it goes into an explanation about how I can remove the wristband at any point, and if I am ever uncomfortable and want someone to stop, just say "red light," and all the guests are aware that they must stop. It has a detailed section about the screening process for the guys, and how most men are repeat visitors. It also states the men use the buddy system so that it's usually two or more men at a time.

Oh god, two men at a time...

My head is spinning by the time I read through it all. My husband knew about this, and he planned to surprise me all along with this offer. I think about this for a few moments and then giggle. Hah, I bet Quentin is super bummed he's going to miss out on seeing me railed by a bunch of guys. Whenever he and I talked about me becoming a hotwife, he said he'd like to see the look on my face as another guy fucked me. There's no way he booked a trip during a freeuse weekend without planning to watch.

I'm still in shock as I flip to the end of the packet and find a small pouch attached to the back cover. Inside are four different colored wristbands with a card explaining what each one is for. The pink wristband is for vaginal penetration, the purple for anal, and the black for oral. The card says I can wear multiple bands, but there's also a green wristband that means 'open,' for women who are willing to take it anywhere the guy wants to stick it.

My entire body shivers as I stare at the wristbands. I've fantasized for years about being gangbanged. I've watched porn where a group of guys use a girl for their own satisfaction, and it's the hottest, dirtiest thing I've found online. But the reality of actually having that happen? That seems impossible and unrealistic.

But...what would be the harm if I did? My husband gave me his permission, and it would be like a dream come true for me. No one knows me here. I can just pretend like it's some sort of roleplay. My pussy buzzes and my nipples ache while a restlessness overtakes me. Yeah, I'm doing it.

Now the only question is...what color wristband am I wearing tomorrow?

Chapter 2

When I wake up the next morning, I spring out of bed. I slept surprisingly well last night, given how long it took my brain to turn off. It was probably the bed. It was like sleeping on a cloud. I force myself to eat something from the breakfast options in the kitchenette; orange juice, a bagel with cream cheese, and some mixed fruit should be enough to keep me fueled until lunch.

My heart pounds in eagerness at the thought of being approached by a man and fucked. I'm nervous. It's been years since I've seen a cock other than my husband's, and now I'm contemplating letting a complete stranger fuck me in a public setting. It seems surreal.

After a quick shower, I put on a bikini and wrap myself in a robe before sitting in front of the vanity table to dry my long black hair. Once it's completely dry, I decide to style it in a loose braid in the back. I put the bare minimum on for makeup since I don't know how today will go. Something tells me it might be pointless to dress up too much. After applying some perfume, I step in front of the full-length mirror.

I'm only 5'3", but even so, my legs seem to stretch for days. I'm proud that I've always stayed in shape by playing so much tennis. I'm definitely a normal woman and have my flaws, but today, I'm excited and radiant. Nothing is going to stop me from enjoying myself.

The only thing left to do is call my husband and tell him what I'm doing and which color bands I'm choosing. As much as I'm turned on by the idea of a bunch of guys using me and taking me wherever they want, I don't think I'm ready for freeuse anal sex. That seems like jumping off the deep end, and I'm not quite that brave. I'll give the guys two holes to use. I can handle that.

I take a deep breath and dial Quentin's number.

When he answers, I blurt out, "I'm doing it."

Quentin chuckles, "Okay. So...what are you wearing today?"

I swallow nervously. "My black bikini."

"That's it?"

I giggle. "Yep, I figured it would make it easier for any guy who wants me."

Quentin growls, "Fuck baby...I'm so hard right now. I wish I could be there to see it."

I smile. "Me too. You'll be the first person I call after."

Quentin laughs. "So, which wristband color are you wearing?"

He sure knows a lot about how this freeuse day works. My pussy throbs at the thought of him planning this trip. He's probably been thinking about this for days. Stupid work. "Pink and black, so they can use my mouth or pussy."

My husband inhales sharply. "I want you to tell me every detail when you get home. Promise."

"I will, honey. I promise." A wave of love for him washes over me.

He sighs and asks in a quiet voice, "Are you scared, baby?"

I bite my lip. "No...I think I'm excited. Nervous...but mostly excited."

"Good," he replies. "You deserve to have a good time. Just relax and go with the flow. Have fun and let them use you. I know you're going to love this."

I smile. "What I know is that I love you."

"I love you so much, sweetheart. Go have fun and call me later."

We blow kisses at each other over the phone before we disconnect.

I'm so lucky. He's the perfect husband for me. He understands and supports me in everything. I couldn't ask for anything more. But now it's time to strut my stuff around the resort and see what happens. My hands tremble as I slide the two colors of wristbands on and let them settle on my right wrist.

I stare at the bands for a moment, and my mind drifts to the first time I hooked up with Quentin. Usually the first time is a little awkward, but he knocked my socks off. He seemed to understand exactly what I needed. We're very compatible in bed—when we have time in our busy schedule—but I've always had a hard time orgasming. I wish I could just have a bunch of orgasms in a row until I'm exhausted...like those porn stars do in the movies where they fuck five or six guys in a row.

A sudden rush of arousal shoots through me. Oh my god, that is actually what I'm going to do today...and my husband approves. My nipples stiffen, and I rub my thighs together. Fuck, I hope they don't waste time talking and just get right to it.

I hope I get a bunch of orgasms.

My clit pulses in excitement. I'm so horny I can't stand it. I'm not sure if I'll be able to wait until someone approaches me. Can I approach the guys?

Shit, the sooner I get out there, the sooner I'll find out. It's time to check out the pool. I slather sunscreen on before grabbing my e-reader and a towel. The day is warm with a light breeze, and I breathe deeply. I'm ready to be a freeuse slut...whatever that entails.

I'm halfway to the pool when a thought almost makes me trip. Oh fuck, what if no one wants to have sex with me? What if the man to woman ratio is off and all the men are busy with other women? I shake my head. No, the resort wouldn't do that. Chances are I'm more likely to be one of the few women wearing wristbands. How many women actually come to this place?

When I get to the pool, it's deserted and my stomach drops in disappointment. Shit, where are the roaming pairs of men? I was expecting to see a bunch of guys waiting in line to fuck the first woman they saw. Where the hell is everyone?

I make my way to a chaise lounge chair and lay out my towel before settling in with my book to wait. I try to relax and read, but my mind races as I wonder where all the men are.

As I'm debating going to the beach, the sound of male laughter draws my attention. Two super sexy guys who are probably in their late 30s walk into the pool area. My pulse speeds up as they look at me. They're both fit with muscular builds. One of them has thick, muscular thighs, and I imagine he could plow a woman for a long time without breaking a sweat.

Butterflies swirl in my stomach as I wonder if they are going to come over here. I try to focus my eyes on my page, but I keep sneaking glances at them. They're both super sexy, and they're wearing matching blue trunks and have similar haircuts. The slightly shorter one has dimples when he smiles. Oh god, I love guys with dimples.

When Dimples looks my way and catches my eye, he smiles. My face flushes as I quickly turn my attention back to my book. I try to read another page, but my mind races as I wonder what's going to happen.

When I peek at him again, he's still watching me. He gives me a wink, and I feel a wave of desire. He needs to come over here and fuck me. My pussy is pulsing, and I'm so horny I can't think straight. I cross my legs and shift positions in a desperate search for relief.

The two guys approach me, and I have a moment of uncertainty. Wait, am I supposed to open my legs as soon as they get here? What's the protocol at a freeuse resort?

They stop next to my chair and Dimples smiles at me. "Hello...I'm Jared. You must be new at the resort."

"I'm Matt." His friend grins at me.

I swallow nervously. "I'm Alyssa."

Jared's dimples deepen. "Are you sure about that?" I'm confused and about to question him when he continues. "Or are you just a toy with no name?"

Time stands still for a moment while my mouth pops open and my entire body buzzes with an illicit thrill. No one has ever talked to me like this before, and if asked, I probably would have said I didn't like it...but goddamn, I like it.

Matt grabs my ankles and tugs me down the chaise lounge. I squeak and almost drop my e-reader.

Jared barks out, "Keep reading, slut. Don't mind us."

Don't mind them? I'm supposed to keep reading? I hold up my e-reader and try to focus on the screen as Jared spreads my legs and kneels between them. His hand slips underneath my bikini bottoms and fingers my pussy, and I gasp at the intrusion but continue pretending to read.

Jared's fingers stroke me, spreading my lips apart and sliding inside me. "Mmm...such a filthy slut. You're soaked already just by the thought of being used."

A zing of bliss swirls in my core from his fingers and his dirty talk. Holy fuck. I wanted someone to use me without wasting time on small talk, but I wasn't actually expecting it to happen.

Matt kneels next to the chair and shoves my bikini top up above my tits, exposing my nipples to the air. Matt cups my breasts, playing with the nipples before leaning over to take one into his mouth. I have to raise the e-reader higher and hold it in the air while Matt swirls his tongue around my nipple.

Every nerve in my body is lit up with pleasure as his skillful mouth makes the words blur on the page. I'm so distracted by Matt I don't realize that Jared has his cock out until I feel him push my bikini bottoms to the side and the tip of it presses against my pussy. I moan as Jared slowly pushes inside and stretches me open. Fuck, he's bigger than I expected, and the fullness makes my head spin as delight swirls in my core.

I try to keep reading, but it's difficult to concentrate on the words when Jared starts to fuck me. At first he's slow but then picks up his tempo. Each thrust sends ripples of ecstasy coursing through my entire body, and I'm moaning and crying out with every whack against my pussy.

Matt chuckles as he moves to the other breast and plays with the nipple with his fingers. "You've got great tits. I like how they bounce while he's fucking you."

As soon as he says that, I imagine what I look like. I'm spread open with my feet on the pavement while a guy kneels between my legs and fucks me. This is obscene.

I'm panting as I look at him and Jared, who's balls deep inside me now. I don't care how this looks, I want more. The pressure intensifies, building with each stroke. I'm so close...I just need something to send me over the edge.

A soft giggle distracts me for a moment as a couple walks past us and a woman murmurs. "Now that looks fun."

Ooooh, shit. There is another woman here. My mind reels knowing someone saw me spread out like this, but I can't think about it too long because Matt slides a hand down to my clit.

As he brushes circles around it, he says, "I know, let's have you read to us. Do it, now."

Oh fuck, I can't do that. I can't even form a sentence...plus I'm reading erotica. Jared's thrusts speed up and Matt rubs harder at my clit until the sensation overcomes any hesitation and I start reading the book out loud to them, my voice wobbling:

> "Have a seat, Miranda. We need to
> talk." Mr. Jacobs's voice is neutral, and
> he doesn't seem angry. The thought

crossed my mind that he might fire me.

I hope he fucks me first.

That's as far as I get before I can't speak. Matt's fingers on my sensitive nub send me flying, and I cry out as the orgasm tears through every nerve ending in my body. I buck my hips wildly as the violent orgasm peaks again and the waves of bliss crash over me.

I'm still gasping from the intensity of my release when I feel Jared tense as he pumps his cum deep into my pussy. He shudders and groans loudly as he collapses on top of me. We both lie there panting in a sweaty heap on the chair.

My e-reader is still in my hands, and I stare at the words on the screen, not really comprehending them. My brain is mush.

I lower the device and notice a small crowd of men has formed around us. A few guys stand nearby with their hard cocks out, stroking them. Matt stands and addresses the guys.

"Sorry boys, I called dibs on this one. You can play with her after." He winks at me, making me blush, right before he pulls me off the chair and carries me over to a nearby metal lattice table. I'm still clutching my e-reader, and he sets me down long enough to bend me over the surface. I gasp when my nipples come in contact with the cool metal.

Matt's voice is gruff. "Keep reading, slut. I was enjoying that story."

Oh fuck. I'm not sure I can read more—especially not with an audience. I take a moment to find where I left off:

> I sit down and cross my legs, letting my
> pencil skirt slide up past my knees.

Matt pulls my bikini bottoms down past my ass and I moan as he slams into me.

"More," he demands.

Shit...fuck...my voice trembles as I continue:

> Mr. Jacobs glances at my legs, so I
> know I hit my target with my chosen
> posture.

Matt goes into a frenzy, whacking against my pussy so hard the e-reader shakes too much to continue. This is so fucked up, but I love it. I want to beg him to never stop.

The world fades away as I immerse myself fully into the moment. I'm not sure how long he pounds into me, but when Matt's fingers find my clit, it sends me into the abyss. Throwing my head back, I scream as I come all over his cock.

I hear him growl with pleasure, and I can feel hot spurts of cum shooting inside me. He grinds against my ass as he finishes. "Ah...yeah. So good."

I'm still trying to catch my breath when I hear a voice behind me. "My turn."

Before I have time to recover, Matt pulls out and another guy slides into my pussy. Who is this? I try to glance over my shoulder, but his strong hand pins me to the table while he hammers into me.

I cry out in bliss as he rams me mercilessly. My nipples are caught in the lattice of the table, and each thrust pulls at them, increasing my pleasure. The guy fucking me leans forward, and his voice is in my ears. "You like it rough like this?" he pants. "I bet you do...you're so wet. You've been dying for this, haven't you? Desperate to have your pussy pounded and filled with cum by strange men?"

I whimper. Oh, yes. Yes. I'm so turned on, it's unbelievable. I didn't even know I wanted this before last night, but this experience is amazing.

"Tell me you want to be our cumdumpster slut."

He's not wrong. I do want it, but I'm so lost in a fog of lust that it's hard to form the words. All I can do is chant, "Yes, yes, yes," as he hammers into me.

I'm completely at his mercy, surrendering to the thrill of being taken in front of an audience. He slides his hand under me and rubs my clit in tight, fast circles. The sensation is too much.

I explode, wracked with pleasure, and I barely understand what I'm saying as I cry out, "Yes! Fuck...please use me...I want it! I'm a cumdumpster. Use me however you want."

I'm a slut. I am. I'm so turned on I'd agree to anything they wanted me to do. The man fucking me roars, and I can feel his cock jerking inside me while he shoots his load. He pumps into me, fucking his cum back into me until he's done.

When he pulls out, I hear Matt's voice behind me. "Good job, babe. That's it for now."

Matt pats me on the ass and helps me stand. My knees wobble, and my head feels like it's going to float away on a cloud of bliss. I look around at the men surrounding me and give them all a loopy smile as I pull the bikini bottoms back into place.

I'm a little unsteady on my feet, but I manage to stand without falling over. "Thanks..." I mumble. I'm not sure how to end that statement. Thanks for using me? Thanks for the fuck? Thanks for the mind-blowing climaxes? I giggle. I guess it was all the above.

Jared smiles at me and holds up my e-reader. "You dropped this," he teases. He winks at me as he hands it over, and I giggle again.

"Have a good day, slut."

I nod and watch Matt walk away with Jared. This place is insane in the best of ways.

I'm still in a state of euphoria, and I can hardly believe what just happened. I just got fucked in a semi-public area by total strangers. Two of them introduced themselves, I guess, but I don't know who that third guy was.

A sudden need to talk to my husband hits me, and I adjust my bikini top, grab my stuff, and make a beeline for my bungalow. As I walk the paved path, I pull out my phone, check the time, and notice it's only been an hour since I last called my husband.

He answers immediately. His voice is husky, like he's turned on. "Hey, baby...did you just get started?"

I smile at his eagerness. "You could say that. I've had sex with three guys so far, and that was just the first hour."

Quentin laughs. "Wow...that's good work. How was it?"

I giggle at the absurdity of that statement. How was it...how was it? "Um...it was amazing."

Quentin chuckles. "Yeah? I knew you would love it. Did they call you dirty names?"

I laugh. "Yes, I got called a filthy slut, a cumdumpster...and maybe other stuff. I liked it."

Quentin groans. "Fuck...that's so hot. What's next on your list?"

I bite my lip and grin to myself. My husband is so naughty.

My mind flashes through what I want to happen next. "I want to get railed...hard."

Quentin's moan makes my clit throb, and he asks, "Do you want more than one guy at once, or one at a time?"

A shiver runs down my spine, and I whisper, "I want to be filled completely."

I can almost see my husband's face as he imagines multiple guys fucking me at the same time. I'm so focused on Quentin I squeak in surprise when someone pulls on the handle of my beach bag. I look over my shoulder and there are two guys behind me. One of them pulls me off the concrete path and into the grass before pressing on my shoulders.

I kneel and blink up at them. Uh...I'm on the phone. Can't they see that?

"Baby, are you still there?" My husband sounds worried.

"Yeah, I'm here. Two men just stopped me in the middle of the path and pushed me to my knees."

"Right now?" His voice is higher pitched than normal, like he's shocked.

"Yeah, I think...oh, one of them just pulled his cock out."

His voice is low. "Where's the other guy?"

"He's kneeling behind me."

"What's he doing?"

"I think he's...Oh fuck..." I whimper as he pushes me forward and I put my free hand down so I'm on my hands and knees, holding the phone with one hand and balancing my weight on the other.

When he yanks my bikini bottom down to my knees, I moan at how filthy this is to be talking to my husband on the phone while some guy is about to fuck me. I can hear Quentin's breathing becoming ragged.

I gasp when I feel the man's hands on my hips and he slides his massive cock into my pussy in one deep thrust. He's bigger than any of the guys who fucked me at the pool, and my vision blurs from the pleasure as he pings every nerve ending inside me.

I whimper, "Ohhh...he just slammed his cock into me."

Quentin groans. "Baby...fuck...that's hot. You have no idea what this is doing to me right now. How does it feel? Describe it to me."

I pant, "He's got a big cock, honey."

He groans, "How big?"

"So huge," I gasp out between thrusts. The guy is really pounding me. "Oh god...it feels incredible."

I'm so wet that I can hear him sliding into me with each thrust, which only adds to the excitement of being fucked while listening to Quentin's heavy breath in my ear.

His tone is insistent. "Tell me how much you like it."

I moan, "Oh, god. So amazing. I wish you were here so you could see this."

When the guy spanks my ass, I cry out and almost drop the phone. Fuck! The second guy stands above my head, jerking his cock, and I keep my eyes trained on his hand moving along his shaft. I lick my lips, anticipating tasting it. I open my mouth and stick my tongue out, hoping he'll blow his load on my face.

Quentin's breath stutters. "Oh, fuck..." he groans. "I can't believe I'm stuck at work."

The guy behind me slams into me repeatedly, and I can feel my tits swaying with each hard thrust. My pussy clenches at the thought of how much of a slut I am right now. The phone is pressed into my ear so hard it hurts, but I don't dare move as the guy behind me whacks against my pussy and the other guy jerks his cock inches from my face.

Quentin's voice is low. "Are you going to suck him off, baby? Let that guy cum in your pretty mouth?"

"Uh huh...I'm gonna swallow it," I whisper.

Quentin growls and the guy above me steps closer, his cock almost touching my face. I tilt my head up, keeping my tongue out and waiting for it.

Quentin groans. "Open wide for him, baby."

The guy in the back pounds my pussy harder, and the second guy aims his dick at my open mouth. He strokes himself furiously, and I watch with fascination.

It's so fucking hot to have my husband on the phone listening to this. The man jerking off over my face groans, and a huge load of cum splatters across my lips and tongue while the guy behind me continues to hammer me relentlessly.

I moan in pleasure as I taste the cum in my mouth and lick it from around my lips, swallowing it eagerly. The guy behind me grunts and gives a final cry as he jerks and blows his load deep inside me.

I'm on fire, and I want more. I need more...

The two guys are done, and the guy behind me stands up. Neither of them says anything as they adjust their cocks back into their pants and walk away.

My body vibrates from being fucked without coming, and then I realize I'm still on the phone. "Honey, you still there?"

Quentin chuckles. "Of course I am. I want to know how many loads of cum you have in you right now, baby girl."

"Four? I think...unless you count the guy who came over my face. But I didn't come just now. I'm still hungry for cock."

"You are?" he moans. "How do you want it, baby? Tell me."

I giggle. "First, I need to get back to my room before more guys find me."

My husband sighs. "Okay, shit. I really need to get back to work for a bit. Call me later with all the details, okay?"

"I will, sweetheart. Love you, bye."

"Love you too, bye."

I disconnect and pull myself up off the grass. I'm still shaky, but I manage not to fall as I pull on the bottom half of my bikini and stumble back to my cottage.

Once I get inside my room, I lock the door for privacy. I'm still dripping with the loads of cum the guys deposited inside me, and my thighs are covered in sticky residue. I'm also a little embarrassed at how slutty I acted. It wasn't just the other guys...Quentin got me all worked up with his comments and encouragement. Fuck, I'm so turned on right now, but I don't want to get myself off, so I decide to take a cool shower to calm down.

After my shower, I'm exhausted. I need some energy for this evening if I want the chance at more orgasms. I face plant on the bed, and within seconds, I'm out like a light.

Chapter 3

I sleep for a solid four hours, and when I wake up, I'm groggy and disoriented. Jesus. What a morning.

My stomach grumbles, and I slip a robe on and dig into the tiny fridge for more food. The resort has a dining room, and I should probably explore that later, but right now I don't want to risk some guys finding me before I get food in my belly. I can't wait to get pounded again. I'm so damn horny, and my pussy aches for a cock.

While I nibble on a cheese, meat, and fruit platter, I scroll through some social media posts and check out what my friends and family are doing this weekend. How would they react if they knew I was getting fucked by total strangers? I don't think anyone would believe what I've done. I really only have one friend I'm close enough to that I'd tell about this adventure. Oooh, hell, I'm going to tell her now and see what she says.

I take a quick picture of the gorgeous view outside the open back door and message it to her.

Alyssa

> The resort is gorgeous, but wait until you hear about the special event this weekend.

She responds immediately.

Mandy

Oh? Spill it.

Alyssa

There's a 'freeuse' day where the guys at the resort can fuck me all they want. Quentin told me to go wild and live my best life.

Mandy

What????? OMG! Are you fucking kidding me?

Alyssa

I'm not. I already had 5 different guys come on me or in me so far today.

Mandy

FIVE? Holy shit. How do you feel?

I giggle, remembering this morning.

Alyssa

Amazing. I need to get back out there. I need another orgasm. I'll chat with you later and tell you all about it!

Mandy

Go! Have fun! Be a super slut. I can't believe you're doing this, but I'm proud of you. You go, girl!

I laugh and set my phone down so I can finish my food before I head out. Just as I take a sip of water to wash down my last bite, there's a knock on the door. I jump, wondering who that is.

Pulling the robe closed, I quickly tie it tight before walking to the door. Right before I turn the handle, the knock comes again, and I hear my husband's voice call out, "Room service."

I squeal and yank open the door. My heart races as I launch myself into his arms. "Oh my god, you came!!!"

I'm so happy to see him. I pepper his face with kisses.

His body vibrates with laughter, and his voice is husky with emotion. "I couldn't stay away. I needed to be here to watch you. I told work they were going to just have to live without me."

My heart melts, and I can't stop grinning. Quentin gives me a devilish grin as he closes the door. I expect him to launch into questions about this morning, but I'm surprised when he spins me around and pushes me face first against the closest wall.

Oh, holy fuck. He's going to use me? Yes, please!

He grabs my wrists, pins them to the wall above my head, and leans forward so his mouth is near my ear.

My heart beats frantically as he whispers, "I thought of other men using you while I was at work, and then I realized...you're mine. Why do they get to be the only ones who are having fun?"

I whimper as his free hand slips between my legs and his fingers slide inside my pussy.

"Fuck, baby...you're so ready for cock, aren't you? Do you know how hard it is to concentrate when all I can think about is fucking this sweet pussy?"

He's breathing heavily, and I push my butt back against his crotch and rub against his erection through his clothes.

Quentin groans, and his voice is thick with arousal. "You want me to fuck you right here against the wall?"

I don't answer him. It's his choice what he does with me. He's the one who told me how freeuse works.

Quentin releases my wrists, and I hear the zipper of his pants. He pushes my robe off my shoulders and then drags me over to the bed. The next thing I know, I'm on all fours on the mattress and he's kneeling behind me as the tip of his cock presses against my pussy.

"You're mine, even if I share you."

I moan loudly. I love this side of Quentin. He's always so controlled and gentle when we're in bed, and it's a treat for me to see this new aggressive and commanding side of him. My entire body tingles in anticipation as I wait for him to fuck me.

When he sinks his cock into me, he's slow and methodical. I moan as he stretches me with his thickness. Once he's seated deep within me, he grasps my hips firmly with both hands and slides almost completely out before slowly pressing into me again with a groan. He does it again, this time picking up the pace slightly, and I whimper in frustration. I want him to pound into me. I want him to fuck me hard.

He doesn't.

He continues to tease me with his torturous, measured strokes, making me beg for more. My voice is strained, and I know I sound desperate. "Please? Oh god, please fuck me hard?"

Quentin's hands tighten on my hips, and he pulls me backwards into his thrusts, slamming his cock deeper into my pussy but still maintaining the steady rhythm. He's in control here, and I'm not. The realization makes me feel like the ultimate fucktoy, and I love it.

My husband's tempo increases as he fucks me, and I push myself back to match his pace. My clit buzzes, and my body is wound so tightly I can hardly stand it.

Quentin groans loudly, and the sound makes me shiver in delight. I love the fact that my body belongs to him right now, and he's the one using me. He's driving me wild with desire. I want more...I need more.

He's caught up in the moment just as much as I am, and he grabs my hair with one hand and wraps it tightly around his fist before pulling my head up. The pain in my scalp sends a surge of pleasure through me as he continues to pound my pussy relentlessly.

"Oh, fuck!" I scream, "Don't stop...please."

My orgasm rips through me like a wildfire, and every nerve ending in my body comes alive at once. My pussy pulses, squeezing his cock as my muscles spasm uncontrollably.

I'm still shaking as my husband groans loudly and blows his load. I can feel his cum coating me as he shoots rope after rope inside me.

I collapse forward onto the bed with my husband draped over my back, both of us panting. Quentin's breath tickles my neck and he places a kiss there.

He murmurs, "That was so amazing, baby. Thank you."

My mind is so fucked, I can't even lift my head as I giggle. "I should be the one thanking you. I've never seen you like this before."

"Like what? Possessive?"

"Mmm, yes. I loved it."

My husband gives me a heated look. "Good, because that's what happens when you let strange men touch what's mine. That phone call was the last straw. I had to be here so I could remind you who you belonged to."

A soft thrill runs through me. "I'm all yours."

Oh, yeah. He can get possessive and fuck me like that whenever he wants. We exchange smiles and lie together as we both recover. When Quentin eventually rolls off me and sits up, his eyes have a naughty twinkle in them. "So, how about you give me a tour of the resort and we see what happens?"

I giggle. "Sounds good to me."

Quentin stands up and adjusts his pants, tucking his cock away. He holds out his hand to me, and I take it, letting him pull me to a sitting position.

I'm dressed in record time—choosing a sundress with no bra or panties, because what's the point? Sliding my feet into my sandals, I follow Quentin out the door. We hold hands as we walk toward the beach and I point things out about the resort. My pink and black wristbands keep catching my attention, and I notice Quentin glancing at them a couple of times.

Neither of us says it out loud, but I can tell we're both wondering how long it'll be before someone uses me.

We pass a few couples on the path, and they smile, but no one tries to talk to us. When we come to some rockery steps with a railing that leads down to a sandy path to the beach, we pause for a moment. Coming up the steps in our direction are two guys.

I assume they won't mess with me since Quentin and I look to be heading somewhere with purpose. We're only a few steps down when they get to us. I gasp in surprise when one of them grabs my wrist and pulls me down another step before bending me over the railing.

The guy addresses my husband. "Sorry dude, just gonna unload. I'll only be a moment."

When Quentin laughs and says, "Have fun," a naughty zing of joy heads straight to my clit.

I grasp the railing with both hands as the guy lifts me off my feet and tips me forward so he can enter me at the right angle.

I moan as his cock slides into me, and I look over my shoulder to see my handsome husband watching with rapt attention and a bulge beneath his jeans. My pussy clenches at my husband's expression, and the man fucks me slowly, as if he's got all the time in the world. Not too long ago, I didn't even know what freeuse was, and now I think I've found my favorite kink. I'm just a slut who wants a bunch of guys to fuck me whenever they want, and having my husband here watching doubles my pleasure.

I can feel the bliss building in layers, and right before I can orgasm, the guy fucking me grunts and thrusts into me hard as he comes, shooting his load deep inside me. I can feel it filling me and spilling out, running down my thighs.

The man eases me down to my feet and pulls my dress over my ass before slapping it and walking away. The other guy gives me a smile before joining his buddy as they continue past us to head toward the main building.

Quentin steps close behind me, and I can feel his hard cock against my lower back through his jeans. He wraps his hand around me, pulls my dress up with one hand, and slides the other one down my stomach and between my legs. He rubs the sticky mix of cum and my juices around, sliding his fingers inside my pussy to tease me while my mind whirls from ecstasy.

I moan as Quentin whispers huskily, "Did you like that, baby? Did you like being fucked by that complete stranger in front of me?"

My pussy throbs from the lack of orgasm, and I whimper without responding. My brain feels fuzzy, and I can't form a coherent answer. Instead, I rock against my husband's fingers, begging him to keep finger fucking me.

He laughs as he withdraws his finger from inside me and pushes me forward until I'm bending over the railing again. When he spreads my ass cheeks, I freeze as I realize what he's about to do. Ohhhh god. Right here? Right now? Quentin's slick finger rubs against my puckered asshole. He circles it, teasing me before he presses in gently.

Quentin's other hand moves to my clit, stroking lightly as I relax under his touch. "Do you trust me, baby?" he asks softly.

I nod as I let my head fall forward, giving in to whatever he wants to do to me.

Quentin continues to rub my clit and play with the rim of my ass while he talks to me in his sexy, soothing baritone. "I want you to enjoy all of this. I want you to experience every pleasure this place has to offer."

He's convinced me. I need someone in every hole. When he removes his hands, he helps me stand up, and I sway against him.

My voice trembles with desire. "We should go back to the room. I want the green wristband."

He chuckles and pulls the green band from his pocket. "No need."

He removes the pink and black bands on my wrist before sliding the green one over my hand, letting it rest on my skin.

I stare down at it. "When? How?"

Quentin pulls me close and kisses my forehead. "I had a hunch you were going to want more."

I can practically hear him smiling, and I'm not sure I've loved him more than I do in this moment. He knows I'm a slut at heart. This resort might be heaven on earth, but having my husband here makes it so much better. I'm going to enjoy every minute left of our trip.

"I love you," I whisper, looking up at him with adoration.

Quentin's eyes shine. "I love you too...now let's go see if someone is tempted to use you by the pool. We can see the ocean tomorrow."

I shiver with excitement when his hand slides down and cups my ass as he guides me down the path to the pool. My pussy buzzes with neediness, and the cum dripping between my legs is a reminder of how filthy I am...filthy in such a wonderful way.

The pool is deserted when we get there, and I'm about to ask Quentin what we should do, when he pulls my sundress over my head. I shiver as the warm breeze caresses my skin and my nipples harden.

"Hey, what do you think you're doing?" I tease him.

Quentin winks. "Getting you naked. I want to see your beautiful tits bounce when someone comes along and fucks you."

Oh, wow. I didn't expect that answer, and my body hums with excitement. I'm worked up, and since we're still alone, I decide to take a dip in the pool to cool off.

Kicking off my sandals, I slip into the refreshing water, moaning as the water laps at my skin. I duck under the surface, feeling the coolness envelop me. The water swirls around me, and I'm hypersensitive to even the brush of water against my sensitive areas. When I resurface, I hear Quentin groan. "Fuck...you're so sexy, baby."

My body responds instantly to his words, tingling with longing. I'm not sure who is going to join us next or where they will want to fuck me, but I'm ready for my husband to see all my holes filled. The thought sends a rush of arousal through my core, making me squirm with need.

If someone had mentioned a freeuse resort to me last week, I might have laughed and asked how you can really have freeuse if the person being used knows it's going to happen and welcomes it. But being here and waiting for someone to come along to use me is a delicious torture. It doesn't matter that I'm all-in and ready to go, just the fact that these are strangers who can walk up to me and just bend me over puts me in the mindset of complete submission to whoever wants me.

And knowing my husband is here and letting it happen? Yeah...this resort is magical.

Closing my eyes, I float on my back and enjoy the feeling of my husband's eyes on my body. I feel sexy and powerful in a way I never have before. Knowing Quentin wants to watch me get fucked by other men gives me a huge confidence boost. I feel like a total slut, and I'm embracing it.

"Wow...she looks delicious," someone says from the side of the pool, and I open my eyes.

The voice belongs to a man who is probably in his early forties. He's with two younger guys. All three are muscular and hot. Neediness swirls in my core as the guys remove their shoes and shirts. The older guy glances at Quentin before he unzips his pants. "Do you want to watch us fuck her?"

Quentin's lips curl up into a sexy smile. "Yes, I do."

The man laughs and walks to the edge of the pool while the two other guys stand and watch.

My heart beats rapidly when Quentin says, "Make her scream for more."

My entire body is thrumming with lust. Three men...this will be intense. How many cocks will I take today?

Once the older guy is naked, he joins me in the pool. The water moves around him, rippling outward as he approaches. He slips his hands under my arms and pulls me close. I'm aroused at the thought of having three cocks inside me while my husband watches, and my nipples brush against his chest as he pulls me to him and kisses me.

His kiss is rough and possessive, and I'm so engrossed in the way his body feels different from my husband's that I don't notice one of the other men got in the pool until he comes up behind me. The older guy stops kissing me and pushes on my shoulder, forcing me to lean back against the dude behind me while the older one hooks his arms around my thighs and pulls me up to his cock. I'm suspended between them in the water, and I gasp when he sinks his cock into me.

I can feel the other man's hard cock digging into my back as the older guy fucks me. The pleasure in my core intensifies, but I'm craving more. I want more than one hole filled.

As if they are reading my mind, the guys stop fucking me and both drag me out of the pool.

"It's time to make you scream for your husband."

The third guy approaches, naked as well, and he's got a bottle of lube in his hands. Oooh, god, I'm going to get what I want. The older guy moves me to a lounge chair. When he reclines, he pulls me on top of him so I'm facing him while I straddle him. He lines his cock up with my pussy and grips my waist, forcing me down on his cock.

Bracing my hands on the chair behind his head, he fucks me furiously. I'm in a daze as one of the others moves behind me and spreads my ass cheeks apart. Oh god...this is it. My body hungers for more as a lubed finger brushes against my ass and slowly sinks in.

I whimper, "Oh...fuck," as I press against his finger eagerly as he prepares me for his cock. As good as what he's doing feels, I'm craving something thicker. When he replaces his fingers with the head of his cock, I almost cheer.

My breathing quickens as he slowly pushes inside me, pausing every few seconds to give me time to adjust to his size. I've never had two cocks at once, and the pleasure of both of them inside me is mind blowing as fiery sparks shoot across my body.

Once he's fully seated, he thrusts into me gently as he sets a rhythm with the guy in my pussy. Each thrust from either of them makes me moan and whimper as delight swirls in my core. I close my eyes, letting the bliss course through every inch of me.

They sync up, pounding into my holes at a rapid pace. The full feeling is so intense, I can't hold in my moans of delight. I can't believe my husband wants me to do this and is watching. I'm married to the most wonderful guy ever for giving me the chance at this much pleasure.

My whole body feels like it's on fire as they continue fucking me. I'm reeling towards ecstasy, and I lose all sense of time as I transcend to a higher plane of joy. Every stroke feels like an eternity, as my body coils, ready to explode.

When the third guy stands next to us and something pushes against my cheek, I open my eyes to see a massive cock waiting for me. Turning towards him, I hum with happiness as my lips stretch around his girth.

He slides down my throat and says, "Good slut...swallow it all."

Mmm, I am a good slut. He rocks into my mouth, and for a minute I revel in the feeling of being completely stuffed. This is exactly what I was hoping would happen, and it makes me feel like I'm just a hole for them to use. The pleasure they're giving me is secondary to the illicit naughtiness of having three guys at once.

I'm almost surprised when the cock in my mouth pulses and the salty taste of his cum coats my tongue. I moan as he shoots more cum down my throat. Fuuuck, this is dirty.

I'm trying to swallow it all down when the cock in my ass suddenly slams against me harder, sending ripples of delight through me. I moan around the cock I'm trying to suck clean as I climax. The orgasm rushes through me in waves before the guy in my pussy rubs my clit, and I peak again. I scream in joy, and my body shudders violently as every muscle contracts. I'm tingling from ecstasy as the guys hammer into me again and again before finally erupting inside both holes.

The world spins, and my vision blurs as their hot cum fills me. Everyone groans as they unload, and I try to imagine what this looks like for my husband. He's got one filthy wife.

It takes a moment for my breathing to return to normal, but when I come back down from the intense high, I feel like I'm floating on a cloud of pure rapture.

"Holy fuck…" I whisper as they slide out of me, one by one.

Within seconds, Quentin pulls me off the guy and wraps me in his arms. He runs his fingers through my hair, tilting my face toward him as he says huskily, "Baby, that was so amazing to watch."

He doesn't give me time to respond before he swings me into his arms and carries me away from the pool. I hear him saying goodnight and thanking the guys as I float along in my happy place. I can tell by Quentin's determined steps he's going to fuck me as soon as we get into our room.

I'm not wrong.

Quentin shuts the door with a foot and strides across the floor straight to the bed. He lays me down gently and doesn't waste any time as he climbs onto the bed and kisses me. His lips move against mine hungrily, as if he wants to devour me, and I sigh in pleasure. When he cups my breast and pulls on the nipple gently, I almost giggle when I realize I'm still naked. I guess my sundress is still at the pool.

He continues to kiss me as he runs his hand over my body. When he slides a hand between my legs and circles my clit with his finger, I moan softly into his mouth, wishing this could go on forever. I need his gentleness after such an intense fucking.

When we break apart, my husband whispers softly, almost like a prayer, "My beautiful slutty wife…that was incredible."

I smile at him as he fumbles with his pants to get his cock out while he continues talking. "You looked so stunning filled by three cocks at once. Your expression was pure bliss."

Mmm, his praise is filthy and I love it. When he settles between my legs, I moan as he slides into me and fucks me slowly. My eyes roll back from delight, and knowing he still loves me after seeing me fucked by multiple guys is a heady feeling.

The orgasm builds inside me as he fucks me faster and harder. When he groans, "God, I love you," the bliss peaks and rushes through me, flooding me with pleasure and washing away everything but this moment with him.

When he feels me coming, it pushes him over the edge, and he cries out with his release, adding another load of cum deep inside me to mix with the other guys' seed. He hammers into me, unloading everything he's got until he shivers and slumps on top of me.

As the rapture fades, Quentin kisses me sweetly before rolling to the side and pulling me close. My head is still swirling from so many orgasms today, but I need to make sure he knows how I feel.

"I love you so much," I whisper. "Thank you for a wonderful trip."

His smile is full of love and admiration, and he kisses me again and murmurs, "You're welcome, baby."

If he ever suggests another freeuse resort trip, I'll jump at the chance but only if he wants to watch again. Life really can't get any better than this.

The End

Her Freeuse Escape

On Display and Public Fun

CHAPTER 1

I click through another webpage on my laptop while my husband Daniel's steady breathing beside me confirms he's asleep, unaware of my late-night research. I type "exclusive adult resorts" into the search bar, delete it, then try "freeuse vacation experiences" instead. There are so many more results than I expected.

What am I doing? I'm the woman who runs meetings with Fortune 500 executives without breaking a sweat, who plans vacations six months in advance with daily itineraries. Yet here I am, obsessively researching at 2 a.m. because I can't stop thinking about my friend Alyssa's recent trip.

My fingers tap methodically against the laptop case. Even in this private moment, I maintain my posture, shoulders back, the screen angled for optimal viewing. Always composed, always in control.

A webpage loads, displaying tasteful images of a Mediterranean-style resort. "Carnal Bay Retreat," the header reads in an elegant script. "An exclusive experience for discerning couples." My pulse quickens as I scan the carefully-worded description that manages to suggest everything while explicitly stating nothing.

Daniel shifts beside me. I quickly minimize the window and shut my laptop.

"Still working?" he mumbles.

"Just finishing up." I slide the laptop onto my nightstand and turn off the light before snuggling on my side next to him. "Go back to sleep."

"You've been distracted lately." His hand slides under my nightgown and curves over my stomach as he caresses my skin. "Something on your mind?"

My throat tightens. We've been married eight years, yet I can't bring myself to admit what I want in the bedroom. I don't usually ask for things—I'm the one who makes what I want happen. And I don't easily disclose insecurities or desires that might make me appear vulnerable.

"Just thinking about vacation options," I say, giving him a half-truth.

"Hmm." His hand slides higher, resting just beneath my breast. "Any particular destination?"

Now. Say it now.

"Actually..." I pause and almost chicken out. What is my problem? This is my damn husband. I should be able to say these things to him. "I've been looking into resorts. Like the one Alyssa visited."

In the darkness, I can't read his expression, and I get a moment of panic. Oh shit, I've miscalculated. I open my mouth to backtrack—

"The sex place?" His voice holds no judgment, just curiosity.

I consider denying it, but stop myself. "Yes. The freeuse resort."

Daniel props himself up on one elbow, now very awake. "Tell me more."

"You're not shocked?" I switch the lamp on, needing to see his face.

He laughs. "Mandy, I know you. You've been different since Alyssa told you about her trip. You've asked her for details three separate times. You've been distracted during sex." He tucks a strand of my hair behind my ear. "I figured you were either interested, or planning to start writing erotica."

"As if I have time to write...."

"So you're interested." His statement requires no confirmation.

I study the sheets as if they're the most fascinating thing in the world. "I found one in Florida. Carnal Bay Retreat. It's part of a collection of resorts that have freeuse days. Very exclusive." I'm retreating to my comfort zone of facts and logistics.

Daniel lifts my chin, forcing me to meet his gaze. "But why? You've never mentioned wanting something like this before."

The question strikes at the heart of what I've been avoiding. "When Alyssa described it—being free to just experience without planning, without being in charge—" I stop, frustrated by my inability to articulate my longing. "Everyone sees me as this competent person who has everything under control. Sometimes I want to just...not be that person."

Daniel's eyes darken. "You want to surrender."

The word 'surrender' makes me shiver. "Yes."

"To strangers?"

"Yes, but while you watch." My face flushes, and I wish I could bury my head into his chest while we have this conversation.

"While I watch," he repeats, his voice dropping an octave.

"Is that—would that be something you'd want?" I hate the uncertainty in my voice.

Daniel doesn't use words to answer. Instead he kisses me until I'm breathless and slides his hand beneath my nightshirt again to play with my nipple.

When he pulls back, lust is written all over his face. "I think the better question is: when can we go?"

Relief floods through me. I reach for him, but he catches my wrists, pinning them gently above my head with one hand. "Tell me more about this place."

"It's on a private peninsula that has a freeuse event for women once a month." I rock against him while I talk. My panties and his boxers are in the way, but I'm enjoying the pings of bliss as my pussy collides with his hardness. I'm already so wet, I could wrap my leg around him and he could slide in easily. "They have different colored wristbands that the women wear, depending on what they're consenting to."

"And what do you want men to do to you?" His lips brush my neck.

"I don't know yet."

"Yes, you do." He nips at my pulse point. "Tell me."

The words stick in my throat. Even here, with my husband, I struggle to voice my desires.

"I want—" I swallow hard. "I want to be used."

Daniel groans, "Keep talking."

"I want men to just take what they want without asking." The confession rushes out, and the words tumble over one another. "To use me without me having to decide or be in charge."

"And you want me to watch you turn into a little slut with these men?" He slides his hand between my legs and moves my panties aside.

"Yes," I gasp. "Just for the weekend."

"You're desperate to be a little fucktoy, aren't you?" He rumbles in my ear as his teeth graze my earlobe. "Say it again. Tell me what you want."

"I want to be used." A bolt of longing zings through me. "I want men to just bend me over and fuck me whenever they want."

Daniel sinks two fingers inside me, and I whimper as I rotate my hips to force his fingers in deeper.

"You're soaked." He pumps his fingers in and out. "You're such a dirty slut for me."

Holy shit, if he keeps up with this dirty talk, I'll bring up fucking other guys more often. He occasionally talks like this, but it's usually after a day of being turned on and he's had a beer to loosen his tongue.

He adds a third finger and my inner muscles clench around him. His thumb circles my clit and sparks dance along my nerve endings.

"Imagine it. Men lining up to fuck you. To fill every hole." He abandons playing with my clit to finger fuck me while his palm slaps my pussy with each thrust. "You're going to be a little fuckdoll for anyone who wants you."

My stomach quivers from delight and I moan, "Please."

He pins my wrists more firmly to the bed, and I squirm from the delicious feeling of being helpless.

But even in this moment, I have an internal director that choreographs my responses as pleasure builds. It's directing my every move like a photoshoot. I've spent my life choreographing every encounter.

Arch your back more. Moan a little louder. Bite your lip—he loves that.

"I'm going to watch them fuck you raw. Turn you into their toy until you're begging for their cum."

Ohhh, god. The thought of being filled by multiple men floods my mind, and my orgasm slams into me. Heat bursts low in my belly, spreading fast, and I cry out as the pleasure rushes through me, too big to hold back. For one perfect moment, my mind goes joyfully blank. This is the only time I ever stop thinking—when I come, and everything else just disappears.

Daniel continues to finger fuck me until the waves of euphoria fade. When he removes his hand from my pussy, he brings his fingers up to my face, painting my lips. I taste myself and moan as his cock probes my pussy.

"Is this what you want?" His voice is softer now. "You want to be my little slut that I share with whoever wants you?"

Mmm, hell yeah. I make sure my voice is clear. "I want that."

In response, he rolls over me, settling between my legs and bracing himself on one arm. He slams his cock deep, and I cry out in raw pleasure. My wrists are still pinned, leaving me helpless beneath him as he fucks me hard. God, I should've shared this fantasy years ago. Getting used by a bunch of men is right up there with my secret craving to be watched by strangers while I'm fucked—and this resort might just give me both.

"You feel so fucking good," he grunts as he chases his orgasm. I can tell he's not going to wait for me to come again.

I put my feet flat on the bed for better leverage as we frantically crash together. He releases my wrists so he can really hammer it home, and the wet, frantic rhythm of our bodies becomes a lewd symphony, spurring him on.

When his hand slides between us again and he fingers my clit, I'm lost. I get a few blissful moments where my brain turns off and my whole body shudders as I climax. The rapture skyrockets me to another plane and fireworks burst behind my eyelids. I cry out when I hit the peak, and Daniel groans as he unloads so much cum inside me, I'm not sure he's ever going to stop.

We ride out our orgasms together, and when we finally come down, he collapses next to me. The sheets are a tangled mess, and I can feel his cum dripping out of me. Mmm, that was wonderfully unexpected.

Daniel snuggles against me and kisses my neck. "Let's look into booking a vacation tomorrow."

I giggle, "I already bookmarked the information."

"Of course you did," he chuckles. "My sweet slut is always prepared."

Mmm, his sweet slut. I like this dirty side of him, and if I have to talk about taking multiple cocks more often to bring it out, I guess a girl's gotta do what a girl's gotta do.

Three days later, I'm in our home office, staring at the application forms on my computer. The questionnaire is far more detailed than I expected, filled with probing questions about sexual preferences, boundaries, and fantasies. I breezed through the logistical parts without hesitation, but now I'm stuck on the section labeled *Desires and Expectations.*

What do I even want? Other than men using me and dirty talk...

On impulse I call Alyssa and spill the tea about booking a trip. It all comes pouring out, and once I slow down, she giggles.

"I didn't know you wanted to be a freeuse slut. But are you sure you're ready for this? It's not exactly a controlled environment."

We've been friends since college, and she knows me better than any-one—except Daniel. "That's the point."

Alyssa is quiet for a moment. "You know, when I told you about my trip, I never expected you'd want the same thing. You were enthusiastic for me to try it, but you're so..."

"Uptight?" I supply.

"I was going to say 'measured.'" She laughs.

I think back to our conversations after her return—how I'd hounded her for details, how each revelation had triggered a rush of exhilaration that I'd carefully concealed.

"I can't get it out of my head," I admit.

"Daniel's on board?"

"Enthusiastically."

She pauses. "But seriously, Mandy, it's intense. You have to really let go."

"That's what I want." And it really is. I want to see if multiple orgasms from a bunch of men can make me stop analyzing everything to death.

"Well then, I hope you find so much pleasure your voice is hoarse from screaming."

Huh, how many times would I have to come for that? We chat some more and when we get off the phone, I focus on the questionnaire.

The cursor blinks at me. "Describe your ultimate fantasy scenario at a resort."

What exactly *is* my fantasy? I catch my reflection in the nearby mirror on the wall and automatically straighten up, brushing a hand over my hair as I offer myself a small, practiced smile. Always presentable, always polished—just the way I like it. Or is it?

Come on, just be honest. No one's going to judge you here. This is exactly why you're doing this.

I take a breath, let my shoulders relax ever so slightly, and turn back to the screen. *No holding back.* I begin to type.

Chapter 2

Daniel pulls into the circular drive of Carnal Bay Retreat and parks the car. My stomach twists as he reaches over and gives my knee a reassuring squeeze. "Well, we're here."

"We are." After several agonizing weeks of waiting, we've finally arrived.

A spark of excitement prickles beneath my skin. How long will it be before someone fucks me? I'm not wearing a wristband yet to signal I'm "open for business," so it won't happen the moment I step out of the car.

Stand up straight when you get out. Smile, but not too eagerly. Look confident but approachable.

The main building is made of white stucco with a terracotta roof and surrounded by large palm trees. It's simple, yet elegant, and the grounds are well maintained. I peer out the car window, trying to decide if it looks like a sex resort. It doesn't exactly scream "filthy things happen here," but since this is my first time visiting a place like this, I'm not sure what would say that.

A porter approaches, tanned and muscular, his biceps straining the sleeves of his polo. When his gaze settles on me, paired with a knowing smile, heat rushes to my cheeks. Is he one of the men allowed to use me? From the way my pussy clenches while my panties grow damp, I wouldn't mind if he was.

Wait—do they have designated men to service the guests? They must, right? All the employees can't be running around fucking people...otherwise, who would actually work?

Just smile at him—not your business smile, your seductive one.

I focus on grabbing my purse instead of gawking at him, but my fingers fumble and I nearly dump everything onto the car floor. I manage to catch it just in time, pulling myself together as the porter opens my door. So much for looking confident—but I still flash him a seductive smile.

"Welcome to Carnal Bay," he says, his focus lingering on me as I step out and straighten my linen dress.

I'm used to guys checking me out—I'm blonde and fit with generous breasts—but this is different. Usually, at work, the guys are covert about it, and no one openly leers. You don't want to mess with the woman in the power suit.

But knowing this guy might actually fuck me makes my skin tingle and my nipples tighten. My steps falter as we approach the entrance. One of my heels catches on the rockery path, and I stumble. I give a small yip of distress, and Daniel catches me before I fall.

"Whoa, you okay?" His eyebrows furrow in concern.

I'm usually graceful, but since I'm practically vibrating from pent-up lust, it's making me awkward. *Come on Mandy. You're not some bumbling intern. You're an executive who dominates at work.*

My grin is sheepish. "Yeah, just excited."

He winks in response, and a blush creeps up my neck. I wanted to not be in control, but this isn't exactly what I had in mind.

The main building's massive wooden doors swing open as we approach, and a second gorgeous male porter ushers us in. The cool air of the lobby is a relief from the humidity. The interior is elegant-casual with limestone floors, whitewashed walls, and tropical arrangements. Again, nothing overtly sexual and I doubt a casual observer would think that I was checking in for a cock free-for-all....At least I hope I am. Just because I'm freeuse doesn't mean someone is going to use me.

I side-eye my husband. I mean, he's here so I'm guaranteed at least one cock. Oh man, that would be hilarious if we paid all this money and no one fucks me but him.

"Mr. and Mrs. Rivera." A woman glides toward us, hand extended, and I bring myself back to attention. "I'm Sophia, your hostess."

Her voice is pleasant and cultured. She's in her mid 50s with silver-streaked dark hair pulled into an elegant chignon. Her white dress clings to curves that put mine to shame. Is being drop-dead gorgeous a requirement for working here?

"Mandy," I say, taking her hand. "And this is Daniel."

Her smile encompasses us both. "Was your journey comfortable?"

"Very," Daniel answers. "The directions were great."

"Excellent." She gestures toward a seating area. "Please, let's sit for a moment before someone shows you to your villa. There are a few details to discuss."

We follow her to a cluster of plush chairs partially screened by tropical plants. A waiter materializes with a tray of beverages.

Sit with your knees bent, legs crossed at the ankles. Back straight but not stiff. Look engaged but relaxed.

"Our welcome tradition," Sophia explains, and Daniel and I each take a non-alcoholic beverage from the selection as Sophia raises her glass. "To new experiences."

I really could have gone with some liquid courage right about now, but Daniel and I made a pact to not drink on this trip. Neither of us want to hide behind the excuse that we were tipsy when we look back on the weekend.

After we all take a sip, Sophia sets her glass aside and produces a leather portfolio. "Now, as you know, today begins our monthly freeuse weekend for women." She extracts a glossy folder and hands it to me. "This contains our schedule of events, a map of the grounds, and your wristbands."

"Tomorrow night is our Roman Bacchanal," Sophia continues. "A favorite among our guests. Attendance is optional, but highly recommended. You can experience Carnal Bay's...atmosphere."

"Roman Bacchanal?" Daniel asks.

I explain. "A celebration inspired by ancient Roman traditions." My marketing brain fills in the details. "Feasting, wine, indulgence."

Sophia's smile widens. "Precisely. Though our version includes modern liberties. Togas are provided in your villa, though many guests choose to attend in varying states of undress."

From what little I know of Roman history, togas were worn by men and sometimes prostitutes. But since I'm not here for historical accuracy, I'm good with modern liberties. A toga seems like it will be easy to remove.

Sophia continues with the orientation. "The information in the folder explains everything, including our wristband system. Pink for vaginal consent, purple for anal, black for oral, and green for open consent to all forms. You can wear any combination that reflects your boundaries."

My throat tightens. Seeing the system laid out makes this very real.

"And the rules?" Daniel asks, his thumb tracing the lines on my palm.

"Simple," Sophia says. "Women wearing wristbands are available for the men here, all of whom have been thoroughly vetted. For everyone's safety, the men always move in pairs or small groups—like a built-in buddy system. And if anything feels off, the safeword 'red light' stops everything immediately."

I flip open the folder with trembling fingers. The black and pink bands peek out from the inside pocket–smooth silicone. Exactly the two colors I'd want to wear. I slip them onto my wrist, one after another, adjusting them so they're both visible. Daniel watches me, his lips curving upward.

Sophia turns to Daniel. "As her partner, you'll receive a tablet connected to our discreet camera system. You may watch from anywhere on the property."

"And privacy?" I manage to ask.

Keep your voice even. Don't let them hear the nervous excitement.

"There is none in the main areas," Sophia answers lightly. "The nature of the freeuse weekend is public enjoyment. However, your room remains private unless you choose otherwise."

She stands, signaling the end of our orientation. "The porter will bring your luggage and show you to Villa 12 now. It has an excellent view of the main courtyard."

The porter returns, joined by another man in the same uniform, and together they collect our bags. As we follow them through the main building, my gaze catches on a mirror mounted on the lobby wall. I take in my reflection—sexy but casual, just the look I was going for. If I were a guy, I'd definitely want to fuck me.

That's right. I look hot and ready. Own it.

Daniel glances at my wristbands, and anticipation coils tighter in my belly. I can't wait until we settle in— I'm already planning to suggest a walk around the grounds, hoping it leads to someone using me.

To distract myself from the growing heat between my legs, I joke with the guys carrying our luggage. "I don't think our two suitcases needed both of you. We didn't pack *that* much for the weekend."

The porter sets my bag down and turns to me, his expression shifting from professional to something more intimate. "They didn't need us both, but someone put her wristbands on already."

My heart rate speeds up. Oh, wow. I'm not even going to be able to unpack first?

Daniel's eyebrows rise, and he watches with interest as the porter turns me towards a side table and bends me over it.

Arch your back just enough. Look back over your shoulder—men love that.

The porter pins my shoulder down and I rest my cheek on the glass surface. His free hand is already sliding beneath my sundress. "This place really is everything we promise our guests."

I gasp as he fingers the lace of my panties. "Did you—are all staff part of the freeuse policy?" My voice catches as he pushes the fabric aside.

"Every one of us." He rubs my clit and my legs part instinctively.

"I didn't think—" My words dissolve into a sharp intake of breath as his fingers dip inside me.

"We provide excellent service. That's why guests choose this resort." The porter's voice drops lower. "To be available whenever, wherever, to whomever. That's why you're here right? To be used like a little slut."

A sudden surge of warmth courses through me as I picture a horde of men using me and calling me filthy things. I wrote down on the visitor questionnaire that I wanted dirty talk, but I didn't expect it before we got to our room. His fingers curl inside me, massaging a spot that makes my vision blur.

"Yes," I sigh, and close my eyes as he finger fucks me. Pleasure builds in my core, and my muscles tighten. This place already gets a five-star review from me.

When I hear laughter in the distance, my head whips up. "Hey, anyone could see us here."

The possibility sends an illicit thrill straight to my clit as I imagine people walking by, stopping to stare at me bent over.

"That's the point." His fingers continue to play with me, eliciting spikes of delight. I can't focus on anything but my impending orgasm. "You like knowing that anyone could walk past at any moment and see you bent over for a guy you don't know, don't you?"

Oh god, he's good. I'm unable to form words beyond a whimpered agreement of, "Yes."

His curled fingers repeatedly hit the pleasure point inside me. I buck into his hand, desperate for more.

"Say it," he demands as he brings his other hand between my legs to rub my clit. "Say you love it loud enough for your husband to hear you."

"I—I love it," I gasp and tense up as he brings me closer to the edge. I have no idea how I got to this point so fast, but I'll do anything to keep his fingers inside me. "I want people to see me like this and know that I'm a slut."

The porter chuckles, as if he's pleased. "That's right. And you'll be thinking about this moment all weekend, knowing you'd get on your knees and beg me to fuck you if I asked."

My mouth pops open in surprise and all I can do is moan as he increases the pace. He's right. I would gladly kneel before him if it got his cock inside me. I'm so close to coming, and my thigh muscles quiver as I wait for the euphoria to overtake me.

Just as I'm about to come, he stops. I whimper in protest, desperate for him to finally give me his cock. I glance back at him, and his fingers glisten as he brings them to his mouth.

He sucks them clean. "Tasty," he says with a satisfied smile. "Now, let's get you to your villa."

What? I look at Daniel in disbelief and I swear to God he's trying to hide a smile. What sort of fucked-up resort is this?

My husband helps me stand and straightens my clothes as if I'm helpless—which to be honest, I basically am right now. My body is about ready to riot without an orgasm. When Daniel's hand brushes across my nipples, the resulting ache earns him a glare. This time he can't hide the upturn at the corner of his mouth. Oh yeah, he's enjoying my pain. But underneath his amusement, I can tell he's turned on—and the bulge in his jeans confirms it.

Compose yourself. Fix your hair. Don't let them see how desperate you are.

The porter is professional now, all evidence of our encounter erased from his demeanor. The second one just stands back and watches, but when I peek at his slacks, there's a pronounced bulge. Before I can tease him and ask if he wants me to blow him, we start walking again.

As we follow the porter, I notice the strategic placement of benches in secluded alcoves. There's an abundance of surfaces at just the right height. They're making this easy for people to have sex in a variety of locations, and to be watched.

Villa 12 sits apart from the others. Our room is decorated with white linens and natural wood and a massive bed dominates the main room. There are sliding glass doors that open to a private terrace that overlooks the main courtyard. Sophia wasn't lying about the great view. If someone was having sex out there, we'd have front row tickets.

"Your welcome package is on the desk," the porter says, indicating a basket filled with snacks, fruit, and what appears to be lube. "Your tablet is charging by the bed—once you turn it on, it'll automatically connect with the observation app."

The idea of being on camera fills me with an intoxicating surge of adrenaline. Not just for Daniel's enjoyment, but potentially anyone with access to the system. I imagine strangers watching me get fucked and commenting on the show. I press my thighs together to ease the sudden ache.

The porters each give me a final smile before they leave, and I stay frozen in place until the door clicks closed behind them.

Once we're alone, I turn to face my husband. "You liked that, didn't you?"

"Which part? The part where you were bent over getting finger fucked, or the part where he didn't let you come?"

Oh yeah, he's in trouble. "Daniel—"

"I loved it." He wraps his arms around me. "Seeing someone else want what belongs to me—what I'm choosing to share."

I give him my best pout. "But I didn't get to come."

"How about this, baby?" He pauses to give me a spine-tingling kiss. Our tongues slide and tease each other, and I imagine forcing him onto the bed and riding him. Who needs the porter anyway? When he breaks off the kiss, I'm ready to shove him down, but his words stop me.

"How about for every orgasm you feel you didn't get this weekend, I'll make it up to you when we get home?"

Oh hey, what's this? I blink at him while my sex-crazed brain considers his offer. So I'll come as many times as I can on the trip, and then my husband is going to give me even more orgasms at a future date? I don't see how this is bad.

"Deal."

He looks like he's about to kiss me again, but instead he steps back. "Let's get some air."

He crosses to the terrace doors and opens them, letting in a warm breeze.

"Come look at this view," he calls.

Is he trying to deny himself? If I were him, I'd be banging me all over the villa by now. I join him outside. Below us, the main courtyard stretches out—multiple pools, cabanas, and lounging areas, all designed with clear sightlines. I imagine it filled with men who will see my wristband and simply take me.

"You're tense," Daniel says, stepping behind me and massaging my shoulders.

"You would be too if you were just left hanging."

"You don't have to participate," he reminds me. "Nothing happens unless you wear the wristband outside our room."

I turn in his arms. "I want this. I'm just..."

When I don't continue he finishes for me. "Scared of not having control?"

"Yeah," I nod, grateful he understands. "Let's look at the pamphlet."

Back inside, we sit on the bed and check out the information about the weekend. The schedule lists various activities tomorrow—naked morning yoga, brunch, pool games, and then the Roman Bacchanal.

Along with the information are the last two silicone wristbands—purple and green. I touch them lightly, imagining each one around my wrist.

"Are you going to keep the black and pink ones on?" Daniel asks, his voice carefully neutral.

I look up at him. "What would you want to see?"

"If it were my choice? Pink and black. Maybe green." He gives me a devilish smile. "I want to see you spit-roasted, but this is your decision."

I imagine being bent over while a stranger takes me from behind, and another man filling my mouth while Daniel watches.

"Yeah, pink and black," I repeat.

"For now," Daniel says. "You can always change your mind. Add the green later if you want."

I laugh lightly. "Let's not get ahead of ourselves."

He kisses me again, possessively, and his hand slides up my thigh beneath my dress. "We have a few hours before dinner," he murmurs against my lips. "How should we spend them?"

Okay, fuck waiting. I push on him and he falls backwards onto the bed. He sighs in pleasure as I straddle him. I have a sudden need to assert control while I still can. Later I'll surrender, but right now, I need to bounce on my husband's cock.

"I have some ideas," I tell him, reaching for his belt.

Chapter 3

After my first orgasm of the trip and an early dinner, I decide it's time to check out the pool area. Before I go, I slip on my white bikini and adjust the pink and black wristbands, making sure they're both clearly visible.

I pause by the mirror and take a long look at myself. *Not bad at all.* I straighten my shoulders, adjust my top for the most flattering fit, and let a sly smile curl my lips. If I saw me walking by, I'd definitely stare.

Blowing a kiss to Daniel, I grin. "See you soon!"

He's eager to watch everything unfold on the tablet, which is just fine by me. Knowing my husband, he's probably scoping out all the camera angles to catch as much action as possible. I'll have to make sure I give him a good show.

Shoulders back. Chin up. Walk with purpose, but not too much urgency.

Dusk is just settling in, and the pool glows under carefully placed lights, turning the water into liquid sapphire. I scan the area, noting sight lines and possible setups. The chairs are the perfect height for bending over, and the steps in the shallow end would give me excellent leverage for all kinds of positions.

Since it's dinner hour, the pool area is empty. So much for finding a bunch of men to fuck me. My carefully planned entrance wasted on an audience of none.

I kick my sandals off and settle onto a lounge, arranging my limbs in what I know is my most flattering pose—one leg slightly bent, arms posed to accentuate my cleavage. My mind is a jumble of concerns. What if no one approaches me all weekend? What if they do and I freeze up? What if I look ridiculous? I should have practiced more poses in the mirror before coming down.

Daniel really isn't getting much of a show from me, but I'm sure someone here is getting a good pounding on screen. The idea of other couples potentially watching guys fuck me from the privacy of their rooms makes me needy and impatient.

Fuck it, I'll go for a swim. At least I can give Daniel something to watch. Just as I sit on the edge of the pool and am about to lower myself into the water, two men approach from the path to the main building.

They're in their mid-thirties, fit, one with dark curly hair, the other with a close-cropped blonde style. They notice me—or more specifically, my wristbands—and exchange a look. My heart hammers and I swirl my feet in the water, pretending not to notice them while being acutely aware of their approach.

Look casual but inviting. Not too eager.

The blonde one is wearing swim trunks and an unbuttoned linen shirt. His friend is in blue board shorts with nothing on top. His chest has just the right amount of hair and I imagine running my fingers through it.

"Mind if we join you?" the blonde one asks, his voice carrying a slight Southern drawl.

"Go for it." I shrug with practiced nonchalance and the blonde one sits down next to me on the edge while the friend hangs back.

They introduce themselves—Tyler is the one who sat down and the brown-haired guy is Justin. We make casual conversation about the weather, and how long I'm staying. Normal chitchat that feels surreal given the context. I answer on autopilot, hyperaware of my body, and the way the water glistens on my legs. I'm performing already, calculating each response for maximum effect.

Am I supposed to be seductive, aloof, or just myself? Should I tell them they should just fuck me? It's not like I'm going to say no...

My skin flushes as I think about Daniel watching on the tablet. Will he be able to see my face when I come? Will he hear every moan, every gasp? But maybe the cameras don't have sound.

"First time at Carnal Bay?" Tyler asks, and I give a soft, playful laugh.

"Is it that obvious?"

The anticipation of what they're going to do—or more specifically how they're going to do it—has my bikini bottoms damp. I cross and uncross my legs, a deliberate movement designed to draw attention.

"Only a little." He touches my knee, and my clit throbs as he drags his gaze over me, heating me up from the inside out. I resist the urge to push my chest out to make my breasts look fuller.

"Did you come here with someone?"

I nod. "My husband. He's...watching." I tilt my head slightly, letting my hair cascade over one shoulder.

"Good. That's what makes this special, isn't it?" Justin finally comes to sit on my other side, effectively bracketing me between them. "Knowing he's seeing everything."

My breath catches, and I twine my fingers together in my lap so they can't see I'm trembling. I need to appear confident, in control, even as I'm supposedly surrendering it.

"You seem tense," Justin says and he leans in and kisses the side of my neck. "That defeats the whole purpose."

Maybe if they'd just fuck me, I'd be able to stop thinking and relax. The words catch in my throat—it feels strange, sharing something so personal to strangers—but I force them out anyway. "I'm just—I'm usually the one in charge. At work, at home. Everywhere."

Justin chuckles. "Well, you aren't here."

I immediately want to challenge him because I still feel very much in charge, but Tyler suggests, "Close your eyes." He kisses my neck and his breath is warm. "Don't think about us. Don't think about anyone else. Just feel."

I hesitate, then let my eyelids fall shut. I'm still directing myself—head tilted, lips slightly parted. Tyler continues to kiss my neck while Justin caresses my thigh, slowly moving higher towards my bikini.

"That's it," Justin croons. "No performance necessary."

Their touches stay light, exploratory, while my mind races in a thousand directions. Should I shift to a better angle for them? Am I supposed to be doing more? What do I look like on camera? Is my stomach flat enough like this?

"You're still thinking too much," Tyler observes. "I can practically hear the gears turning."

I laugh despite myself. "Sorry. I'm trying." I force my shoulders to relax, consciously unclenching my jaw. This isn't a board presentation. This is supposed to be surrender.

I sense Tyler's movement and I hear a splash. We're at the shallow end so the water would only be up to his waist. He hooks his fingers into my bikini bottoms and I shift from side to side so he can remove them. It takes extreme effort to not watch him as he parts my legs.

Knowing he's looking at my pussy makes something shift inside me. The constant internal narrator quiets slightly, but doesn't disappear.

"Beautiful." Tyler hums the word, and heat ripples through me as I spread my legs for him.

I moan when he explores the crease of my thigh and his fingers brush my pussy lips. Tyler slides a finger inside me and spreads my wetness to my clit. His strokes make me wiggle against his hand. Nothing is going as I expected, but I'm not complaining.

Justin runs his fingertips from my shoulder to the swell of my breast and my nipples harden, begging for his touch. He pulls my bikini top up and his thumb grazes my nipple. A zing of pleasure heads straight for my clit. Everything they're doing is like a delicious tease that makes me feel more alive.

When Justin tweaks my nipple almost painfully, I gasp. I'm so turned on, the world is a little hazy. He tugs on my other nipple and I bite my lip to hold back my moan. He's hurting me, but it's a pleasurable pain. I wonder if I should let myself be loud—Daniel would probably enjoy hearing me.

"I think..." Justin pauses to pull on my nipple again. "The slut is warmed up. What do you say?"

A surge of heat rushes through me. Oh yeah, I'm warmed up.

Tyler chuckles. "I think you're right." He slides his finger out of me, and I feel a pang of emptiness. But before I can process it, he pulls me into the water with him. The water is the perfect temperature, but it's still a contrast to my overheated skin.

Justin gets up and walks over to the stairs leading into the pool. He sits on one of the steps above the water and takes his cock out of his shorts. "Bring her over here. I want to use her mouth."

Oooh, here we go. Tyler picks me up bridal style and carries me over to Justin. When he sets me down, Justin spreads his legs and I crawl between them. He's high enough on the steps that I have to kneel on one of them. My legs are in the water, but my ass isn't.

I arrange myself carefully—back arched just enough, head at the optimal angle for both pleasure and visual appeal no matter where the cameras are located. Justin holds onto the base of his shaft as Tyler guides my head to it. I part my lips, eager to taste my first cock at the resort. The tip is already slick with pre-cum, and I open wider, taking him in.

My tongue swirls around his shaft, feeling every ridge, every vein. His pre-cum tastes different from Daniel's, which makes this feel dirtier. Daniel better be watching this. I'm being a slut, and I love it.

Tyler pulls my asscheeks apart and angles me so that I'm fully exposed to him. I moan around the cock in my mouth as I imagine he's about to fuck me from behind.

"You should see yourself," Tyler says. "On your knees, cock in your mouth—you're a natural fucktoy."

Knowing that I'm letting two guys I don't know use me makes my head spin, and I feel like this is what I was meant to do. I can't believe how much I'm enjoying this. He's right–I am a natural fucktoy and it's liberating.

Justin tangles his hands in my hair, guiding me up and down his cock. "Suck harder, slut. Give me the best blowjob of your life."

He fucks my mouth and I gag a little. He's not being overly forceful, but it's just enough to make me feel like he's controlling me and making me do what he wants. I don't want him to stop.

Tyler's fingers caress the curve of my ass, dipping between my legs. He finger fucks me with two fingers, stretching me open. "The slut is ready for my cock."

Justin tugs my head up and his cock pops out of my mouth. I gasp for breath, a string of saliva connecting my lips to his shaft. "Tell us what you are," he demands.

I hesitate, my mind racing. Tyler's fingers are still inside me, curling, hitting that spot that makes me writhe as the pressure increases. "I—I'm a slut." The words tumble out. "I'm a fucking slut!"

When Tyler thrusts particularly deep, my mind goes blank for three marvelous seconds.

Justin gives me a wicked grin as he strokes his cock. "That's right. And what do sluts do?"

"They—they fuck and suck."

Tyler finger fucks me faster and harder, and I moan.

"That's right...fuck and suck," Justin says. "And we're going to use your holes because you aren't even really a slut. You're just two holes waiting to be filled with cum."

Oh god, he's right. If there were more men here right now, I'd beg them to line up and use my holes however they wanted. Hell, if I was wearing the green wristband, I'd beg someone to fuck that hole too.

Tyler continues to pump his fingers in and out of my pussy as the rapture builds. I won't be able to hold back my release, and I don't intend to.

"Now say it again." Justin tightens my hair in his fist and pulls my head back, forcing me to look up at him. "Tell us what you are."

"I'm just two holes for cum," I gasp out, the admission making my pussy clench with desire.

Justin's grip tightens as he pushes my head back down to his cock. "Now do your job so I can blow my load down your pretty little throat."

I eagerly take him back into my mouth as Tyler removes his fingers from my pussy. The head of his cock nudges my entrance before he slams into me. I'm shoved forward onto Justin's cock and the bliss is so intense, I almost come right then. For a brief moment, my mind quiets again from the overwhelming sensation of being filled from both ends.

"Fuck, this hole is tight." Tyler drives into me and each thrust makes me tremble from joy.

Suddenly, I really am nothing but two holes as Justin grips my head, guiding me to match their rhythm while they take their pleasure from me.

"Such a good fucktoy," Justin groans, and I suck harder on his cock in response. Daniel better not be missing this, and I hope he's got his cock out. I imagine how we must look on camera—me sandwiched between two men.

"Fuck, I'm close," Tyler grunts, his thrusts growing rougher. He drives into me hard, his cock throbbing as he spills hot cum inside me, tipping me over the edge. Rapture crashes through me as I moan around Justin's cock, trembling with pleasure.

Justin holds my head still as he thrusts into my throat. "Swallow it all, slut," he commands, and his cock spasms as his cum coats my throat and tongue. I swallow as quickly so I don't lose a drop.

When they both pull out of me, I'm still trembling with aftershocks of pleasure. Justin scoops me up from the water, cradling me to his chest as he carries me to the lounge chair and eases me down gently. Tyler disappears for a moment before returning with bottled water.

He opens it for me and puts it in my hand. "Drink up. We won't leave you until we know you'll be okay."

I hold in a giggle and take a sip. When I rest back and close my eyes, the water bottle is removed from my hand. I'm floating in a haze of happiness when I hear the slap of leather on the pavement.

"Hi guys. I'm her husband. I'll take it from here."

My bikini top is still pulled up and my bottoms are by the edge of the pool. I'm wet, and I'm sure my hair is a mess. I crack an eye open and beam at Daniel. "Hi!"

He leans down and gives me a thorough kiss that makes my insides simmer. "Hi, my slut."

Yeah, he's definitely earning himself a reward today.

The guys say their goodbyes to us, and Justin winks at me before they both turn and head down the path. There's a lingering warmth in my cheeks and a neediness between my legs.

"Ready to go back to our room?" Daniel asks, and by his tone I can tell he's turned on. Oh yeah, he saw the entire thing.

I nod, still feeling a bit dazed. He helps me up and holds me steady as I put my bikini bottoms back on and adjust my top. He wraps a towel around me that he must have brought with him.

Once my sandals are on, I lean into him, inhaling his familiar, comforting scent. I just got spit-roasted by two guys, and now it feels like I'm home as Daniel slings his arm around my waist. As we walk, his thumb strokes my hip and my desire grows.

Back in the villa, Daniel takes me straight to the bed. He sits down, pulling me to stand between his legs. "Tell me what you felt."

Oh god, how do I even begin to explain it? "It was like I was completely out of control, and it was incredible."

It might have been brief, but those few moments when my mind finally went quiet...that was something else entirely.

His voice roughens with hunger. "And what are you now?"

"Oh..." I feel myself blushing. "You could hear us too?"

"I heard everything." His gaze is unyielding, coaxing the truth from me.

"I'm a slut. Your slut."

A slow smile spreads across his face. "That's right."

He slides his hands up to cup my breasts, and I moan as he plays with my nipples.

"And what does a slut need?" His voice is husky, and I arch into his touch.

"She needs to be fucked by her husband."

He chuckles. "That's right, my love. And I'm going to fuck you. But first..." He rises to his feet and turns me toward the bed.

When he bends me over, I brace my palms against the mattress to steady myself. He tugs my bikini bottoms down, baring my still-wet pussy.

"First..." He trails his fingers along my soaked folds. "I want to watch my cock slide into your well-used pussy. I want to see their cum dripping out of you as I fuck you."

Oh god, that's hot. I glance back at him and give my ass a teasing wiggle. After the experience I just had, the filthy words slip out easier than I ever imagined. "Then do it. Fuck your slut. Use me like the fucktoy I am."

He pulls his shorts down and when the tip of his cock nudges at my pussy, I face forward and just enjoy the moment. He rubs my clit with the head of his cock before sliding in. I moan loudly when he bottoms out, and I can tell I'm going to come quickly.

He leans over me, grabbing my swinging breasts and pulling at my nipples while he fucks me. I can feel wetness leaking out of me, and I imagine it's Tyler's cum as a surge of delight ripples through me.

"That's it," Daniel growls. "Take my cock like the good little slut you are."

I moan, the sound caught between a gasp and a cry as I come undone. For a glorious moment, my mind goes completely silent before I chant, "Fuck me, fuck me," as I slam back towards him, greedy for every moment of bliss.

"Fuuuuck, Mandy," He groans and explodes inside me. He spasms and jerks, mixing his cum with Tyler's.

When he's done, he withdraws and we collapse onto the bed into each other's arms.

"My good little slut," he says, his voice soft and sated.

If I had known he was going to fuck me a bunch this weekend, I would have been even more eager to get here. This is the best of both worlds. Is he going to keep going crazy after other guys use me? It's wonderful.

I smile as my eyes flutter closed. Yep, I am his slut. And this slut still has another day to try to find that elusive moment when my mind finally, completely shuts off. I drift off to sleep, eager for what tomorrow will bring.

Chapter 4

The next day, Daniel and I have breakfast in the dining room at the main building. He enjoyed watching so much last night that he wants to do it again today. After we eat, I slip away from the table, leaving Daniel chatting with another couple.

I have a plan. There are plenty of intriguing areas at the resort, but when I looked at the map this morning, something called 'The Secluded Grotto' caught my attention.

As I stroll through manicured gardens, I daydream about what someone could do to me in all the hidden alcoves on the property. The morning is warm and I'm wearing a sundress with no panties—easy access. My pink and black wristbands are clearly visible. I'm impatient. This is our last day and I need more cocks.

The path descends between two large boulders, and I hear the sound of trickling water before I see the source. The grotto opens up—a natural stone enclosure with a small waterfall feeding into a pool. Lounges surround the water, and discreet lighting illuminates the space despite the overhead canopy of trees.

I pause at the entrance. Three men occupy different spots around the pool. One is sprawled out on a chair reading—he's shirtless, his shorts riding low on narrow hips. Another floats lazily in the water. The third stands near the waterfall, adjusting something on the wall—a control panel of some kind.

They notice me simultaneously. The shift in energy is immediate—their casual postures tightening with interest, and they track my movements as I step fully into the grotto.

"Good morning," I say, hiding my anticipation behind my marketing executive voice. I'm a woman on a mission to get fucked, and hopefully these guys provide.

The man by the waterfall approaches first. He stands close enough that I catch his scent—clean, with hints of sandalwood.

"I'm Miguel." He gestures to the others. "That's Chris in the pool and Ben on the lounge."

I sound surprisingly breathy when I introduce myself. "I'm Mandy."

Miguel smiles and slides his hand down my back before moving lower to cup my ass. "The grotto has some interesting features. Would you like a tour?"

"I'd like that." I don't add what I'm really thinking: as long as it ends with a cock in me.

Miguel guides me toward the waterfall. "The water temperature is adjustable," he says, motioning to the control panel. Then he gestures to the curved alcoves carved into the wall, each one deep enough to fit multiple people, with cushions tucked inside. "These are designed for privacy...or for certain positions," he adds, his tone suggestive.

"The acoustics are great too," Chris adds, emerging from the pool. Water streams down his chest while his shorts cling to his powerful thighs. "Sounds don't carry beyond the grotto."

I notice small cameras around the space, and my clit throbs at the sight of them. Someone could be watching right now—Daniel, other guests, maybe even staff. The thought of being their entertainment, their live sex show, gives me a naughty thrill.

"This dress looks lovely," Miguel says as he fingers the thin straps on my shoulders. "But it's unnecessary."

He slides the straps down my arms and I remain still as he undresses me. The fabric pools at my feet, leaving me naked except for my sandals and the bands around my wrist.

"Beautiful from behind as well," Ben comments, approaching me.

Hands touch me from multiple directions—Miguel traces my collarbone with his fingers, while Ben palms my ass and Chris plays with my nipples. I stand still, fighting the urge to tell them where to touch me.

"Do you know how the resort makes sure you get what you want?" Miguel asks, his lips brushing my neck.

What? No—how would I know? My mind scrambles for an answer, but I come up empty. When I stay silent, he goes on, his voice a dark, teasing purr. "We're given pictures of all the women guests and their list of what they want done to them."

Of course. I mean, I filled out the questionnaire when I booked, so I should have guessed there was a system behind it. But somehow, it hadn't crossed my mind that the staff would have studied my answers so thoroughly. They know. They *really* know. My throat tightens, and I swallow hard, suddenly unsure what to say.

He kisses the other side of my neck. "As soon as you walked into the grotto, I already knew you were Mandy—the fucktoy slut who wants to be used by every man she can possibly take."

Hearing him say it out loud sends a zing of pleasure straight to my clit. Miguel's voice is hypnotic, sinking under my skin. "You want to stop thinking all the time. Let's see if we can help with that."

He guides me toward one of the alcoves and pushes me down onto the cushion. The space is big enough for several people to share, and I lie back.

"Sometimes the body needs to overwhelm the mind." Miguel kneels in front of me and prods my legs open.

His breath is hot against my inner thigh, and I can already feel the wetness pooling between my legs. He doesn't tease or build up slowly—he dives right in, his tongue flat and firm as it drags over my clit.

"Fuck," I gasp, my body jolting upward.

He holds my hips firmly. "Stay still," he orders, his voice muffled. "You're not going anywhere until I say so."

The other men join me in the alcove, their hands roaming over me. Ben cups my breast and plays with my nipple, while another hand, rougher and more insistent, grips my jaw and turns my face towards him.

"Look at me," Chris demands. "I want to see your face when you come."

Miguel's tongue works my pussy relentlessly, and each lick is a jolt of pleasure. I'm quickly coiling tighter and tighter. Ben pinches my nipples, rolling them between his fingers until my breasts feel heavy and full. Chris's grip on my jaw tightens, his thumb brushing over my bottom lip.

"You like being watched, don't you?" Chris murmurs. "You're on camera and the entire resort could be watching this right now."

My breath is ragged and I can't answer. It's true. Even though it was a fantasy of mine, I didn't even know how much I'd enjoy knowing that someone other than Daniel might watch me. The cameras transform this private moment into a performance, and I'm the star. My body responds to the invisible audience, growing wetter, more sensitive with each passing second.

For a brief moment, as Miguel's tongue works me over, the constant commentary in my head falters before the familiar voice returns.

Gasp and show your pleasure. Make him know you like it.

He flicks his tongue faster, his hands sliding under my ass to lift me closer to his mouth. When he sucks on my swollen bundle of nerves, I detonate. I cry out as ecstasy makes my entire body undulate. Miguel doesn't let up, and he licks me through the cascade of bliss. Ben's fingers tighten on my nipples, sending a sharp burst of pain that only intensifies the delight.

When my orgasm finally subsides, I'm panting and limp. Miguel sits back with a smug grin, his lips glistening. Oh yeah, he knows he did a good job.

If someone had asked me a week ago if I thought the guys would go down on the women here, I would have said it was doubtful. But in my post-orgasmic haze it's crystal clear that this weekend might be about using the women, but it's really all about our pleasure. Every woman should spend a weekend here–hell, multiple weekends. This is my new favorite vacation destination.

"We're not done with you yet." Chris's tone leaves no room for doubt.

He releases my jaw and shoves his shorts down, then covers me with his weight, pinning me. My breath catches as he pushes his knee between my thighs, opening them wider. His thick cock probes my entrance, and my desperation builds.

Oh god, I want this—*need* this.

When he drives into me, I gasp. He feels impossibly thick–maybe thicker than anyone I've fucked before. My moan bounces off the grotto walls, loud and shameless, as he fucks me with furious intensity. Each thrust sends a jolt of wild pleasure through me, rattling my bones, scrambling my thoughts until there's nothing left but the feeling of him pounding deep inside me.

"Do you like my cock?" he grunts. "Do you like knowing your husband is listening to you moan like a little slut for someone else?"

"Yes," I confess breathlessly, my cheeks flushing with arousal. I cling to his shoulders as he takes what he wants. The sound of flesh meeting flesh fills the air, punctuated by his harsh breaths and my continual moans.

"Fuck yes," he hisses, his pace quickening. "Take every fucking inch."

I frantically meet every thrust. When he rocks against a particularly good spot, I whimper, "Please."

"Please what? You want to come? Earn it."

I wrap my legs around his thighs and close my eyes as he pummels into me. He's fucking me so hard, I feel like a rag doll being tossed around. I'm writhing and I cling to him as I'm lost in a sea of bliss.

"Come for me, you filthy little slut."

I convulse as ecstasy short circuits my brain. My mind goes completely blank. No direction, no analysis—just pure, raw pleasure flooding my body. Then awareness returns and he's filling me with his warm seed.

Before I can even process what's happening, I'm rolled onto my stomach. Ben moves behind me, and then I feel him slide his cock deep inside my pussy. Pleasure surges through me, drowning out the voice in my head once again, and for a few heavenly moments, I exist only in my body.

"There she goes," Miguel hums approvingly. "Our mindless fucktoy."

The truth of his words jolts me, snapping me back to awareness—but the pull of that freedom, of being nothing but sensation, is too strong to resist. It tempts me, lures me back toward that perfect, empty state.

Another orgasm crashes into me like a freight train, tearing a scream from my throat.

"Fuck, fuck, fuck," Ben chants, and he drills into me a few more times before roaring as he unloads, adding his cum into my already well-lubricated pussy.

He rolls off me and I moan softly as I'm flipped over again. Miguel is standing next to me, jerking off. I giggle as three shots of cum hit my stomach. He strokes himself, milking out every drop and I move my fingers down to lazily swirl the cum around on my skin.

For a moment, the four of us are quiet. I'm completely happy and sated. It's crazy how an orgasm can quiet my mind.

Miguel breaks the silence first, and his voice is soft and teasing. "You're a mess."

"Mmm hmm, but so good," I giggle.

Chris hands me a cold bottle of water from somewhere. The service at this resort is wonderful. I could come here whenever I needed to unwind.

"Are you going to be okay?" Chris asks, and I know someone would stay with me if I wanted them to.

"I'm fine. I'm going to rest for a minute."

They leave me to recover, and I sit in the alcove, sipping water, processing what just happened. The breakthrough moments when my mind went silent replay in my memory—precious seconds of only physical existence.

I hear footsteps and Daniel is walking towards me. "I saw every filthy moment."

He sits next to me and kisses me. When we break apart, I sigh, "I'm glad."

"You were so beautiful, baby."

His praise warms me, and I yawn. "I think your beautiful slut needs a nap already."

"Yeah," he kisses my temple. "My baby needs to be ready for the Roman Bacchanal tonight."

I might not have been able to fully let go while the guys fucked me in the grotto, but I can tell I'm getting closer to complete surrender. Maybe if something wild happens at the party, I finally can.

Daniel helps me to my feet. "Let's go take a nap together. I'm not going to fuck you again until later tonight."

His statement makes me giggle as I slip my dress back on. If he wants to deny himself the pleasure, I won't stop him. Plus, I might be too tired unless he just ruts away while I sleep. My pussy briefly tries to stir alive at the thought.

Yep, I'm still a slut.

CHAPTER 5

The gossamer toga they've provided for tonight's Bacchanal barely qualifies as clothing. The white fabric is so sheer the pink areolas of my nipples are visible. I don't want anything to stop a cock from sliding into me, so I don't wear panties beneath the thin fabric.

I braided my blonde hair into a crown, the tight plaits keeping the strands off my neck, though I can feel the occasional loose tendril brushing my shoulder. I've paired the toga with flat sandals that I can remove easily. For once, I don't check my reflection before we leave. There's no need—tonight isn't about how I look, it's about how I feel.

Daniel entwines his arm with mine and we follow a torchlit path to the courtyard being used for the event. When we get there, I'm impressed—flowing white drapes create the illusion of intimacy, with lounging areas surrounding a central space.

In the middle of the courtyard, a raised platform holds a woman stretched out for all to see. She writhes beneath two men, her moans echoing through the night air. I can't look away–the arch of her back, the way her fingers clutch the marble as pleasure overtakes her.

There's a sharp, insistent throb between my legs. I can almost feel the hard stone beneath my own skin, the intensity of being the center of everyone's attention as dozens of strangers watch the men fuck me. I've never admitted it to anyone, not even Daniel, but being observed has always been a feature in my deepest fantasies.

I want that.

The possibility fills me with a desperation I can't shake. I want to be the one shamelessly sprawled out while every eye in the courtyard watches. I want to feel the exhilaration of being on display. Desire threatens to consume me, and I can barely keep my feet from moving toward the platform.

The woman moans again. She's on her hands and knees now as a guy fucks her ass. A bolt of arousal shoots straight to my core, and my hand instinctively goes to my wrist. No green band. I wore the pink and black again, thinking it would be enough. But now—now I want more.

"That's where I want to be," I whisper, nodding toward the slab.

Daniel's fingers tighten around my arm. "I'd love to see you up there. I wonder how they choose the woman."

Sophia appears beside us. "That honor is reserved for our most adventurous guests." She gestures toward it. "Would you like to take a turn there when she's finished?"

"Yes." The word pops out without hesitation.

"Perfect. Enjoy yourself, and I'll come find you when it's time."

As she glides away, Daniel kisses my forehead. "Someone is feeling brave tonight."

I give him a smile as I take in the scene around us. A woman kneels before three men near a fountain, sucking their cocks in turns while her partner watches. Another couple has abandoned their clothing, and he's fucking her against a pillar while her legs are wrapped around him.

I don't know why I want to be in the center of everything. Fantasizing about it and actually doing it are very different things. I enjoy the attention of being the boss at work, but I didn't know it would translate to wanting people to watch me getting railed in multiple holes.

A swell of lust and determination drifts over me. "It's just something I need to do."

I'm already imagining myself up there and my analytical mind kicks into high gear, planning how I'll move and perform.

Daniel pulls me into his arms. "You're thinking too much."

"Maybe." I don't want him to question me too much, so I try to distract him. "Hey, does this seem like an orgy to you?"

He looks around and snorts. "Yes, except none of the men are playing together."

Oh, he has a good point. I read in the brochure that they have other monthly freeuse weekends for various desires. I bet some of them get crazy...though having a platform for a woman to be ravished upon isn't exactly tame.

The screams of pleasure from the woman as she's getting fucked in the ass make me whisper to Daniel, "I wish I'd worn the green band."

Daniel laughs, slipping his hand under his toga. I know he's wearing shorts beneath it since he didn't want to free-ball it.

"You mean this?" He holds up the green wristband.

My eyes widen. "You brought it?"

"Yep, just in case my slut wanted it in all her holes."

Okay, yeah, he's the best husband ever. I pull the black and pink bands off and exchange the green one with him.

He gives me a sly grin. "Now you're truly free to do whatever you want."

The weight of the band feels like permission to surrender completely. This is what I want—what I *need*. And now, nothing's holding me back... well, except for one thing. I could really use a drink. Being a slut is thirsty work.

I tug Daniel over to the refreshment table, and admire the marble surface as we approach. The male bartender smiles as I pick up a glass of grape juice. The tart sweetness slides down my throat while Daniel chats with the bartender.

A firm hand lands on my shoulder, making me gasp in surprise and drawing Daniel's attention. I glance over my shoulder—it's Miguel from earlier. He guides me forward until I'm against the table. I quickly set the glass down, and the bartender whisks it away without a word, as if this happens all the time.

Before I know it, I'm bent over—just a dirty plaything for him to use. My gaze drops to the marble beneath me, the veins in the stone swirling like my scattered thoughts. I clutch the edge of the table as Miguel yanks my toga up to my waist.

"I didn't get to use your pussy and I regretted it," he says as an explanation, and I rest my head on the marble as his hard length slides inside me.

The pleasure makes me gasp, and I clench around him instinctively. He immediately sets a steady rhythm, each thrust shoving me forward slightly. The fabric of my toga is so thin that my nipples brush the cool marble as he fucks me. Sparks of pleasure ripple through me as the delight builds in my core.

I surrender fully to the feeling of being used. I might never have this experience again, and I want to savor it. Each thrust hits a magical spot deep inside me, a pleasure that grows and grows but never quite gets me there.

When Miguel speeds up his thrusts, I know he's close. He finishes with a low groan, his body shuddering. When he pulls out, I straighten up slowly, a trickle of cum trailing down my inner thigh. Holy fuck, this is dirty. Ugh, and I was so damn close to coming.

He straightens his clothes and smiles at me. "Thanks for the second chance."

I barely get out a, "You're welcome," before he turns and heads off.

Daniel kisses my forehead. "You okay?"

"Yeah," I say, though the word feels inadequate. I'm more than okay. I'm restless, eager, and thrumming with unspent energy. "I'm ready for my turn on the platform."

He hugs me tightly. When his hard cock brushes against my stomach, I can't resist rubbing him through his toga and shorts.

"Behave." He grabs both my wrists, pulling them up and holding them between us.

Sophia materializes beside us again. "Mandy, they're ready for you."

Oooh, it's showtime. My heart races as Daniel takes my hand. Each step toward the marble slab feels momentous, and desire simmers in my veins. I've never had sex in front of an audience before this weekend, and doing something this public seems like jumping into the deep end. But I'm ready for it.

"Just relax and enjoy," Sophia says as we reach the platform. "Daniel, you can watch from here." She indicates a cushioned area right next to where I'll be. It's practically within arm's reach with an unobstructed view. "And these gentlemen have expressed interest in joining you."

Five men stand nearby—all attractive, all clearly aroused beneath their togas. I recognize Tyler and Justin from the pool earlier. The others are new faces, new bodies.

I kick off my sandals and the marble is cool beneath my bare feet as I climb the steps. Without prompting, I untie the knot at my shoulder, letting my toga fall to the ground. I'm naked now except for the green wristband, and I lie back on the stone.

Stomach in. Arch your back just enough. Legs at the most flattering angle.

The first man approaches, naked. He kneels between my legs without a word, spreading my thighs wider. I look toward Daniel and blow him a kiss. He's already got his hand beneath his toga and I can see it moving as he strokes himself. Dang, he's not wasting any time. I get a little zing of lust from knowing he's going to touch himself while these men use me.

The man's mouth latches onto my pussy and I moan in surprise. He licks me like he's starving, alternating between giving his attention to my pussy and then twirling his tongue around my clit. He works me into a frenzy, and I lift my hips to meet his mouth, my body already begging for more. This guy is a master at oral. He knows exactly what he's doing, with the way he sucks my clit between his lips and teases me with his tongue.

"Fuck, you're dripping," he growls. "Such a dirty little slut for us, aren't you?"

I moan in response as another man kneels near my head. His cock is inches from my lips, and I open wide. He slides inside my mouth, and I savor the salty taste of his precum. He's rock hard, the veins pulsing beneath my tongue as I lick the sensitive underside. His cock twitches in response, and he grips the sides of my head to control the rhythm.

"That's it, fucktoy," he rasps. "Show me how much you love sucking cock."

I do enjoy sucking cock. There's nothing more powerful than making a guy come with my mouth. I relax my throat and my lips stretch around his girth. He groans, and I hollow my cheeks, sucking harder as he steadily thrusts into my throat.

The man between my legs redoubles his efforts, plunging his tongue deep while his fingers spread my pussy lips wide. Air sweeps over my slick folds, making me shiver. His thumb finds my clit, circling it in slow, relentless strokes, and sparks of pleasure ripple through me.

"Fuck, you taste good." His breath is a warm puff against my wet flesh.

His tongue fucks me with long strokes. I can feel every flick, every greedy suck as he devours me. The wet sounds of my sucking and the man's tongue lapping at my pussy are loud enough that Daniel can probably hear them—a symphony of filth.

Keep your neck at this angle. Use your hand like this. Make eye contact—men love that.

My internal director continues as Justin begins caressing my breasts and pulling on my nipples. Tyler strokes himself, waiting his turn.

"Look at you," Tyler murmurs. "Still a good little fucktoy."

I'm performing well—I know I am. Their groans and praise confirm it. But I'm still *performing*.

The man between my legs stands and pushes my knees toward my chest. As I'm folded up like this, he has total control over depth and speed. He slides inside me and when he bottoms out, stars pop on the edge of my vision. I moan around the cock in my mouth and I feel a mental shift. Suddenly, I'm not thinking about every move. I'm feeling–experiencing–just being in the moment.

"Fuck, you feel so good," the guy in my pussy grunts as he hammers into me. "Such an eager little slut."

I can't say anything since my mouth is full, but when the guy fucking my pussy groans loudly, I feel his warm cum coating my insides. How many loads of cum is this now since breakfast? Three in my pussy–four? How many in my mouth? I don't even know.

The men trade places. Now Tyler fills my mouth while Justin fucks my pussy. A third guy takes over playing with my breasts, pinching and pulling hard enough to make me whimper.

"You like that, don't you?" he says, twisting my nipple. "You're a little pain slut."

Oh, fuck. I think I might be. The other men surround me. The sensations are overwhelming now. Rough hands roll me over, force me onto my hands and knees. A thick cock slides into my pussy from behind. Another probes my mouth, demanding entry. I open wide, taking it deep into my throat. Hands grip my waist, my hair, my breasts—every part of me. This is exactly what I wanted, what I craved.

"Look at you," one of them growls. "Fucked and filled like the dirty little slut you are."

A hard thrust makes me cry out, and I realize I'm not in control here. I really am their fucktoy. My pleasure builds, drowning out everything but the need to be used. I imagine Daniel watching and stroking himself. I want him to enjoy seeing me like this, completely at their mercy.

"Spread her ass," another voice demands, and cold lube drips between my cheeks. A finger circles my tight hole, bearing down, stretching me. I gasp as I adjust to the feeling of a finger in my ass, and the cock in my mouth explodes. I swallow all I can, but when he pulls out, saliva mixed with cum drips down my chin.

"Relax, slut. You're going to take my cock in your ass while they fuck your pussy and mouth."

The finger withdraws, and for the briefest moment, I'm left achingly empty—every hole wanting, desperate. I don't even have time to mourn the loss before the man playing with my ass stands on the platform and I feel him crouching over me.

The blunt head of his cock presses against my tight rim, inching in slowly, stretching me wider with every breath. *Oh god.* I brace for the burn, tensing on instinct, as I clench around him. I force myself to relax, to open. *Take it. You can take it.*

And I do.

My muscles give way, surrendering to the slow, steady invasion, and heat floods through me. Before I can even settle into the stretch, the other cock drives back into my pussy, harder this time. The dual onslaught steals my breath, sends my mind spinning.

Then there's another cock at my lips, and I don't hesitate—I open eagerly, hungry for more, for *everything.* I suck him deep, my tongue swirling greedily around the thick head, as my body is used front and back.

"Nothing like a tight ass," the man behind me groans. "Feel that, slut? That's all your holes filled."

I can't respond–the bliss is beyond anything I've ever felt. My world narrows to the fullness, and the pleasure borders on pain. The courtyard buzzes with low voices as strangers watch. I imagine them greedily tracking every thrust. I've never felt more free. More present. More myself.

I force myself to look, needing to witness their attention. Dozens of faces stare back—some with parted lips, others with flushed cheeks. A woman whispers to her partner while pointing at me, and knowing that I'm the subject of their conversation makes my pussy clench around the cock inside me. I've spent my life performing at work, but never like this, never so exposed.

And in that moment, I come undone. The climax is a massive explosion, and ecstasy consumes me from the inside out. I twitch with such force that the guys have to shift their positions to keep fucking me.

The pleasure is never ending as I scream around the cock in my mouth. The men fuck me through the bliss and when one guy fills one of my holes with cum, another guy immediately replaces him.

Time loses meaning. Men come and go. I'm moved around, filled again, used in ways I've only fantasized about. Fingers grip my hair, my breasts, and my nipples while I revel in every nasty thing they do to me. Cocks fill my mouth, my pussy, my ass, pounding me, using me until I'm a sweat-slicked, trembling mess.

At some point, I'm aware of Daniel approaching. The knowledge that he's been watching everything—seeing his wife become a spectacle for strangers—intensifies every moment.

He strokes my face tenderly. "You're my gorgeous, filthy slut."

Then he's gone, returning to his seat, leaving me with these strangers who still want to fill me with their cum. And I take it all, my mind blank, my soul alive.

I lose count of the number of times I come, and I don't know how many men use me. It doesn't matter.

When the final wave of pleasure crashes through me, I give in completely. My body arches off the slab, and a sound I don't recognize tears from my throat. Nothing exists beyond this moment.

There is only sensation.

Only surrender.

Later—minutes or hours, I can't tell—Daniel helps me get down. I'm covered in drying cum and more drips out of me.

"You're so beautiful," he whispers as he wraps my toga around me, not bothering to adjust it properly.

When my legs shake and it's difficult to take a step, he picks me up. I wrap my arms around him, boneless and sated.

As Daniel holds me, I realize what I've discovered extends beyond sex. That voice in my head has controlled every aspect of my life. The freedom I found in those moments of silence is something I can take back with me, and truly experience life rather than just direct it.

But first, this slut needs her husband's cock inside her. "Take me to our room and fuck me."

CHAPTER 6

Daniel carries me inside the villa, kicking the door shut behind us. His mouth finds mine in a hungry, desperate kiss. I cling to him, my fingers digging into the muscles of his shoulders. He tastes like grape juice and desire, and I can't get enough.

"Mandy," he moans against my lips. "Watching you tonight—"

"Mmm, I was your good slut."

"You were."

He carries me to bed and sets me down, pulling off my hastily-wrapped toga before laying me back. Then he's sliding my thighs open, exposing my pussy.

"You were so fucking sexy. The way you'd moan and whimper as they fucked you."

My heartbeat kicks into overdrive at the memories of being completely, utterly used.

"I need you," I whisper. "Just you."

He sinks to his knees in front of me, and his breath is warm as he leans in. He doesn't touch me with his mouth, but instead, he stares at my pussy.

"God," he murmurs, and I swear I hear awe in his voice. "You're absolutely drenched."

I squirm under his scrutiny from a mix of embarrassment and arousal. "Because of you. Because you watched me."

His fingers trace the seam of my pussy, teasing me with his feather-light touch. "I can't believe how much cum you took. It's fucking incredible."

He slides one finger inside me, then another, moving slowly. The wetness makes obscene sounds as he finger fucks me, his gaze never leaving my pussy. Holy fuck, this is dirty.

"Daniel," I moan, desperate for more.

He curls his fingers inside me, finding that spot that makes my vision blur. The room fills with the sounds of my ragged breaths as the pleasure builds with each thrust of his fingers.

"Come for me," he commands. "Let me see it."

I come hard, convulsing as my pussy grips his fingers. Wetness coats his hand as he strokes me through my orgasm. When I'm a trembling mess beneath him, he finally pulls his hand away.

"Now it's my turn."

All I can do is lie there and welcome him into my arms. Within moments he's naked and thrusting into me. He's crazed as he jackhammers my sodden pussy.

"Fuck, you feel so good," he moans. Knowing I'm full of so much cum sends a zing of delight through me.

He sets a punishing pace, driving into me again and again. The bed creaks and the sound of our bodies slapping together echoes through the room.

There's another orgasm building as my husband turns feral and growls, "This pussy belongs to me."

His fingers dig into my hips and each thrust is brutal, claiming, as if he's trying to fuck the memory of every other cock out of me.

"Say it," he groans. "Tell me who you belong to."

"You," I gasp, my body quivering with the force of his thrusts. "I belong to you."

He's relentless, and he snarls, "That's right. This pussy is mine. Always has been. Always will be."

Holy fuck, who is this man? This is incredible. I can barely breathe, I'm overwhelmed by the sheer magnitude of his need to own me.

"You're my little slut, aren't you? My fucktoy. My dirty little wife."

I moan, "Yes, your dirty wife."

His cock swells inside me, his veins dragging against my sensitive inner walls. "You love being used. Love being filled with cum, over and over again."

"Yes, yes, yes!" I cry out, my nails clawing at his back. "Love it. Need it."

He suddenly slows down and fucks me with long, slow thrusts. "You're a greedy little thing, aren't you? Can't get enough cock. Can't get enough cum."

My muscles tighten with every filthy word. "Please," I beg, though I don't know what I'm asking for. More of him. More of this. More of everything.

"You want to come again, don't you? Want to come all over my cock like the good little slut you are."

"Yes," I whimper and try to meet him thrust for thrust. "Make me come. Please, make me come."

He slides his hand between us, and rubs my clit exactly how he knows I like it. I'm trembling and my toes curl as he speeds up his thrusts again.

"It's time for my fucktoy to come."

He slams into me and I squeal as my climax obliterates everything from my mind. My vision goes white, the world reduced to the swirling pleasure between my legs. I scream his name, my pussy clamping down on his cock.

"Fuck yes," he roars, his body tensing above me. He slams into me one last time, burying himself deep. The heat of his cum fills me, mixing with the others', claiming me completely. Each spurt of his cum creates a shockwave of pleasure, and I shake with the force of it.

When he's done unloading, we collapse together, our bodies slick with sweat and trembling with exertion. He keeps his cock buried inside me, as if he can't bear to let me go.

"Mine," he murmurs. "You're mine, Mandy. Always."

"Always," I whisper back, basking in the warmth of his possession, and knowing that just as much as I'm his, he's also mine.

He rolls off me, but his arm stays locked around my waist, pulling me tight against him. His heat surrounds me, and my mind wanders, already imagining the way I'll tell my friends about this place. No one will believe me unless they come and see it for themselves.

But that's for tomorrow. Tomorrow, I'll tell the world.

I think back to the deal he made me yesterday—promising to make up for every orgasm I felt I missed on this trip. He's probably feeling pretty smug right now, assuming he's off the hook.

Maybe I'll let him think that.

Or maybe I'll wake him up in the morning with his cock in my mouth and remind him, properly, that he still owes me. And I expect him to pay up. *Hard.*

As I drift toward sleep in Daniel's arms, I realize I've found what I truly came here for—not just the thrill of being used by strangers, but those perfect moments when the constant voice in my head finally went quiet. For the first time ever, I'm simply *being.*

What an amazing journey.

The End

Her Freeuse Retreat

Hotwife Shared in Public

CHAPTER 1

"You will not believe the weekend I just had." My friend Mandy leans across the table, her voice a conspiratorial whisper.

I arch a brow and set down my iced tea. "Judging by that tone, I'm guessing it wasn't spent organizing your sock drawer."

"Not exactly." Mandy drops her gaze to the table, fingers tracing the rim of her margarita glass. "Daniel and I visited a resort on the coast. Think 'luxury meets freeuse fantasy'."

My pulse stutters. "Freeuse?" I know exactly what it means thanks to our mutual friend Alyssa who visited a freeuse resort last year. I just didn't expect to hear Mandy, of all people, use the term casually during lunch. She's always in control, and I can't imagine her letting go.

"Yep, it was..." She searches for the right word. "Liberating."

Images flood my mind: men's hands gripping my hips, a stranger pressing me against a wall while others watch, fingers tangling in my hair as I'm kneeling. My skin prickles with heat, and I take a sip of my iced tea to try and cool down.

Mandy looks at me and laughs, delighted. "You're blushing."

"I'm always blushing. It's my default state." I fan myself with a cocktail napkin. God, I hate how transparent I am. Miles says he can read my every thought through the changing colors on my face.

She tilts her head, seeing through my bullshit like she has since we shared a dorm room at college. "You spend your days hanging racy sculptures and paintings without batting an eye."

I busy myself folding my napkin into triangles. "Looking at art isn't the same as doing something in real life." I'd sooner die than admit how often I've imagined being the subject that inspired the artwork.

"Maybe." She nudges my ankle beneath the table. "But just imagine it, Brooklyn. Being watched, praised, and desired. It's perfect for that secret exhibitionist hiding under those buttoned-up cardigans you like to wear."

I'm suddenly glad I left the cardigan in the car. "Right. The exhibitionist in me who still changes in the bathroom stall at the gym." Who keeps the lights off in the bedroom, and never does anything where someone might hear us, let alone see us. The idea is ridiculous. Absurd. Completely at odds with everything I've ever done.

So why is my heart racing at the thought?

"Come on, you get that telltale sparkle in your eye every time we wander through those interactive exhibits with the live models." Mandy waves her hands as she speaks. "Look, I'm not trying to drag you off to a freeuse resort or anything. I'm just saying it was incredible for me. For once, my brain finally switched off. So don't knock it until you try it."

God, what would that feel like? To become the experience itself instead of merely observing it? Miles and I share a good sex life. It's comfortable, loving, and predictable. We move together in a well-rehearsed dance, each knowing exactly which steps lead where. But to have such freedom, and to let others watch....That's something else entirely.

I'm about to ask how much this paradise costs—my salary barely covers rent and student loans—when Mandy's phone buzzes.

"Shit, work emergency." She grimaces, gathering her purse. "Text me if you want more dirty details."

"Maybe I will." I say noncommittally, but curiosity is already gnawing at me, and I know I'll text her later tonight, probably after Miles falls asleep.

After she leaves, my thoughts wander. Would it be weird to go to a resort like the one Mandy went to? Not that I'd seriously consider it, or have the financial means to make it happen. Plus, Miles and I have only joked about me sleeping with other guys. Those late-night whispers when we're fucking and he's asking if I've ever thought about another guy touching me. But that's just fantasy talk. We're not actually adventurous like Mandy and Daniel, or Alyssa and Quentin.

But what is it about these resorts that has two of my closest friends raving? Am I missing something fundamental about life that they've discovered? The thought follows me back to the gallery, nagging at the edges of my mind.

When I get back, the afternoon chaos is in full swing. We're setting up a new installation, and there are crates splintered open and bubble wrap everywhere. One of the staff and an intern are maneuvering a massive, mirrored sculpture toward the center floor. The piece is pure voyeurism with angled panes reflecting anyone who approaches. It catches the light like liquid silver.

"Careful with the corners," I call out, then pivot straight into a solid wall of tailored gray suit.

"Brooklyn." Julian Roche steadies me with a hand on my arm. "Always in motion."

My face heats instantly. "Oops, sorry. Didn't mean to try and knock you over."

Like I could knock Julian over. Julian, with his silver-streaked hair, and the kind of fit body that comes from tennis and sailing rather than a gym membership. He and his wife, Celeste, are two of our top donors and, according to gallery gossip, rich enough to buy the building we're standing in without checking their bank balance.

I tuck a wayward strand of brown hair behind my ear. "You're early for the preview. I wasn't expecting you until later." My voice comes out steadier than I feel. Something about Julian always makes me feel awkward.

"Couldn't stay away." His gaze drifts to the mirrored sculpture.

"How's Celeste? She texted me last week about having to miss the opening." I can feel the color in my cheeks fading, and I relax now that my initial physical reaction to him calms down. Celeste is brilliant, elegant, and refreshingly down-to-earth despite their wealth. She's been my mentor since I started working at the gallery and is always championing my more daring exhibitions when the board gets nervous. "She mentioned a trip?"

"Yes, an island retreat she visits several times a year." Something shifts in his expression—a subtle knowing that makes my pulse speed up. "She'll be disappointed to miss this. Mirrors are a particular fascination of hers."

I switch into curator mode, grateful for the professional shield. "The artist wants viewers to confront their own voyeurism."

"Your instinct for the provocative is why Celeste insisted we support your career."

I feel deeply grateful. Their patronage helped me get this job when I was barely qualified on paper.

"Speaking of provocative," he continues, running a finger along the mirror's surface—those strong fingers. "The retreat Celeste visits is rather focused on that concept."

"Oh?" I try to sound polite, and attempt to pull my gaze away from his hand. The way he's stroking the artwork makes me imagine men stroking me while I watch in a mirror. My body buzzes and I can tell I'm going to turn beet red if I don't get my thoughts under control. What is wrong with me today? First Mandy, now this conversation. Everything is making me think about sex.

He catches my gaze in the mirror. "It's a private retreat in the Grenadines. She says it's a masterpiece of human desire. Watching and being watched. Glass walkways, rooms designed as living galleries. People are free to partake in carnal delights."

My mouth goes dry. I can almost feel the tropical breeze and hear the ocean. "Sounds relaxing." The lie sits awkwardly on my tongue. I'd be a nervous wreck in a place like that, wouldn't I?

"I'm not sure Celeste would call it relaxing, but she thought you'd enjoy the artistry of the resort."

Heat crawls down my spine. "She did?"

"She's always saying everyone should experience being art." His eyes crinkle at the corners. "Especially those who surround themselves with it every day."

Oh God, how did the conversation go in this direction? "I'm not—I don't—" I stammer, not even sure what I'm trying to say, and then force a laugh. "I just hang the paintings, Julian."

I'd sooner walk into traffic than admit that sometimes, late at night, I imagine what it would be like to be one of the models in our live exhibits, admired and desired.

He grins. "Celeste swears every woman deserves a weekend of exploration. My wife is rarely wrong."

Before I can form a coherent reply, he's already strolling toward the office wing, leaving me staring at my flushed reflection in the sculpture's mirror. The woman looking back at me seems different somehow—curious...tempted.

I shake my head and turn away. What the actual fuck? First Mandy at lunch, now Julian and Celeste? Is the universe trying to tell me something? Or do I just give off some vibe that screams "secretly wants to be watched having sex"?

Well, the universe is wrong. And I need to work on getting rid of whatever's causing that vibe. Me going to an adult resort and sleeping with other people? Never in a million years. I'm not sexy enough to be on display, and I'm definitely not the type who knows how to flirt and attract guys. The idea is crazy.

So why can't I stop thinking about it?

CHAPTER 2

Later that night after dinner, I change into my nightshirt and sprawl on the sofa with Miles. It's our usual routine. He scrolls through architectural photos on his tablet while I nurse a glass of cheap red. The pictures on his screen flash by, the sleek buildings with dramatic angles, abandoned factories with light streaming through broken windows. They're all part of his latest commercial project. As an architectural photographer, he has an eye for spaces that most people overlook.

My earlier conversation with Mandy still buzzes in my head, demanding to be shared. "So I had lunch with Mandy today. She told me about this resort she visited."

"Yeah?" Miles doesn't look up, but his thumb pauses on the screen. It's a subtle tell that I've caught his attention.

I spill everything—freeuse, public sex, Julian's comments, Celeste's apparent endorsement, and how the universe keeps tossing the idea in front of me. The words tumble out faster than I can filter them. I'm flushed by the time I finish.

Miles sets the tablet aside and turns his full attention to me. "So basically, these retreats are fancy sex resorts?"

"I guess?" I mumble, picking at a loose thread on the throw pillow. "Very expensive and exclusive ones."

"And you're curious about it." Not a question. His gaze fixes on me with that penetrating intensity that makes me feel transparent.

"I'm completely mortified." I take another gulp of wine, welcoming the bitterness. "Julian Roche of all people practically suggested I should go show off my body in public. Can you imagine?"

Miles's lips quirk up. "Ah, yes, Julian. Should I be jealous that he's inviting my wife to a sex resort?"

"Don't be ridiculous." I swat his arm. "He wasn't inviting me. He was talking about his wife."

"The same Julian and Celeste Roche who sent you those expensive art books. The people you get all flustered around."

"I do not get flustered!" But my voice rises an octave, betraying me.

"Brooklyn." Miles pulls me closer, his fingertip tracing my jaw. "You almost stutter whenever you mention them. It's adorable."

"They're important patrons." My skin tingles under his touch.

"And apparently people who think you should explore your exhibitionist side." His gray eyes soften behind his glasses. "Which, if I'm being honest, is something I've noticed too."

I gape at him. "I've never said anything about being an exhibitionist."

"You didn't have to." His thumb brushes my lower lip, sending a bolt of electricity straight to my core. "I've seen how you look at those performance pieces. How you linger at installations where the audience becomes part of the exhibit."

"That's just professional interest," I insist, but a recognition flutters in my stomach. It's something I don't want to acknowledge.

"Remember our beach trip last year? You begged me to keep the curtains open."

"That was one time. And the nearest house was like half a mile away." My protest sounds weak even to me. My thighs press together, fighting the growing ache between them.

"And remember when I said someone might be watching from the cliffs—that they might see you spread out on the bed, taking my cock." His hand slides up my thigh. "You screamed when you came and said you've never orgasmed so hard."

My clit throbs at the reminder and my breath catches as his hand creeps higher. "Even if I were curious, we can't afford some billionaire sex island."

"I see. So the expense is your only objection?"

I roll my eyes. "You're ridiculous. We're not going to a sex resort." But even as I say it, I imagine strangers touching me and fucking me while Miles watches.

"Hey, you're the one who said the universe was sending you messages. If the universe wants to provide the trip, I'll be there with you."

His fingers keep inching up and they're almost to my pussy when something in my chest unlocks and a wave of love for him washes over me. But instead of saying how much the idea thrills me, I snort. "Okay, sure. As soon as the universe drops an all-expenses-paid trip in our laps, I'll go."

"Maybe the Roches want to take you to one so they can use your delectable body." Miles wiggles his eyebrows, his hand now resting on my pussy, my panties the only thing between him and my wetness.

"Shut up!" I laugh, but my mind races with possibilities—not about the Roches, but about other men fucking me while Miles encourages them. "You're terrible."

"And you're turned on." He tugs me into his lap, the hard ridge of his cock pressing against my pussy as he slides his hand beneath my nightshirt. He traces the underside of my breast, making me arch into his touch. "And I'm very curious to watch my sexy wife discover a new side of herself."

Sexy... right... He kisses my neck, and as his teeth graze my sensitive skin, I close my eyes and imagine being gorgeous enough for strangers to want me and line up to wait for their turn. The fantasy sends a rush of wetness between my legs, and I grind against Miles, suddenly desperate for more than just talking.

"Tell me more," I whisper. "Tell me what you think I want."

Miles growls against my throat, and he cups my breast fully. "I think you want to be the center of attention. You want men's eyes on you, their hands on you." He pinches my nipple and I moan. "I think you want to be used and admired, all while knowing I'm there, loving every second of watching you with them."

I grind against his cock. "And you'd be okay with that? With sharing me?"

"Brooklyn." he breathes my name like a prayer. "I've been trying to get you to consider it for years."

His confession ignites something primal in me. I fumble with his jeans, desperate to get his cock out. He helps me, and once it's free, I push my panties aside and press the tip of his cock against my entrance.

"Maybe we should pretend someone is watching us, and practice for when the universe delivers that trip." I tease myself with just the tip, circling it against my clit before sliding it back to my entrance.

Miles grasps my hips, his eyes darkening behind his glasses. "Practice makes perfect."

He groans as I sink down onto him. I brace my hands on his shoulders as I begin to rock against him.

"Imagine we're in one of those glass villas," he whispers. "People walking by, stopping to watch you ride me."

I daydream of strangers pressing their faces to the glass, their eyes hungry as they watch Miles's cock disappear inside me. I moan and increase my pace, my body tightening around him.

"You'd like that, wouldn't you?" He pushes my nightshirt up and I lift my arms so he can remove it before I grip his shoulders again. He focuses on my breasts, pinching both nipples simultaneously, and I cry out. "You'd like them seeing how beautiful you look when you're being fucked."

"Yes," I moan, finally revealing how much I enjoy the thought. "I want them to watch."

Miles sits up straighter, wrapping an arm around my waist to hold me close as he thrusts up into me. The new angle massages a wonderful spot inside me, and I throw my head back, riding the wave of delight.

"That's it, baby. Let them hear you." His free hand tangles in my hair, pulling just enough to make my scalp tingle. "Show them how good it feels."

I abandon myself to the fantasy, imagining eyes on us from every direction. In my mind, I'm an art piece on display. The thought pushes me closer to the edge.

Miles's thrusts become more urgent. "Touch yourself," he commands. "Let them see you make yourself come on my cock."

My hand slips between us. I'm so sensitive I almost come as soon as I touch my clit. I circle it, matching the tempo of my hips as I ride him.

"That's it," Miles encourages, his voice strained with the effort of holding back. "Show everyone how gorgeous you are when you come."

The pressure builds until it snaps. The pleasure crashes through me, and I moan as my body clenches around him in rhythmic pulses. Miles follows a moment later, groaning as he empties himself inside me.

As we come down, I slump against him and giggle.

"What?" he asks, brushing a strand of hair from my face.

"Nothing. Just wondering what happened to my predictable sex life."

He kisses me gently. "It's still here. We're just adding new dimensions, like when I photograph a building from a different angle and suddenly see something I never noticed before."

I rest my head on his shoulder, feeling content and oddly liberated. "I love you."

"I love you too." He strokes my back lazily. "Enough to share you with the world, if that's what you want."

I don't answer, but the possibility settles into me like a seed taking root.

A week later, an email pings my phone while I'm eating breakfast. My stomach flips as I read it.

> Subject: An invitation to be seen.
> From: Celeste Roche.
>
> Julian mentioned you might be curious, and curiosity should never go unfed. I'm extending a personal, all-expenses-paid invitation for you and your husband to Infinite Gaze Retreat in the Caribbean. Trust me, every woman deserves the chance to experience this.
>
> It's a freeuse resort. Look that up if you don't know what it means and let me know if you want to go.

Below her signature is a digital brochure filled with glass villas, infinity pools, couples strolling through exquisite gardens.

Holy fuck, it's an actual freeuse resort like the one Mandy and Alyssa went to? I set my phone down and stare off into space, trying to imagine what it would be like. That's different from just a casual sex resort where people hook up with other people. Yeah, I can't do this. Right? I'm not the type to let other guys fuck me whenever they want. My hands tremble and I have to remind myself to breathe. An invitation doesn't mean we're going...

But even as panic rises, an undeniable throb of my clit contradicts my hesitation. I want to say yes.

CHAPTER 3

Miles left for work already, and it's a busy day, so I don't have time to talk to him about the invitation until later. I pounce on him as soon as I get home and thrust my phone at him.

"Read this email," I squeak in nervous excitement.

He takes it with him to the living room and sits down on the sofa before scrolling through the message twice. "Private villa. All expenses paid." He looks up with a smile. "Well, that takes care of the money issue."

"Was that really the only thing stopping us?" I mutter.

"Come here." He sets the phone on the coffee table, and when I get close enough, he pulls me down next to him. "Give me your gut reaction. No overthinking."

"My gut is currently hiding under the bed with a blanket over its head." I pull my knees to my chest, making myself small. "Half of me wants to delete the email and pretend it never happened. The other half can't stop picturing other men fucking me while you watch."

"If you want to do it, I'm in."

I meet his eyes. "I'm terrified and stupidly turned on by the whole idea."

"So tell Celeste we accept. Would it be so horrible if we went there and you didn't fuck anyone else? It looks like a gorgeous vacation spot. And it's free."

Heh, he's got a point. "Okay, I'll email her."

The arrangements are surprisingly easy. The Roches really are paying for everything and Miles and I are both able to get time off from our jobs on short notice. Crazy enough, when I tell Alyssa and Mandy about it, I find out this resort is part of the same group of resorts they went to that do freeuse weekends. Talk about a small world.

Three weeks later, luggage covers our bedroom floor. I fold breezy linen sundresses and pack exactly one modest swimsuit since I doubt I'll have the nerve to swim naked. Miles walks in and sets a small bag from my favorite lingerie shop onto the bed. Inside is a sheer cream set.

I hold it up, the fabric nearly invisible between my fingers. "This wouldn't hide a freckle, let alone my entire body."

"That's the point." His eyes take on that focused look he gets when framing a shot. "You'll look gorgeous in it."

I swallow hard, nervousness warring with desire in my brain. "Fine. Into the suitcase of questionable decisions it goes."

We fly commercial to Barbados, then board a charter seaplane. Infinite Gaze Retreat rises from the turquoise water like something from a dream. The villas with walls of glass nestle into the lush green hillsides, and the infinity pools seem to spill directly into the ocean. Even the arrival pier is transparent, and my sandals click on the panels while colorful fish dart beneath my feet. The resort is designed to avoid barriers to block people's sight. I don't even want to know how much this is costing the Roches. I'm not going to think about it and just enjoy the trip.

A concierge in a crisp uniform hands us small boxes containing welcome packets that I know include wristbands to indicate what I'm consenting to for freeuse—black, pink, white, and green. My pulse jumps erratically as I clutch the packet.

Our villa stands on stilts over the water, a glass prism catching every ray of sunlight. The walls switch from opaque to transparent by an app on a tablet in the room. Mirrors hang from the ceiling, turning the massive bed into a stage where every movement becomes visible from multiple angles.

Miles sets down our bags and stretches, rolling his shoulders. "I could get used to luxury like this."

"Is this place a bit much? This seems over the top."

"Hey, just enjoy it. We'll never be able to afford a trip like this again." He picks up the tablet beside the bed and taps the privacy controls. Suddenly, the walls clear completely. Outside, another couple crosses a distant walkway. The woman is completely naked, her body glowing in the late afternoon sun. She's gorgeous and I can't look away.

Miles steps behind me, his hands circling my waist. His mouth is close to my ear. "Remember, you're in control here. You choose what you want to do. I support you fully."

Tipping my head up, I watch our reflection in a mirror on the ceiling. I'm both the viewer and the viewed, and I look turned on. "Mmm, and what if I only want to fuck you and enjoy this luxury resort?"

Miles spins me around and kisses me, before saying, "No rush tonight. Let's just observe and tomorrow you can be a freeuse toy, if you want it."

But I can feel the island humming with energy around us. A yearning deep in my soul awakens. Observer, yes, but I'm hungry for more. It's a desire I've kept hidden for so long.

Tomorrow I'll let other guys fuck me.

CHAPTER 4

The resort brochure unfolds in my hands like a treasure map to forbidden pleasures. Miles stands behind me, his chin resting on my shoulder as we study the layout. "The Living Gallery, The Watchers' Club, observation towers...." I trace each location with my fingertip. "This place is definitely designed for voyeurism."

"Architectural genius," Miles murmurs, his photographer's eye approving of the overall vision. "Where should we start?"

"Wait, we should probably read through the rules first." I pull out the welcome letter from the packet. "Let's make sure we understand how everything works before we wander into something we're not ready for."

Miles scans the page from over my shoulder. "It's only a freeuse event for women this weekend. Any worker or guest who is allowed to use the women wears a yellow wristband after they pass the resort's screening process."

We knew this already, but seeing it laid out still makes me nervous and excited. That screening process was no joke. Miles and I spent nearly two hours filling out their detailed questionnaire about sexual preferences, boundaries, and medical history. Miles and I had laughed about some of the more explicit questions, but now I understand the thoroughness.

When you're running a place where strangers can touch each other, you need to be careful about who you let in.

He continues reading. "All the wristbands are color-coded. No wristband means you're just observing. White means you allow people to take photos of you. Pink allows consent for vaginal sex, black is for oral, and green means—" he pauses, his eyes darkening, "—any hole."

Heat rushes to my face. I wasn't expecting the option of letting people take pictures of me, and I'm definitely not that brave.

I put the map and letter away. "Let's go out and get the lay of the land."

We slather on sunscreen, and once we're ready to explore, we take a glass walkway that curves around the hillside. The Caribbean sun beats down, warming me through my dress. Below us, the sea crashes against rocks in a hypnotic rhythm. But it's not the view that catches my attention—it's the naked couple on a deck beneath us.

The woman kneels before a seated man, her head bobbing between his legs while he reclines, one hand tangled in her hair. I can see everything through the glass floor; the flex of her jaw, the tension in his thighs, the way he wraps her silky blonde hair around his hand and guides her movements.

"Oh!" I stop short, nearly causing Miles to collide with me. "Should we—I mean—are we allowed to just watch?"

Miles grins. "They wouldn't be outside if they didn't want it."

It still feels weird, so I continue walking, but I can't tear my eyes away from the scene below. "Do you think they know we can see them?"

"I don't know. They seem a little busy."

He's right, and I giggle as we continue along the path. We spot more naked couples, and sometimes groups, engaged in various sexual acts. There's a woman bent over a balcony railing while a man takes her from behind, her pink bracelet catching the sunlight as she grips the rail and moans with each thrust. A woman and a man intertwine on a daybed beside a pool, her wearing a green wristband as a man watches from nearby, stroking himself openly.

The women all look so comfortable in their skin, with their toned thighs, flat stomachs, and breasts that don't sag without a bra. I glance down at my own body, hidden beneath my modest sundress. It would be wonderful to be that confident. My stomach isn't perfectly flat, and my breasts aren't impressive. Will anyone even want to fuck me tomorrow if I wear a wristband?

"I feel like I'm inside one of our gallery installations," I whisper to Miles, pushing away my insecurities.

"Except you can't hide behind your curator clipboard here."

We reach a clearing with several chairs surrounding a central platform. A woman with long dark hair and a pink bracelet lies face up and spread-eagled on the platform while a man slowly circles her, trailing a feather up and down her sides. Her body is exquisite. She has long, lean limbs and full breasts. Three other couples watch, sipping colorful cocktails.

"Want to sit?" Miles gestures to an empty double lounger.

"Sure."

We settle onto the cushions. A server appears almost immediately, offering drinks from a tray. I accept something blue and fruity, grateful for something to occupy my hands.

On the platform, the man has replaced the feather with his mouth. He works his way up the woman's inner thigh while she writhes beneath him, moaning loudly. Her confidence and the uninhibited sounds she makes are mesmerizing. I could never be that bold, that free with my body. Could I?

"God, she's gorgeous," I blurt out before I can stop myself.

"Not as gorgeous as you."

I snort. "Uh huh. I'm just as hot as that woman who's being eaten out in front of strangers."

"Hotter." His hand lands on my knee, squeezing gently. "And you could be that woman tomorrow, if you wanted."

I take a long sip of my drink. "I'd need about three shots of liquid courage first."

The woman on the platform cries out as she comes, her back arching dramatically. The audience applauds—actually applauds. There's no hint of embarrassment on her face, just pure satisfaction.

"Performance art at its finest," Miles whispers in my ear.

My tension eases, and I joke, "Think the gallery would fund this kind of exhibition?"

"Not in a million years."

We spend the next hour observing, commenting, and occasionally laughing as new women take their turn on the platform. With each scene, each orgasm witnessed, something inside me uncoils. The initial shock fades, replaced by a growing, insistent throb between my thighs.

A woman passes by us, completely naked except for a green bracelet and a body chain that accentuates her curves. She has stretch marks on her hips and a small pouch of softness at her belly, but she moves with such confidence that she's radiant. Men turn to watch her walk by. Maybe perfection isn't required here, just willingness.

"Ready to explore more?" Miles asks, noticing my restlessness.

We wander toward "The Living Gallery." It's a circular building with glass walls that houses what can only be described as sexual exhibits. Inside, women in various states of pleasure are displayed like living art installations. One stands shackled against a wall while a man holds a vibrator between her legs, her body trembling. Another reclines on a dais surrounded by mirrors, touching herself while observers circle her, some taking photos with her clear consent shown by a white bracelet alongside her green one.

In one corner, a woman who must be at least fifty, with silver streaks in her hair and laugh lines around her eyes, straddles a young man, riding him while onlookers watch. Her body shows the signs of age and childbearing, and she's undeniably sexy. Something about her confidence makes her the most beautiful woman in the room.

"This is—" I can't find the words. My pussy pulses with each new sight, each moan that reaches my ears.

"Inspiring?" Miles suggests, his hand sliding to my lower back.

"Overwhelming," I correct him, though inspiration is definitely part of it. "These women are so comfortable being watched and desired."

"You could be too." His lips brush my ear. "You already are desired."

We move to a quieter corner of the gallery where a woman with a pink bracelet sits on a man's lap, facing away from him. His cock disappears into her as she rises and falls in a slow rhythm. What captures my attention is the bliss on her face. She doesn't look like a model. Her thighs dimple slightly, and her breasts aren't perfectly symmetrical, but she's captivating in her authenticity.

"She's not performing," I whisper to Miles. "She's just enjoying it."

"That's what makes it so good. Real pleasure is more compelling than a performance."

My panties are soaked now, and my nipples are hard. Miles notices and slides his hand around to cup my breast.

"Careful," I say, though I make no move to stop him. "We're still in the observation phase."

"I'm observing how turned on you are." His thumb circles my nipple through the dress. "How your breathing changes when you watch someone come. How you press your thighs together when a woman moans."

I step away, needing space to collect myself. "Let's check out the restaurant. I need food and maybe another drink."

The restaurant occupies the central pavilion, with floor-to-ceiling windows overlooking the bay. Even here, sex is on display. A woman kneels beneath a table, her head moving between a seated man's legs while he calmly cuts into his steak. At another table, a woman straddles her partner, riding him slowly while they share a dessert, feeding each other bites between kisses.

"This gives 'dinner and a show' a whole new meaning," I quip as we're seated at a table near the window.

Miles's voice is husky. "I'm more interested in the appetizer you've become. You're vibrating with arousal."

"Shut up," I mutter, but there's no denying it. Every nerve ending in my body feels electrified. "Is it that obvious?"

"Only to me." He reaches across the table for my hand. "I know every tell, remember? The flush on your chest. The way you bite your lower lip. How you keep crossing and uncrossing your legs."

I roll my eyes, but I can feel my face blazing. "Fine. Yes. Watching people fuck is turning me on. Happy?"

"Ecstatic." His thumb traces circles on my palm. "Because watching you get turned on is my favorite thing in the world."

After dinner, we stroll along the beach as the sun begins to set. The day's activities haven't slowed—if anything, the approaching darkness seems to embolden the resort guests. On a nearby deck, a woman leans over while two men use her, one fucks her mouth while the other pounds into her from behind.

"Jesus," I breathe, unable to look away. "Do you think she knows them?"

Miles shrugs. "Maybe. Maybe not. That's kind of the point, isn't it?"

We find a secluded spot on the beach and sit on the warm sand. Miles wraps his arm around me, and I lean into his solid frame.

"So." His voice vibrates against my ear. "Thoughts so far?"

I consider the question, watching the waves lap at the shore. "It's like I've been looking at erotic art my whole career, thinking I understood it. But this—" I gesture vaguely at the resort. "This is experiencing it instead of just observing it."

"And?"

"And it's fucking hot," I giggle softly. "Way hotter than I expected."

"Any regrets about coming here?"

"Not yet. But ask me again tomorrow when I'm wearing a bracelet."

He laughs. "Which one are you going to wear?"

The choices have been in the back of my mind all day, and I've been weighing my courage against my desire.

"Pink and black," I say finally.

Miles raises an eyebrow. "Not white?"

I punch his arm lightly. "Let's not get ahead of ourselves, photographer boy. Baby steps."

"Pink and black it is." He kisses my temple. "And remember, just say 'red light' if you want everything to stop."

I'm grateful for the reminder of the safeword that the resort abides by.

As darkness falls completely, the resort transforms. Hidden lights illuminate the walkways with a soft glow and music drifts from the central pavilion where a party is starting. We make our way there, drawn by curiosity and the pulsing beat.

The pavilion has become a nightclub, bodies moving together on the dance floor. Unlike any club I've been to, here the dancing quickly evolves into more. A woman dances between two men, their hands roaming freely over her body before one pushes her to her knees. She sucks him off right on the dance floor. Another woman is bent over a high table, her dress pushed up as a man thrusts into her from behind.

"Want to dance?" Miles asks.

"No, let's watch a bit."

We find space at the bar, ordering drinks and swiveling our stools around to observe the increasingly uninhibited crowd. A woman climbs onto a table a few feet away, removing her top to cheers from onlookers.

"Look at her." I'm transfixed by the woman's blatant sexuality.

Miles's hand slides up my thigh under my dress. "I'm too busy to look."

"What're you doing?" I don't stop him as he traces the seam of my panties, finding the damp fabric.

"Just checking how wet you are." He presses against my pussy through the thin material. "And the answer is 'very'."

I feel like I should tell him to stop since we're in public and surrounded by strangers. But the exhibitionist thrill that's been building all day crests within me and I spread my legs.

"That's it," he encourages, and slides his fingers beneath the fabric to stroke my pussy.

I rock my hips as I watch the woman on the table get fingerfucked by a guy. Miles circles my clit with his thumb, and I bite my lip to keep from moaning.

"No one's watching us," he whispers. "Not yet, anyway. But they could be."

The thought makes me quiver with lust. I'm already so close, wound tight from hours of visual stimulation.

"Should I make you come right here? Give everyone a preview of what they might get tomorrow?"

"Yes," I gasp, past caring that we're surrounded by people. "Please."

His fingers work faster, his thumb pressing harder against my clit. I fix my eyes on the various erotic scenes around us. There's a woman on her knees servicing multiple men, taking one cock after another into her mouth. Another being fingered on the dance floor. Each image spirals me closer to my orgasm.

A movement catches my attention—a man leaning against a column across the room. He stares directly at me, at Miles's hand disappearing beneath my dress. His hungry gaze locks with mine and my breath catches. He doesn't look away, doesn't pretend he isn't watching.

Miles massages a pleasure point inside me. "Someone's enjoying the show."

The stranger's lips curve into a smile as if he could hear what Miles said. The connection with this watching stranger gives me a naughty thrill. My orgasm crashes into me as ecstasy rockets through my core. I cry out, not caring who hears me as I ride out the climax, my eyes never leaving the stranger's until the final wave subsides.

When I come back to myself, I realize a couple at the end of the bar was also watching us. Heat floods my face, but it's not embarrassment—it's excitement.

"Take me back to our room," I tell Miles. "I need you inside me. Now."

He grins, withdrawing his hand and licking his fingers clean. "As you wish."

We practically run back to our glass villa, shedding clothes as soon as the door closes behind us—which is, admittedly, an amusing display of modesty considering we're at a resort specifically designed for exhibitionists. Miles presses me against the clear wall, face first. My breasts smash against the glass. We're fully visible to anyone who might pass by.

"Do you want me to make the windows opaque?" he asks, his cock hard against my ass.

I glance out at the starlit night, at the distant figures moving along illuminated paths. The thought of someone seeing us makes my pussy clench with renewed desire.

"Transparent. Let them watch."

As Miles slides into me, pinning me against the glass, I finally understand what Mandy meant about liberation. Tomorrow I'll wear my bracelets and step fully into this new experience. But tonight—tonight I'm already becoming art.

CHAPTER 5

I wake before Miles, sunlight streaming through the glass walls of our villa like a crystal drop from a chandelier casting rainbows everywhere. My body aches pleasantly from last night when I slip from beneath his arm and pad to the bathroom.

My reflection catches me off guard in the floor-to-ceiling mirror. Naked, I look...ordinary. I'm not like the women I saw yesterday embracing their bodies and sexuality. My breasts are smaller than I'd like, with pale pink nipples that pucker in the cool morning air. My hips are slight, and I lack the hourglass figure that so many people find sexy. The softness of my lower belly refuses to disappear no matter how much I exercise and eat healthy.

I press my palm against that soft spot as I critically catalog every flaw. Would men here even want me? Miles's desire I understand since he loves me and has seven years of history with me. But strangers? What would make them choose me over the beautiful women I saw yesterday?

Ugh. I need to stop this. I'm not here to hide.

I trace the curve of my hip, trying to see myself through different eyes. My skin is smooth and flushed with sleep. My wavy brown hair falls past my shoulders in a tousled mess that looks almost intentional. My legs are long for my height, and my ass—I turn slightly—yeah, that actually looks pretty good.

The wristbands sit on the counter, innocent and terrifying. I pick up the pink one, the weight of it nothing compared to what it represents. Permission to be touched, to be filled, to be used—flaws and all.

I put the pink and black wristbands on. The silicone feels cool against my pulse point. This weekend is about pleasure, not perfection.

When I return to the bedroom, Miles is awake, propped up on one elbow watching me. He notices the bands on my wrist.

"Pink and black looks good on you," he says, voice still rough with sleep.

I lift my chin. "I'm going to dive right in. No point coming all this way just to observe."

He pulls back the sheet, patting the space beside him. "Come here first."

I shake my head. "If I get back in that bed, we'll never make it to breakfast."

"Would that be so terrible?"

"I'm starving." I move to the closet, aware of his eyes tracking me. "Besides, I thought you wanted to see me take a bunch of other cocks."

He laughs. "Good point," and climbs out of bed.

I select a gauzy white sundress that falls to mid-thigh; conservative by resort standards but revealing enough to make me feel like I'm participating. I don't put panties or a bra on, and the fabric of the dress is so thin, my nipples are visible through it when I turn back to Miles.

"You're perfect. Beautiful and accessible."

I pick at the hem of my dress. "If anyone wants to actually fuck me."

"You're gorgeous, and if they don't make a move, that's their loss. Either way, you and I are going to have fun tonight —watching or showing them what they're missing.

His compliment warms me, and once he's dressed I follow him through the resort grounds. The path winds between lush tropical plants, opening to reveal views that stop me in my tracks—not just of the turquoise ocean beyond, but of bodies entwined.

"There are so many people here," I whisper, pressing closer to Miles. "I didn't expect this many."

He squeezes my hand. "I didn't either."

I count at least a dozen couples or groups visible from our path alone. A blonde woman bent over a railing gasps as a muscular man thrusts into her from behind. Twenty feet away, a petite Asian woman kneels in a garden sucking on a guy standing in front of her while another man photographs them from different angles.

"Look at all the yellow bands," I say, noticing the bright markers on wrists as we pass by. Near a small reflection pool, three men wearing them observe a woman being pleasured by another man. "Are they all guests, or staff?"

"Both, I think," Miles says. "The brochure mentioned that some staff are here specifically to provide services, but guests can wear yellow too if they want to be the person using others."

My pulse quickens with each scene we pass. Miles's hand rests at the small of my back, a constant reassurance of his presence. I find myself cataloging details like I would at an exhibition—the curve of a spine, the grip of fingers on flesh, the expressions of abandon.

The dining pavilion comes into view, an architectural marvel of glass and timber. It's half-full when we arrive, the atmosphere more subdued than last night but still charged with erotic potential. A woman sits on a man's lap at one table, slowly riding him while she sips her coffee and chats with companions as if nothing unusual is happening. At another table, a staff member with a yellow band takes a customer's order while simultaneously directing a kneeling woman's movements as she sucks his cock.

"How do they get any actual work done?" I whisper to Miles, fascinated by the server's multitasking ability.

"Efficiency," he replies with a grin.

A greeter leads us to a table with an ocean view. I settle into my chair, hyperaware of the activities continuing around us. A woman at the next table stands to leave, and a man with a yellow band stops her, bends her over the table, and enters her from behind. She moans softly as he uses her, their breakfast dishes still on the table.

We order fresh fruit, pastries, and strong coffee. I'm spreading jam on a croissant when a tall man with salt-and-pepper hair approaches our table. He's handsome in that distinguished way that comes with age and confidence, a yellow band prominent on his wrist.

"Good morning," he says, his accent vaguely Mediterranean. "Welcome to Infinite Gaze. I'm Victor, the hospitality manager here." He straightens the cuff of his linen shirt. "I personally oversee our guests' comfort and... satisfaction during their stay."

He's so sexy that my mouth goes dry, but I manage to say, "Is it obvious we're new?"

"Only in the most charming way." He extends his hand. "Part of my job is identifying first-time visitors who might benefit from a proper introduction to our amenities."

"Brooklyn," I reply, and when I take his hand my pink and black wristbands are visible on my wrist. "And this is my husband, Miles."

Victor nods politely to Miles before returning his attention to me. His gaze flickers briefly to my wristbands. "Brooklyn. A beautiful name for a beautiful woman."

Before I can respond, he places his hand on my shoulder, his thumb stroking the bare skin. The touch is casual, as if he has every right to touch me. Which, given my bracelet and the consent that comes with it, he does. My heart hammers against my ribs.

Victor moves behind my chair, both hands now on my shoulders. His touch is firm but gentle as he massages the tension from my muscles. I close my eyes, letting myself focus on the sensation of unfamiliar hands on my body.

"Relax," he murmurs, close to my ear. "You're safe here."

His hands slide lower, brushing the sides of my breasts through the fabric of my dress. I inhale sharply, my nipples hardening in response. I open my eyes and Miles is watching intently.

Victor continues his exploration, one hand moving to cup my breast while the other trails down towards my pussy. He pinches my nipple lightly, drawing a gasp from me. The dining pavilion fades from my awareness until there is only Victor's hands, Miles's eyes, and the growing wetness between my legs.

"Stand up," Victor instructs, his voice low.

I obey without thinking, rising from my chair on shaky legs. He leads me a short distance from the table, turning me to face Miles. With one arm secured around my waist, his other hand moves beneath my dress.

"Your husband is watching," he whispers. "Show him how much you enjoy being touched by another man."

His hand slides up my thigh, finding my bare pussy. I should be mortified since we're in the middle of the dining pavilion, surrounded by other guests, but instead, I'm dizzy with arousal.

"She's soaked," Victor tells Miles, who watches with lust written all over his face.

Victor's fingers circle my clit while he pulls down the top of my dress with the other hand, exposing my breasts. Cool air hits me, followed by the searing gazes from nearby tables.

"Look at them watching you," he murmurs. "All these people see how beautiful you are when you're touched."

His words ping my brain with delight. This is so fucking dirty.

Victor increases the pressure on my clit, and I rock my hips into his hand. My eyes lock with Miles's. I need the reassurance that he's okay with what's going on, and all I can see radiating from him is joy and lust.

"Are you going to be a little slut and come for us?" Victor growls into my ear, and suddenly my thighs quiver and shocks of delight rush through me as I climax.

I cry out and tremble against Victor's solid frame. He holds me upright as my knees threaten to buckle.

When I can stand on my own again, he steps back, helping straighten my dress before retrieving a handkerchief from his pocket to clean his hand. He places a chaste kiss on my cheek. "A beautiful beginning to your day. Enjoy your breakfast."

He heads off through the crowd of diners and I return to my seat on wobbly legs, my face burning.

Miles reaches across the table to take my hand. "That was hot."

I'm breathless and giddy. "And unexpected."

"But good?"

I take a gulp of water before I reply. "Oh god, so good."

We finish our breakfast in charged silence, both of us processing what just happened. My body still hums with pleasure, and my mind races. It's still morning. What else is going to happen today?

After breakfast, we explore the island some more, and discover an area where several small beaches nestle between rocky outcroppings. Each cove is designed for different activities. There's one that features padded platforms for group encounters, another has swings and harnesses suspended from sturdy trees.

We pause at a particularly beautiful spot where the sand is fine and white. A wooden deck extends over the water, with lounge chairs arranged for sunbathing. Several people are already there, most completely naked.

"Want to sit for a while?" Miles asks.

I nod, suddenly eager to feel the sun on my skin. We claim a double lounger on the deck, and Miles helps me apply sunscreen.

"You should take this off," he suggests, tugging at the strap on my shoulder. "Avoid tan lines."

I know he doesn't really care about the tan lines, and the old Brooklyn would hesitate, make excuses. But this new slutty me nods and pulls the dress over her head.

Miles grins. "That's my girl."

We settle down, adjusting the chair so it rests flat. Miles is on his back while I lie on my stomach beside him. The sun warms me, and I close my eyes, drifting in a pleasant haze. Nearby conversations blend with the sound of waves lapping against the deck pilings. Occasional moans drift from a nearby couple, but I'm too relaxed to look.

My mind is drifting lazily, and the next thing I register is a hand on my ankle. Not Miles's hand since his arm is still draped across my lower back. I lift my head, blinking in the bright sunlight.

A man kneels beside me, his hand sliding up my calf. He's younger than Victor, maybe early thirties, sun-bronzed and dark hair. His eyes —a startling blue against his tan—meet mine as his hand continues its upward journey.

"You looked too delicious to pass up," he says, his voice carrying an Australian accent.

Miles stirs and lifts his head. The stranger nods to him. "Mind if I play with her a bit, mate?"

"Have at her. The louder she moans, the better," Miles replies.

My husband's words send a spike of desire through me and I can feel the wetness between my legs. Dang, he's really getting into the whole 'sharing his wife' deal. I'm surprised I'm not nervous, but the morning's experience with Victor has left me relaxed and feeling bold...not to mention incredibly horny.

The stranger's fingers reach the sensitive spot behind my knee. His smile is wicked as his hand continues up my thigh. "I'm Joe, by the way."

"Brooklyn," I manage as his fingers glide closer to my pussy.

"Brooklyn," he repeats, as if tasting the word. "Let's see what Brooklyn likes."

Without warning, he grasps my shoulder and hips, flipping me onto my back. The sudden movement startles a laugh from me, which turns to a gasp as he spreads my legs.

"Much better," he says, positioning himself between my thighs. "Now I can see all of you."

I'm completely naked on a public deck, legs spread for a stranger while my husband watches right next to me. People turn to observe, their interest obvious.

Joe's hands push my thighs even wider. "Look at this pretty pussy. All wet and ready."

Before I can respond, he lowers his head and gives a long lick, his tongue sliding between my folds. I arch my back and cry out in bliss. Holy fuck, some dude is going down on me in public. His tongue is insistent, circling my clit before dipping lower to tease my entrance.

Miles murmurs beside me. "So hot."

I'm beyond words as Joe's tongue works magic between my legs. He devours me like a man starved. When he slides two fingers inside me, I moan loudly enough to draw even more attention.

"That's it," Joe encourages against my pussy. "Let everyone hear how good it feels."

The pleasure builds in layers, and I'm vaguely aware of people gathering around, watching intently as this stranger brings me to the brink of orgasm.

Joe lifts his head, his chin glistening with my arousal. "I think she's ready for more, don't you?" he asks the onlookers.

Someone voices their agreement while Miles says, "Fuck her hard."

His crude encouragement sends a shock of delight through me. Joe stands and pulls down his shorts to free his cock. It's thick and curved upward. He strokes himself a few times, his eyes focused on my pussy.

"Time to show everyone how much of a slut you are," he says as he kneels between my legs.

"Yes," I gasp, beyond caring about anything except the need pulsing in my clit. My gallery curator persona that's always composed and analytical, dissolves as the craving to be watched overtakes me.

Joe's cock juts proudly as he settles in above me. He grips the back of the lounger with one hand, creating a frame around my body and displaying me to our audience. With his other hand, he guides himself to my entrance, the blunt head pressing against my wetness.

He pushes inside with one powerful thrust. My pussy stretches around his thickness, and I cry out from pleasure. My hands fly to his forearms and I cling to him. He's bigger than Miles and the difference is noticeable and thrilling. My body struggles to accommodate him, sending electric pulses of pleasure-pain up my spine.

"Fuck, she's tight," Joe announces to the audience, his voice carrying across the pool deck. "Her pussy's gripping me like a fist."

His vulgar words make me shudder in delight. I've never been described this way—as a physical sensation rather than a person. In this moment, I love it.

He begins to fuck me in deep, measured thrusts. The wood creaks beneath us, a rhythmic counterpoint to my increasingly desperate moans. Miles rolls onto his side to make room and his eyes remain fixed on the point where Joe's cock disappears into me. His gaze feels like a physical touch.

"You like being fucked in front of all these people?" Joe asks, his pace increasing, hips snapping forward with greater force. "Being used like the little slut you are?"

In my professional world, those words would trigger immediate offense. Here, with my legs spread and a stranger inside me, they send me barrelling toward my climax. The contradiction thrills me. How I can be both the woman who analyzes provocative art and the woman who becomes it?

"Yes," I moan, my voice breaking on the single syllable. "I love it."

"Tell them," he demands, his hips slamming against mine, the impact jolting through my entire body. "Tell everyone watching."

I turn my head, taking in the ring of faces. The emotions on their faces range from aroused to fascinated. Not one shows judgment. Only appreciation.

"I love being fucked like this," I moan, abandoning the last of my inhibitions. The words feel foreign on my tongue but undeniably true. "I love being watched. I love being used."

My declaration sends Joe into a frenzy. He straightens up and grabs my legs, pushing them back toward my chest to change the angle. The position exposes me completely. His cock is deep inside me, touching places that make my vision blur at the edge from pleasure.

Miles leans closer, his breath warm against my ear. "You're beautiful like this," he whispers. "So fucking beautiful."

The combination of Joe's cock stretching me open and Miles' words in my ear sizzles my brain. My thighs begin to tremble. A woman in a red bikini has moved closer, her hand now between her own legs as she watches.

"Gonna fill this tight pussy," Joe grunts, his rhythm becoming erratic. Sweat beads on his forehead. "Gonna make you come while everyone watches."

The pressure builds inside me, coiling tight at the base of my spine. I'm vaguely aware of someone kneeling beside us for a better view, of hushed conversations about my body, my responses. I'm being consumed and devoured by their collective gaze. And I'm coming undone because of it.

When Joe reaches down and rubs my clit, I shatter completely. My orgasm tears through me, and I scream my pleasure to the open sky. It's an experience unlike anything I've ever felt before —all these people watching, the scent of the ocean, the breeze, it all culminates in me coming harder than I have in months. Bliss wracks my body and I become a fucktoy, ready for all the delights the island has to offer.

Joe follows moments later, his cock pulsing inside me as he empties himself with a groan. He collapses on top of me, his weight pressing me down as we both struggle to catch our breath.

When he finally pulls out, a smattering of applause breaks out from our audience. Joe stands and grins, tucking himself back into his shorts and taking a playful bow.

"Thanks for the fun," he says, casually as if we'd just shared a drink rather than the most public sex of my life. "Have a good trip."

As he walks away, I become aware of the wetness between my thighs, the pleasant ache in muscles unused to being folded like origami paper.

Miles looks at me with a mix of awe and desire as he brushes hair from my sweat-dampened forehead. "You okay?"

I laugh, the sound bubbling up from the newly-liberated place inside me. "I'm better than okay. And I'm a messy canvas."

Miles kisses me softly as he slides a hand down to my well-used pussy. "The most beautiful exhibit in the whole resort."

I moan as he rubs my clit, but before I can start building up to another orgasm he pulls his hand away. "Let's explore some more."

As we gather our things and I put my sundress back on, I can feel Joe's cum dripping down my inner thigh. This is nasty in such an amazing way. The day is only half over, and already I've been transformed.

CHAPTER 6

The afternoon sun beats down as Miles and I walk hand in hand through the resort. I'm grateful for the sunscreen we've been applying generously. Joe's attention on the deck was just the start. Since then, I've had encounters with several men: I was fingered by a silver-haired businessman against a garden wall, a college-aged guy made me kneel and suck him off by the reflection pool, and someone whose face I never saw who fucked me hard against a railing.

The Living Gallery is ahead of us, and through it, I can see figures arranged on pedestals like statues, their bodies adorned with paint and light. They're getting set up for tonight's viewing.

Miles nods towards the building. "Want to visit again tonight?"

I squeeze his hand. "Actually, I was thinking..."

"What?" He turns to me, his eyes bright with curiosity.

I bite my lip. "What if I participated instead?"

"You want to be one of the exhibits?"

"Is that crazy?" I search his face for judgment but find only excitement.

"It's hot as hell." He pulls me close and slides a hand down to cup my ass.

Nerves flutter in my stomach. "I'm not sure I'm brave enough."

"Yesterday you weren't sure if you were brave enough to do anything in public, and look how that turned out."

He's right. Each boundary I've crossed has only led to more pleasure, more freedom. My body buzzes with the possibility as I say, "According to the brochure, participants need to arrive an hour before the show opens, so we need to hurry."

Miles grins. "Then let's get going."

We stop in at the villa and Miles pulls out the lingerie he bought me. "Put this on."

"You sure?" I ask, but I'm already stripping off my sundress.

Miles watches hungrily as I slip into the lingerie. The fabric whispers against my skin, cool and weightless. "Perfect. Now everyone will see what I see."

I study my reflection in the mirror. The cream color complements my light tan and from a distance people won't realize how sheer it is. My nipples pucker visibly through the fabric, and the panties cling to the curves of my ass.

"Do you think many people will fuck me?" I ask, suddenly insecure. "There are so many gorgeous women here."

Miles steps behind me, his hands sliding around to cup my breasts through the delicate fabric. "They'd be fools not to."

We make our way to The Living Gallery, and as we walk, I notice more people than usual watching us—or rather, watching me. Two men are sitting in chairs by a small pool and one actually stops mid-conversation to stare as we pass. A woman nudges her partner and whispers something that makes him turn and look. The attention makes my pussy tingle.

A muscular guy greets us at a check-in desk near the entrance and introduces himself as Xavier. He's wearing tight black shorts that do nothing to hide his impressive physique. His smile is warm as he looks me over, eyes lingering on my wristbands and the sheer lingerie.

"Brooklyn, right? I was told to take good care of you." His voice is rich and deep.

"What?" I'm startled that he knows my name. "How did you—"

"Celeste is one of our favorite guests here. She requested that I make sure you have the best spot." He gestures to the room. "Ready?"

My heart flips with nervous excitement. The reality of what I'm about to do strikes me. I'm going to be displayed for strangers to touch, taste, and possibly fuck. The thought makes my pulse race.

"How does it work exactly?" I ask, grateful that my voice doesn't betray my nerves.

Xavier retrieves a small gold pot and a brush from under the desk. "Tonight is called the Golden Hour. We highlight your body with edible body paint, and you become an exhibit that everyone can enjoy. When we open the doors, the viewers decide what they want to do with you."

Miles and I exchange grins, and I say, "Let's do it."

Xavier's eyes darken as he takes in the cream lingerie. "Beautiful choice. We'll leave this on. The contrast with the gold paint will be captivating."

He leads me to a preparation area where three other women are being painted by more workers. One has intricate patterns covering her entire naked body, another is being adorned with tiny jewels along her spine. A third woman—older and curvy–is having her nipples gilded with gold leaf.

"You're new," she says when she notices me watching. "First time as an exhibit?"

I nod, suddenly shy despite everything I've done today.

"It's addictive," she warns with a wink. "Once you've been art, it's hard to go back to being just a person."

Xavier directs me to a padded bench and begins his work. The brush tickles as he paints gold across my collarbones, then down between my breasts. He moves my lingerie out of the way so he can circle my nipples with the brush, adds delicate swirls along my rib cage, then asks me to stand so he can continue down my body.

The paint is cool as he traces the curve of my hip bones. He dips the brush into the hollow beside my hip, then follows the edge of my panties with a thin golden line. The intimate attention makes my breath catch.

"Spread your legs," he instructs, kneeling before me.

I comply, feeling Miles's eyes on me as Xavier paints a line up my inner thigh, stopping just short of where the fabric covers my pussy. The brush strokes are professional, yet undeniably erotic.

"Turn," he says, and I present my back to him.

He paints down my spine, across my shoulder blades, and along the curve where my ass meets my thighs. By the time he's finished and I've adjusted my lingerie, I'm hypersensitive, every nerve ending awake and hungry for touch.

"Perfect," Xavier says, and steps back to assess his work. "Now for your position."

He leads me to a pedestal that's about waist high and in the center of the room. The spotlights will illuminate me from all angles. Miles follows, his eyes never leaving my painted body.

"This is one of our premium spots," Xavier explains. "You'll be visible from every entrance."

He boosts me up to sit on the platform. Around us, other exhibits are being arranged. There's a woman on all fours, her ass in the air, and another woman standing with arms outstretched.

"We'll bind your hands," Xavier says, reaching for a soft gold rope hanging nearby. "Nothing too restrictive. You can release yourself if needed. Hands in front, please."

I extend my wrists toward him, watching as he crosses them before looping the rope around them with efficiency. The binding is snug but not uncomfortable.

He moves to the wall where a lever protrudes from a recessed panel. With one smooth motion, he pulls it downward. The rope tightens and lifts, drawing my bound wrists upward until my arms stretch above my head. My body straightens in response, chest thrust forward, back arched.

Wow, I really am the exhibit. The strategic spotlights, the body positioning, the sightlines. The pink and black wristbands remain visible as a clear signal of what's permitted.

"Remember," he says quietly when he comes back, "your bracelet means they can touch without asking, but you can use your safeword at any time. Your husband will be right here."

Xavier leaves us and Miles brushes his lips against my cheek. "You look incredible," he says. "Like a fantasy come to life."

I lean into his touch. "I can't believe I'm doing this."

"Having second thoughts?"

I search my feelings. Twenty-four hours ago, I would have been horrified at the thought of being displayed like this. Now, my body thrums with anticipation.

"No," I say, surprising myself with my certainty. "I want this."

Miles kisses me softly. "I love you so much, you know that, right?"

"I know. That's why I can be this brave with you. Because I trust you completely."

Around us, the final preparations are underway. The anticipation builds as staff members move to the doors to open them. I can hear voices outside as people wait for the exhibition to open. My heart pounds, and my pussy throbs with each beat. I've never been so aware of my body.

Miles stands next to my pedestal, close enough that I can see him but not so close that he'll deter interaction. He gives me a reassuring wink.

The gold paint has dried, leaving a delicate shimmer that reflects light through my sheer cream lingerie. I sit casually, legs dangling from the pedestal's edge, feeling my pussy getting wetter with each passing second.

This is it. In moments, strangers will look at me, touch me, taste me, use me—and I'll let them.

A chime sounds, and the doors open. People filter in, and their eyes land on me and stick. I've never been looked at like this before—not as a person to talk to or even a woman to desire, but as an object of pure appreciation. It should feel degrading. Instead, it feels like power.

The first touch comes from a man with tanned skin and salt-and-pepper hair. He runs his hand up my calf, looking at Miles. "May I taste her?"

My breath catches when Miles says, "Go ahead."

The man leans forward and takes my gold-painted nipple into his mouth through my lingerie. His tongue swirls around it, and I gasp in joy, arching toward him.

A second man moves behind me, his hands sliding down to cup my pussy. He pushes past my panties and spreads my pussy lips open, showing everyone how wet I am. I should be mortified, but instead I rock against his hand, wanting more.

"Look how wet she is already," the man announces to the growing crowd. "She's dripping for us."

A third man approaches. As he moves to take off my panties, I lean from side to side to assist him, and once he guides them down my legs, they fall to the floor. He runs his fingers through my folds, collecting my wetness and inserts two thick digits inside me. A spike of pleasure makes my knees weak. If I wasn't already seated, I'd probably have trouble standing. I pull against the rope, not trying to get away but needing something to anchor me as the delight builds.

"Fuck," I gasp, as he adds a third finger, stretching me wider. "Oh god, right there—"

The man strokes me faster. His voice is deep and commanding. "Show everyone how much you love being our gallery piece."

My orgasm engulfs me like a tidal wave, making me cry out and shake. Someone claps, and others join in. I laugh, breathless and high on endorphins.

Then I see them—Celeste and Julian Roche, watching from behind everyone else. Surprised delight pulses in my core. They're dressed in casual resort wear. Celeste is in a crisp linen blouse and flowing pants. Julian wears a light button-down with the sleeves rolled to his elbows and tailored shorts. Despite the relaxed attire, they maintain an effortless elegance that sets them apart from the crowd. Celeste's eyes are bright with approval; Julian looks like he wants to devour me.

He approaches Miles. "Your wife is stunning. May I?"

Miles's jaw tightens for a second. This is the first time I've seen him hesitate. He glances at me.

I nod.

"Yes," Miles says, looking back at him.

I never imagined Celeste and Julian would show up this weekend, but somehow it seems fitting. Fuck, this is filthy. I'm eager for Julian to do whatever he wants to me.

Julian steps between my legs and leans down, bringing his face level with my pussy. He licks a slow stripe through my folds and groans like he's tasting something exquisite. "Better than the finest wine," he murmurs against my sensitive flesh before diving in, eating me with the confidence of a man who knows exactly what he's doing.

His tongue is relentless, circling and flicking my clit while he grips my thighs hard enough to leave marks. I'm vaguely aware of other men touching me—hands on my breasts, fingers tracing the gold paint, someone stroking my hair—but Julian's mouth demands my attention.

My second orgasm builds faster than the first. Julian's tongue is expert, alternating between broad strokes and precise flicks until I'm gasping and pulling at the bindings. Miles stands behind me and holds me steady as I explode, my whole body convulsing.

Julian stands and wipes his mouth with the back of his hand, looking pleased with himself. "Magnificent. A true masterpiece."

Celeste approaches and whispers in my ear. "He's fabulous with his tongue, isn't he?" Before I can respond, she giggles and says, "Enjoy the rest of your trip."

Celeste and Julian disappear into the crowd, and a younger man steps forward next. He's muscular with dark hair and eager eyes. "She needs to be fucked," he announces.

I couldn't agree with him more. I feel drunk on pleasure and exhibition.

He moves between my legs, and suddenly I realize this platform really is at the ideal height. The man hooks a hand under my thigh as he guides his cock to my pussy.

"She feels good," he groans.

He pulls me off the pedestal so that I'm hanging by my wrists while he supports me with his hands under my ass. I wrap my legs around him and he bounces me on his cock, using his strength to lift and lower me. My breasts jiggle and each thrust drives him deeper, hitting places inside me that make stars explode behind my eyelids. I'm aware of every pair of eyes on us.

"Look at her take it," someone murmurs.

The man fucking me increases his pace, his breathing becoming ragged. "Gonna come," he groans, a second before his cock pulses and he empties himself inside me. When he sets me down, I can feel his cum dripping down my thigh. Before I can catch my breath, another man steps forward, his cock already in hand.

"My turn," he says, and slides into my pussy.

His cock is thick and curved, hitting different spots from the last man. The obscene, wet sounds of his cock moving through the previous man's cum should embarrass me, but instead it pushes me toward another orgasm. This man fucks me harder, one hand tangled in my hair, the other grasping my hip hard enough to bruise.

Miles moves to where I can see him, his eyes locked on mine. "I love you," he mouths, and the pride mixed with raw lust in his expression sends me over the edge again.

I come around the stranger's cock as he continues to pound into me. He follows moments later, adding his load to the mess already inside me.

When another man approaches with his cock out, I'm still shaking from my orgasm. The rest passes in a haze. Cock after cock sliding into me, filling me with cum. Hands caressing every inch of me. At some point, my mind retreats into a primal headspace. All that exists is this feeling of pure bliss and utter surrender.

At last the lights dim and people filter out. Xavier unties the rope and I sway as Miles wraps his arms around me, holding me close. I bury my face against his neck as he says, "Let's go back to the villa, baby. Get some food in you."

I agree softly, and Miles helps me down. He picks my panties up from the floor and holds my hand the entire way back to our villa.

When we get there, Miles turns the walls opaque as I collapse onto the bed, my body humming with pleasure. My muscles ache in places I didn't know could ache, and my pussy feels satisfyingly sore. Miles brings me a glass of water, and I gulp it down, suddenly aware of how thirsty I am.

"Hungry?" he asks, brushing hair from my face.

I nod, realizing I'm starving. "Ravenous. Apparently being fucked by a bunch of men burns a lot of calories."

Miles laughs and taps on the room's tablet, ordering from the resort's room service menu. While we wait, he runs a bath, adding fragrant oils that fill the bathroom with the scent of jasmine and vanilla.

"Come on," he says, helping me sit up. "Let's get you clean."

The water envelops me as I sink into the tub. Miles kneels beside it, using a cloth to wash away the gold paint and the evidence of multiple men from my skin. His touch is gentle, reverent almost.

"How do you feel?" he asks, his voice soft.

I sigh, "Wonderful," and it's true. It's been a great day so far.

A knock at the door signals our food has arrived. Miles helps me from the bath. I wrap a plush robe around me while he takes care of room service.

We eat on the terrace. We have fresh seafood, tropical fruits, and crusty bread with olive oil. I devour my food, my body demanding fuel.

"So..." Miles says. "Julian and Celeste."

I nearly choke on a piece of mango. "God, I almost forgot they were there."

"Really? Because Julian eating you out seemed pretty memorable to me."

I kick him under the table, but can't help laughing. "Okay, fine. It was unexpected."

"And?"

"And what?"

Miles raises an eyebrow. "And how was it? The great Julian Roche going down on my wife."

My face flames as I remember Julian's mouth on me. "He was...skilled."

"I noticed. Is that going to make things weird at work?"

I take a long sip of water, considering. "Maybe? But probably in a good way." I set down my glass. "Celeste has always treated me like I belonged in their world, even when I felt like an imposter. Now it's like...I don't know. Like we share a secret language."

"The language of public orgasms?"

I throw a grape at him. "Shut up."

He catches it and pops it in his mouth, grinning. "Seriously though, you're okay with everything?"

"Weirdly, yes." I pull my legs up, wrapping my arms around my knees in my usual comforting position. "It actually makes me feel more confident. Like, how can I be embarrassed about hanging artwork of couples fucking now?" He smiles in understanding, and I reach for his hand across the table. "Thank you for encouraging this. For knowing what I needed before I did."

He brings my knuckles to his lips. "I'm having an amazing time."

We finish our meal as darkness falls, the villa's automatic lighting creating a soft glow around us. Once we're finished and go inside, Miles pulls me against him, his hands sliding beneath my robe.

"What do you want to do now?" he asks and kisses the sensitive spot below my ear.

"I want to go to the pool party later." And then I give a big yawn. "But I want a nap first."

Chapter 7

I decide to be daring and I don't wear my bathing suit to the pool. The night air feels like silk against my exposed body. In the distance, music from the party pulses in rhythm with my racing heart. After a full day at this resort, I'm a sexual goddess in her element.

"Nervous?" Miles squeezes my hand.

"Excited. Horny as hell." I squeeze back. "You?"

"Same. Plus proud. Of us. Of you."

The Prism Pool comes into view. It's a massive infinity edge overlooking the ocean, with glass walls that extend below the waterline creating an aquarium effect for viewers in a room below. About thirty people are already gathered around, some standing with drinks in hand, others sprawled on cushions. A man has a woman bent over the bar at the far end, her moans carrying across the water. Another woman is on all fours getting railed while two others wait their turn behind her.

The regular lights dim, and underwater LEDs kick on, sending blue and purple lights dancing across naked flesh. My pink and black wristbands are on display, advertising my availability to anyone watching.

I step down the first stair leading into the pool, dipping my toes in the water. Several men turn toward me, their gazes tracking my movements. One nudges another, nodding in my direction. Yep, I really am a goddess.

I dip underwater, feeling the warm currents caress my body. Through the glass floor, I can see more silhouettes gathering in the viewing room beneath me, their faces turned upward, drinks in hand, watching the show. I'm not sure how much they can see through the water, but I'm on display from every angle. The thought makes my clit throb.

I surface with an arch, letting water stream off my breasts. Miles joins me in the water and swims to meet me. He backs me against the pool wall, his hand moves between my legs.

"You're so amazing," he says as he circles my clit. Pings of bliss make me cry out.

The lights fade from blue to green to red, painting our bodies in jewel tones. Someone in the crowd claps. The sound breaks through my haze, reminding me we're not alone. Instead of making me shy away, it makes me bolder. I spread my legs, hopefully offering the people below a better view.

A man with broad shoulders and a closely trimmed beard wades toward us. He doesn't speak, just raises an eyebrow at Miles in silent question.

Miles nods and steps aside. "She's all yours."

The stranger turns me around and I cling to the side as he grasps my waist. The blunt head of his cock presses against my entrance, thicker than any cock I've had so far today, and as he pushes in slowly, it's an exquisite unfamiliar stretch.

"God, this pussy feels good," he groans as he pulls all the way out and thrusts back in.

I glance around through half-lidded eyes. A man is fingering his partner while they watch us. Another couple is fucking on a nearby lounger. We're creating a chain reaction, and it's intoxicating.

I continue to hold onto the side of the pool as the man behind me picks up his pace. Water sloshes rhythmically with each thrust.

"Fuck her harder," someone calls out, and a ping of lust ripples down my spine.

Another naked guy sits down on the edge of the pool next to me. One of his arms is covered in tattoos, and he strokes his cock. The guy fucking me from behind pulls me over so my face is by the man's cock. I part my lips, and without a word, the tattooed guy guides the tip into my mouth.

I turn my head as best I can to peek at Miles. His eyes are glazed over from passion and it makes my pussy tighten around the cock inside it.

The tattooed man groans as I hollow my cheeks around him, my tongue working the sensitive underside of his cock. His hand tangles in my wet hair, guiding my rhythm to match the thrusts coming from behind.

My orgasm builds like a wave gathering force. I'm suspended between these two strangers, filled completely, on display for everyone around the pool and those watching from below. The man behind me reaches around to find my clit, and a burst of delight zings through me. I'm lost in a sea of bliss as he slams into me one final time.

"Fuuuck," he groans as he fills me with cum.

I moan around the cock still in my mouth, the vibrations pushing the tattooed man closer to coming.

"Where do you want it?" he grunts, his thrusts becoming erratic.

Miles answers for me. "On her tits."

The tattooed stranger pulls out of my mouth and I stand up a moment before streams of hot cum land on my breasts. The visual of my body marked by a stranger is the right kind of filthy for my brain.

The crowd cheers, and Miles and I smile as we climb out of the pool. "Let me get you a towel," Miles says, but before he can move away, a familiar figure approaches us.

Victor, the hospitality manager, moves with that same confident stride I noticed this morning.

"Enjoying the pool party finale?" he asks, his accent making the simple question sound like an invitation to something forbidden.

"Very much," I reply, suddenly aware of how exposed I am. I'm dripping wet, completely naked, and my pussy still throbs from the attention in the pool.

Victor steps closer. "I've been watching you all evening. You're quite the natural exhibitionist."

"I'm discovering that about myself."

I'm not even surprised when he takes my arm and leads me over to a glass-topped table. The surface is cool against my palms as I lean forward. Victor kicks my feet wider apart, exposing my pussy to anyone watching from behind. Miles circles to the other side, standing where he can see my face.

Victor's hands grasp my hips, his thumbs pressing into the dimples at the base of my spine. He slides one finger through my folds to gather my wetness, and I gasp as he pushes that finger inside me, testing my readiness. The knowledge that we're being watched—that my surrender is on display for everyone at the party—only heightens my arousal.

"Please," I whisper, pushing back against his hand.

"Please what?" Victor withdraws his finger, leaving me empty.

"Please fuck me," I say, loud enough for those closest to hear.

Victor immediately thrusts into me smoothly until he's balls deep. I whimper from pleasure and jiggle my ass as spikes of bliss ripple down my legs.

"Look at your husband," Victor commands, his accent thickening with desire. "Let him see how much you love taking another man's cock."

I lift my gaze to Miles's face. His breathing is shallow and quick. The muscle in his jaw ticks with tension. It's not jealousy, but restraint, and I can tell he wants to fuck me.

Victor sets a punishing pace, each thrust driving me forward against the table and my breasts swaying with each impact. More people come to watch, their whispers and occasional groans forming a soundtrack to my pleasure.

"Such a little slut," Victor growls as he wraps my hair around his fist. He pulls, forcing my head back. "Taking my cock so well in front of all these people."

In this moment, I am a slut, and I love it. I'm free, uninhibited, and displayed.

"Harder," I demand. "Fuck me harder."

Victor grants my request. His hips slam against my ass, the sound of wet skin slapping together echoes across the pool deck. My orgasm builds rapidly, coiling tight at the base of my spine. When Victor reaches around to rub my clit, I detonate as wave after wave of pleasure crashes through me. I scream, the sound tearing from my throat and I don't try to muffle my euphoria.

Victor's rhythm falters as my body squeezes him. With a guttural groan, he pulls out, stroking himself rapidly before coming across my lower back in hot pulses.

The crowd claps. It's absurd and perfect. My legs tremble as Victor steps back, his hand giving my ass an appreciative farewell squeeze.

Before I can even catch my breath, another man takes Victor's place behind me. He pushes into me.

"Fuck, she's so wet," he grunts, and I laugh in delight. I'm filled full of cum and even I can tell how messy I am.

Miles moves closer. "How does it feel being passed around like this?"

"Amazing," I gasp as the new man establishes a rhythm that makes my toes curl. "I never knew—oh god—never knew it could feel like this."

The man behind me slaps my ass, the sharp sting jolting me. "You like being our little freeuse slut, don't you?"

"Yes," I moan, the admission freeing something primal inside me. "Use me. Do whatever you want."

A man approaches, completely naked. He stands next to the table with his cock in his hand. "Suck me."

I turn my head and open my mouth, getting filled from both ends again.

As the guy fucks my mouth, the man behind me increases his pace. "Gonna fill this pussy up," he grunts, driving deep one final time before unleashing ropes of sticky cum deep inside me.

When he withdraws, his cum drips down my thighs. A new guy takes his place. This guy's cock is curved in a way that rubs a delightful spot perfectly.

The party becomes a blur of sensation. Men take turns with my pussy while others use my mouth. At some point, I'm lifted onto the table and I'm on my back looking up at the stars while men fuck me.

Miles never leaves my side, sometimes stroking my hair, sometimes whispering encouragement, always watching with that mixture of pride and desire that makes me feel both protected and exposed in the most delicious way.

I lose count of my orgasms. Each one blends into the next until I exist in a constant state of pleasure, my body no longer my own but a conduit for everyone's enjoyment—including mine.

As the night wears on, the crowd thins. Eventually, I find myself lying on a plush lounger, cum leaking from my well-used pussy, my jaw aching pleasantly. Miles sits beside me, gently wiping my face with a cool cloth.

"Ready to head back?" he asks, his voice tender.

I nod, suddenly aware of how thoroughly exhausted I am. My muscles ache and I'm covered in cum.

Miles helps me to my feet, supporting me when my legs threaten to give out. As we make our way back toward our villa, several people we pass nod in admiration.

"You were the highlight of the finale," one woman tells me as we pass. "Absolutely breathtaking."

I blush, still capable of that despite everything I've done tonight. "Thank you."

Back in our villa, Miles turns on the shower, adjusting the temperature. He helps me step inside, my legs still unsteady.

I lean against the cool tile wall, letting the hot water cascade over me. I close my eyes as the evidence of other men swirls down the drain.

I'm not surprised when the shower door opens. Miles steps in and turns me to face him.

"I couldn't stay away," he says, voice rough.

I reach for the soap. "Let me just—"

"No." He pins my wrists against the tile. "I need you like this."

His mouth crashes against mine, his tongue pushing past my lips, reclaiming territory that's only ever been his. I moan into the kiss, arching against him.

"Do you have any idea what it did to me?" His teeth graze my earlobe. "Watching you take all those men?"

His cock presses hard against me, and I roll my hips, seeking friction. "Show me."

Miles growls and lifts me against the wall. Water streams over us as I wrap my arms and legs around him.

"Mine," he says, pushing inside me with one powerful thrust.

I whimper, oversensitive from all the cocks I've taken today, but still desperate for him. My husband. The only one who truly knows me.

"Yes," I gasp, locking my ankles behind his back. "Yours."

He fucks me with an intensity I've never felt before. He's claiming me, erasing every other touch with his own. His fingers dig into my flesh, his mouth leaving a trail of bites along my neck.

He pants, "So fucking beautiful. But this—" He punctuates the word with a particularly deep thrust. "This pussy is mine."

The possessiveness in his voice sends a fresh wave of arousal through me. I rake my nails down his back, leaving marks of my own.

"Tell me you're mine," he demands as he gets close to coming.

"I'm yours," I gasp, my head falling back against the tile. "Always yours."

My orgasm builds with startling speed and it's different from the others. This one belongs only to Miles. I scream as pure joy ripples from my fingers to my toes. I'm trembling, my body quivering with the force of my climax.

He follows seconds later, burying himself deep as he comes with a hoarse shout. We stay locked together, water streaming over us, until our breathing slows.

When we've come to our senses, he sets me down and reaches for the shampoo, working it gently through my hair.

"How do you feel?" he asks, his voice softer now.

I'm floating in the haze, and I can't keep the smile off my face. "Used. Sore...complete."

He kisses me softly, and an understanding flows between us. "You were magnificent. I've never seen anything more beautiful than you surrendering to pleasure like that."

"I never thought I could be that person," I confess as he rinses the suds from my hair.

"You've always been that person." His hands are gentle on my tender skin. "You just needed permission to let her out."

When we get out of the shower, he wraps me in a towel, and I realize he's right. The Brooklyn who arranges art has always been this Brooklyn—the one who became the art tonight.

The freeuse weekend is over, but we aren't leaving yet. It will be just me and Miles, enjoying each other for two more days. When we return to our regular lives, I'll curate exhibitions again, Miles will photograph buildings, and we'll go back to our comfortable routine. But something fundamental has shifted inside me. I don't have to hide who I am anymore, and the knowledge of that will change everything.

The End

Her Freeuse Break

A First Time Hotwife Adventure

CHAPTER 1

I adjust the vase of tulips on the dining table for the third time, rotating it two degrees to the left.

The light needs to be just right for my social media post later. My pulse quickens with familiar anxiety—if I don't get the perfect shot, my engagement will tank.

"Babe, they'll be here any minute." Austin stands in the dining room entryway, watching me fuss. "Everything looks great."

The word makes my stomach twist. Great isn't good enough. I'd prefer something a little more enthusiastic. I grab my phone and snap a quick overhead shot of the table. The white plates on the light wood look stunning with the expensive linen napkins I bought specifically for today's content.

But something's still off.

"The shadows are all wrong." I move the wine glasses half an inch. "And I haven't posted anything today. The algorithm will bury me if I don't—"

"Jenna." Austin's voice cuts through my spiral. "Put the phone down."

"This is my work," I snap, my shoulders tensing. "You wouldn't tell someone to stop working in the middle of a project."

He doesn't respond and continues observing me while I take another picture. His expression remains neutral, but I feel his judgment like a weight on my chest.

Finally, he opens his mouth to say something, but the doorbell saves me.

"They're here!" I trill, dashing to answer it.

When I open the door, Brooklyn looks different and it catches me off guard. She's always been pretty, but tonight she's radiant. Her posture is straighter, her smile more genuine. Even her eyes seem to sparkle.

"Jenna!" She pulls me into a hug that's warmer than her usual reserved greeting. "You look amazing."

I'm wearing a cream silk blouse and charcoal gray high-waisted trousers—an outfit I spent forty minutes styling and photographing earlier, complete with my nude pointed-toe pumps, and delicate gold layered necklaces. Brooklyn's in a simple sundress that probably cost half what my blouse did, but she looks infinitely more comfortable.

Her husband Miles follows behind her, carrying wine. He looks more relaxed too. Austin shakes his hand, but his attention keeps drifting back to Brooklyn. It's not sexual—more like he's trying to figure out what's different with her.

"Your place is gorgeous as usual," Brooklyn says, admiring the open-concept living area. "Very you."

Very me. What does that even mean anymore?

We settle on the large, circle couch with our wine. I resist the urge to photograph the scene—four attractive people, expensive bottle, ideal lighting. My followers would eat it up. But Austin's earlier comment telling me to put the phone down echoes in my head, so I leave my phone on the coffee table.

I slip my shoes off and tuck my legs under me. "So tell me about this Caribbean trip. You never gave me details."

Brooklyn and Miles exchange a look. Quick, but I catch it. What secrets are they hiding?

"It was educational," Brooklyn says, laughing. "Definitely not your typical resort experience."

"Educational how?" Did they go on nature hikes? Somehow I can't imagine Brooklyn doing that.

Miles takes a sip of wine. "Let's just say we learned some things about ourselves."

"You're being very mysterious." I glance at Austin, who's watching this exchange with interest. "What kind of resort was it?"

Brooklyn bites her lip. She always does that when she's deciding whether to share something. Miles gives her a tiny nod.

"Promise you won't judge?" she asks.

"When have I ever judged you?" The words come out automatically, though I immediately think of all the times I've mentally critiqued other people's choices. But Brooklyn's different; I've known her since college and she's one of my best friends.

"It was an adult resort," she says finally. "Like, very adult. They had these special events…"

"Wait, like the resort Mandy went to?"

Mandy is another college friend of ours, who recently went to a freeuse resort and had a mind-blowing experience. She came back a changed person and is still raving about the experience.

"Similar concept, but a different place." Brooklyn's cheeks flush pink. "I was…available for the other guests to use."

The word 'use' sends heat straight between my legs. I take a large gulp of wine, hoping it'll explain the flush creeping up my neck.

Austin shifts on the couch beside me. Wait, he better not be imagining other men using Brooklyn.

"That sounds…" I struggle for what to say that won't reveal how interested I am. "Intense."

"It was incredible," Brooklyn says, and there's an openness in her voice I've never heard before. "I've spent my whole life curating everything—my career, my image, even my relationship with Miles. But all the walls came down."

"Weren't you scared?" I ask.

"Terrified," she says. "But also more alive than I'd felt in years. There's something about surrendering control completely that makes a person realize how much pleasure they're capable of experiencing."

I stare at her. Wow, she's like a new woman.

Beside me, Austin has gone very still, but when I peek at him, his eyes are on me. The fire in his gaze makes my hand tremble, and I set the wineglass down on the coffee table. My pussy hums with unexpected arousal.

Austin clears his throat, and shifts the conversation to vacations in general. I listen with half an ear, lost in the fantasy of a freeuse resort. Being used. Having no control. Not worrying about how I look or what people think.

"Jenna?" Austin's voice brings me back. "You okay?"

"Fine," I say quickly. "Just hungry."

But I'm not fine. I'm wet and confused and desperately turned on. The idea of being nothing more than a hole for men to use, having my carefully maintained image completely destroyed... Holy fuck, where did this desire come from?

The rest of dinner passes in a blur. I can't stop asking questions about the resort—how it worked, what the other guests were like. Brooklyn answers freely while Miles squeezes her hand in support. Austin doesn't say much, but every time I ask Brooklyn another question, he's watching me.

When they finally leave, my heart races as I close the front door.

"That was an interesting dinner," Austin says behind me.

I turn to face him. His hands are in his pockets, and he's studying me with an unreadable expression. I'm not sure what to say to him since I don't want to admit I've been fantasizing about fucking other men.

"They seem happy," I manage.

"They do. And Brooklyn seems different. More uninhibited."

The word hits like a slap. Uninhibited. He doesn't have to say it, but that's everything I'm not.

"Jenna," he says softly. "What are you thinking about?"

I could lie, make a joke, change the subject. The safe response sits right there on my tongue—something about how nice it was to catch up with old friends.

But I'm so tired of safe responses.

I take a shaky breath while my heart hammers. What if he thinks I'm disgusting? What if this ruins everything between us?

"I'm thinking about what Brooklyn said," I say. "About surrendering control."

"What about it?" That neutral tone of his that I dislike.

My cheeks burn. I can't look at him directly, so I focus on the top button of his shirt instead. "I keep imagining…God, this is so embarrassing."

"Tell me." His voice is gentler now.

I fidget with my sleeve, and hope this isn't a mistake to say. "I'm thinking about how it would feel to be used like that. To not have to worry about being perfect."

I wait for him to look at me like I'm broken or perverted. Instead, he wraps his arms around my waist.

"Keep going," he says, and kisses the skin below my ear.

A flush spreads through me—part arousal, part mortification. "I can't believe I'm saying this out loud, but…" I squeeze my eyes shut. "I want to just be a hole for someone's pleasure."

Oh god, that sounds so slutty. Austin's grip tightens, pulling me close, and his hard cock under his jeans brushes against my thigh.

He kisses my neck below my ear. "So you want to be just a hole for a line of men to use?"

Goosebumps rise across my skin and I shiver. "Yes. I want to be used and degraded. I want men to take turns with me while you watch."

He groans. "Fuck, Jenna."

Oooh, he likes this idea, me being passed around having orgasm after orgasm and getting all dirty. I reach down and rub his cock through his jeans. "Tell me what you'd want to see them do to me."

He inhales sharply and his control snaps. He pushes me to the wall, kissing me with a hunger that borders on desperation.

When he pulls back, his eyes glitter with lust. "I'd want to see them bend you over and fuck you while you beg for more. I'd want you on your knees with your mouth full and your perfect hair ruined."

"Yes." I paw at his belt. "I want to be nothing but a set of holes for them to use," I say again. The more I repeat it, the more I want it.

We crash into the bedroom, stumbling into furniture. Austin rips my silk blouse open—buttons flying everywhere. My carefully-styled hair tangles in his fingers as he yanks my head back to expose my neck. Holy fuck.

His teeth scrape my skin, and my pussy throbs with need. I don't even flinch when my expensive trousers land on the floor in a crumpled heap. For the first time in years, I don't give a single shit how I look. I just need to be fucked. Now.

"Tell me how you want to be used," he growls.

My breath comes in quick bursts as he unhooks my bra. "I want to be fucked by strangers who just take me." Hearing my own filthy words sends a bolt of electricity straight to my clit. "I want to be on my knees, sucking on a line of cocks. I want them to cover me in cum."

He groans and forces me onto the bed, pinning my wrists above my head. He grinds against my thigh, but his jeans are in the way of him fucking me.

"You want to be a little slut?"

Holy shit, we've never done dirty talk like this before. I love it. I writhe beneath him and moan, "Yes. Just a fucktoy for anyone who wants me."

He lets go of my wrists and props himself up. There's lust mixed with something deeper in his gaze that makes my chest ache. "You're so fucking beautiful when you talk like that," he murmurs. "So filthy and real."

Real. The word sends a rush of heat through me. I grab his shoulders and pull him in for a fierce kiss. Our tongues clash as we devour each other, and he squeezes my tits like he can't get enough of me.

I can tell when he's lost his patience, and he pulls my panties down. I help kick them off and then we both attack his clothes. Once he's naked, he spreads my legs.

"Look at you," he says, voice thick with desire. "So wet and eager."

"Please," I beg, lifting my hips to tempt him. "Please fuck me."

He teases my entrance with the tip of his cock before slamming into me. The intense stretch makes me cry out. "Fuck!"

"Is this what you want?" He drills into me steadily. "To be turned into a little slut who can't think?"

"Yes. Oh god, yes!"

He grasps my hair, tipping my head back. He sucks on my neck, sending a tingle of bliss down my spine. "You're mine," he whispers. "Mine to love, mine to share."

The thought of him sharing me sends me spiraling. I can picture it vividly—on my knees, surrounded by strangers, their hands and cocks all over me. It's filthy and wrong and everything I want.

"Yes," I moan, my body quivering with each thrust. "I'm yours. Share me. Let me be a dirty little slut for you."

He pulls my thighs up as he pounds into me. I hold onto his shoulders as the tension builds, rapture coiling tighter in my core.

I'm chanting, "Fuck me, fuck me," and right before I climax, he gives a final hard whack, groans loudly, and explodes. His warm cum fills me as ripples of pleasure run up and down my body.

When he's done unloading, he collapses on top of me before rolling to his side. We're both trembling and he pulls me close. Uh...I think he just fucked me silly. I giggle at the thought and float in a haze of contentment.

"I love you." He brushes his lips against my forehead. "And I'll do anything to make you happy. You know that, right?"

"Mm hmm, and I love you," I whisper and close my eyes, letting peace wash over me.

Tonight was unexpected, but I'm more relaxed than I've been in ages.

And starving for more.

Chapter 2

I wake up with my pussy still humming from last night. Did Austin and I really fantasize about me being used by strangers? The memory sends a rush of desire through me and I fight the urge to play with myself. I can hear the shower running, so I know I have a few minutes, but I reach for my phone instead.

I check engagement and respond to comments before mentally planning today's content. I'm about ready to work on a post, but my fingers freeze over the screen.

I didn't document last night, and didn't take any pictures other than the one table shot. Last night would have made for great posts today, but I don't regret it. Austin's greedy kiss, the way he fucked me, and the dirty talk—none of that would've happened if I had been busy trying to capture the evening so I could post about it.

I scroll through my past content, and it's just the same recycled bullshit I put up every week. Morning routine. Outfit of the day. Inspirational quote over some sunset stock photo.

The comments are all the same hollow praise. "Goals!" "Living your best life!" "So aesthetic!"

My stomach churns. What the hell am I doing with my life? But at the same time, I know I need to post something–and soon–to make up for the oversight last night. It doesn't make my stomach feel any better.

When Austin comes into the bedroom with a towel around his waist, I'm staring at my phone like it personally offended me.

"What's wrong?"

"Ugh, I need to film my morning routine." The words taste like ash. "And I haven't posted anything inspirational this week. My engagement is down three percent."

He sits on the bed beside me. "What would happen if you didn't post anything today?"

I look at him like he's crazy. "I'd lose followers. The algorithm would—"

"No." His voice is gentle but firm. "What would actually happen to you? To your life?"

I open my mouth to argue, then close it. Nothing real would happen, but the void of not posting terrifies me.

"I don't know how to not perform anymore," I whisper.

Austin kisses me softly. "When you're ready for a change, I'll help you."

I smile at him and climb out of bed. But even after we have breakfast together, I can't let go that easily. After he heads to our home office to work, I set up my ring light and try to film content. The morning routine video I've done hundreds of times somehow feels impossible.

"Good morning, beautiful people!" I chirp at the camera, then immediately stop recording.

I sound like a robot programmed to simulate enthusiasm.

Take two.

"Hey everyone, hope you're having an amazing..." I stop. Delete.

Take three.

I don't even get the first line out before I'm grimacing at my fake smile.

Twenty minutes later and I'm hurling my phone onto the bed before collapsing beside it. I'm frustrated and scream into my pillow.

Austin appears in the doorway. "Jenna?"

"I can't do it anymore." My voice is muffled by the pillow. "I can't pretend to be this perfect person who has her shit together."

The bed dips as he sits beside me and rubs my back in slow circles. "So don't."

"It's how I make money. It's who I am."

"No." His voice is firm. "It's what you do. It's not who you are."

I lift my head to look at him. "Then who am I?"

He doesn't answer right away. "I don't know," he says finally. "But I want to find out. And so do you."

The skincare brand video I'm supposed to create today weighs on my mind, and suddenly everything feels impossible. The weight of it all—the constant pretending, the fake smiles, the lies—crashes over me.

I turn and collapse into his arms, the sobs coming hard and fast. "I'm a fraud," I cry into his shirt. "I'm selling this perfect life that doesn't exist. I hate my morning routine. I don't even use half these products I promote."

He holds me tight as I fall apart.

"It's like I'm suffocating," I continue. "Like I'm trapped in this fake life and I don't know how to get out."

"Then let's get you out."

I blink at him through my tears. "What do you mean?"

"Let's take a real vacation. No phones. Just us."

The idea terrifies me. "I can't just disappear from social media. I'll lose everything I've built."

"What if what you've built is a prison?"

Is he right? When was the last time I felt as happy as Brooklyn looked last night?

"Where would we go?" I ask softly.

"Anywhere you want. As long as you unplug completely."

I consider Brooklyn's stories about surrendering control. Being nothing but a body existing purely for pleasure. My pussy aches just thinking about it.

"What about a freeuse resort?"

Austin goes very still. "You want that?"

"Brooklyn mentioned there's a whole network of these places. Different types of experiences." I play with the collar of his shirt. "I want to go somewhere I can't control anything."

"You really want to be used by strangers?"

I can't tell what he's thinking, but I'm too desperate to care. "I want to find out who I am when I'm not trying to be flawless," I blurt out. "I want to be fucked until I can't think about followers or engagement."

Austin tightens his arms around me. "Are you sure?"

"Yes. And no. I'm intimidated by the idea, but I don't want to keep living like this."

My tears dry up as he studies me and says, "Okay. Let's do it."

"Really?"

"Really. But I have conditions."

The commanding edge in his voice makes my body tingle. "What conditions?"

"No phones except for emergencies. No social media. No documenting anything for content." His eyes are intense. "Can you handle that?"

The thought of being completely disconnected makes my chest tight with panic, but underneath the fear is something else. Relief.

"I can try."

He kisses my forehead. "Good girl."

Fuck, I love when he talks to me like that. The praise sends warmth pooling low in my belly, and suddenly I'm eager to plan the trip.

That evening, we research resorts while curled up on the couch. Austin's laptop sits between us, and every image we find turns me into a thirsty slut as I imagine guys lining up to use me in each location.

"Here," Austin says, showing me a website. "Aqua Paradiso Resort."

The website has beautiful photos of tropical beaches and elaborate water features, but the language is carefully coded. 'Adult-only environment. Clothing-optional areas. Special events for adventurous guests.'

"Hey, look at this," Austin continues. "They have a strict phone policy. All devices are secured in individual lockers upon check-in. Guests may access them for thirty minutes per day maximum."

My palms start sweating. Thirty minutes. Hell, I usually spend four hours a day on my phone.

"And here's what we're looking for," he says. "They host monthly events for guests interested in alternative relationship dynamics."

I squint at the screen to read the information. The next event for women is in three weeks. A Saturday dedicated to consensual use scenarios with experienced facilitators and screened guests.

"Experienced facilitators," I laugh. "Code for men who know exactly how to fuck every hole."

"Only if you want them to."

I don't hesitate. "Right. Only if I want it."

Austin closes the laptop and pulls me closer. "So am I booking the trip?"

I kiss him deeply and murmur, "Yes, please."

That night, we fuck with a new passion.

"Tell me again," I gasp as he pounds into me. "Tell me what you want to see them do to me."

"I want to see you stop thinking," he growls. "I want to see you come so many times that you forget everything."

"Yes," I moan in delight as he repeatedly hits that perfect spot deep inside me. "I want to be nothing but holes for them to use."

"Fuck, Jenna." His thrusts becomes more urgent. "You're going to be such a gorgeous slut."

As he shoots ropes of cum deep inside me, my body convulses and I come so hard the ecstasy wipes my mind clean.

Later, lying in sheets that definitely aren't photo-ready, I stare at the ceiling and try to imagine what it's going to be like at a freeuse resort where I can't control everything.

It terrifies me.

It also might save me.

CHAPTER 3

The taxi winds through lush Costa Rican mountains, and I grip Austin's hand as we approach Aqua Paradiso Resort. My phone dings in my purse—probably social media notifications I should check—but I ignore it. In twenty minutes, it'll be locked away anyway.

"You okay?" Austin asks, squeezing my hand.

"Anxious," I admit. "But good anxious."

The resort entrance is understated—no flashy signs, just carved wooden gates that open to reveal manicured gardens and glimpses of blue water beyond. There's butterflies in my stomach when we pull up to the main building. This is exactly what I need, even without the freeuse day.

At check-in, a woman introduces herself as Carmen and explains the policies. She's in her early forties with kind eyes and the sort of confidence that makes me immediately jealous.

"First time with us?" Carmen asks, sliding two key cards across the marble counter.

"Yes," Austin answers when I seem to have lost my voice.

"Well, we're delighted to have you join us. I see you've already completed all the preliminary online forms we emailed."

My mind flashes back to the questionnaires we filled out three days ago. Pages and pages of likes, dislikes, hard limits, soft limits. Checkboxes for every sex act imaginable—some I'd never even heard of before. I remember blushing as Austin watched me check 'Yes' next to things like 'multiple partners', 'public use', and 'dirty talk'.

"The consent forms were thorough," I say, my cheeks warming at the memory.

"They have to be," she replies with a knowing smile. "Especially for our one-day freeuse events. We take consent and boundaries extremely seriously here."

I nod, remembering the medical forms too. The entire process had been surprisingly clinical, but also reassuring. These people aren't messing around.

"Your preferences have been logged in our system," she continues. "There are colored wristbands in your room for the freeuse day tomorrow. The ones you choose to wear will communicate your boundaries to our facilitators and other participants. Nothing happens that you haven't consented to, but if you ever need something to stop, we use 'red light' as a safeword."

I had read about the safeword in the paperwork, and excitement surges through my veins. Holy fuck, this is really happening.

Carmen produces a small lockbox with our room number on it. "Phones and smart devices go here. You can access them for thirty minutes daily if needed."

My chest tightens as I stare at the box. I usually check social media every fifteen minutes and I'm uneasy at the thought of being so disconnected.

"What if there's an emergency?" I blurt out.

"Our staff can find you, and we have your emergency contact information." Carmen smiles. "Trust me, most guests find the digital detox more freeing than frightening."

Austin places his phone and watch in the box without hesitation. I clutch mine for another second, then force myself to let go. The separation feels physical, like missing a limb.

She hands us a pamphlet. "Here's information about tomorrow's special event. Participation is entirely voluntary, and you can change your mind at any time."

The pamphlet contains no explicit photos, just elegant descriptions of 'consensual scenarios' and 'exploration of power dynamics.' But my pulse quickens reading about the colored wristband system.

Pink for vaginal access. Black for oral. Green for anal. Purple for anything goes. Workers and vetted guests who can use the women wear yellow wristbands.

My pussy gets wet as I imagine wearing the purple band. Would I really do that? Let strangers fuck all my holes?

"The water park facilities are closed in preparation for the event," she continues. "Tonight, feel free to explore and get comfortable with the environment."

Our suite is on the fourth floor of the resort. When we open the door, I smile at how perfect it is—a spacious room with a king-sized bed draped in crisp white linens, natural wood furniture, and floor-to-ceiling windows that flood the space with light. There's a rainfall shower visible through frosted glass in the bathroom, and a deep soaking tub built for two. The room smells faintly of vanilla and something tropical.

I instinctively reach for my phone to capture this gorgeous view, my hand patting my pocket before I remember—no phones allowed at the resort. For a split second, I feel that familiar panic of not being able to document the moment, to share it with the world. But then I take a deeper breath and really look around, committing every detail to memory instead of through a screen.

Our view overlooks the main pool area and beyond that, the elaborate water park that drew me to this resort over other options. From our balcony, I can see a lazy river, a water slide, and various pools.

"It's beautiful here," I say as Austin wraps his arms around me from behind.

"How're you doing without your phone?"

I consider the question honestly. "It feels like something is missing, but it's also lighter somehow. Like I don't have to perform."

"You never have to perform for me."

"I know. But I do it for myself too. Constantly." I turn in his arms. "What if I don't know how to have fun anymore?"

He kisses my nose. "I'm sure all the cocks flying at you tomorrow will distract you."

"Hey!" I slap his chest and laugh. "I doubt there'll be enough guys here to have cocks being thrown at me. You're just being silly."

He gives me a smug look. "We'll see."

What if he's right? My body tingles with anticipation. What if tomorrow I'm surrounded by so many men wanting to use me that I get tired of it? Wait, is that even possible?

Nah, not when it's freeuse for only one day.

That evening, we explore the resort. The restaurant overlooks the ocean, and I actually taste my food without photographing it first. Other guests seem relaxed in a way that feels foreign—couples talking without checking devices, people reading books–actual physical books–by the pool.

I study the women we pass, wondering which ones will be participating tomorrow. That blonde with the perfect tits? The brunette with legs for days? Will they be my companions in this adventure?

After dinner, we walk through the water park area. Even though it's closed, security lights illuminate the elaborate setup. The lazy river curves through multiple sections, with platforms and seating areas along the banks.

Austin studies the tiered ledges overlooking one section of the river. "A lazy river doesn't seem like something people would watch. Isn't that more for the person floating down it?"

I follow his gaze, my mind racing with possibilities. There has to be something people would want to see, or maybe it's just a bunch of sexy half-naked women that's the draw.

"I can't believe we're actually at a freeuse resort," I whisper.

"What part scares you most?"

I think about it. "What if I don't like it? What if no one wants to fuck me? What if—"

He cuts me off with a kiss that starts gentle but quickly deepens. Suddenly I'm fisting his shirt and wishing we were in our room. His tongue explores my mouth possessively, and I feel myself getting wet.

When he breaks the kiss, we're both breathless. "And what excites you most?"

"The opposite. What if so many guys want to fuck me that I can't handle it? What if I love being used like a slut and don't want normal again?"

He laughs as we continue walking, passing the storage area where I glimpse inflatable pool floats half covered by tarps. Wait, is that a pink unicorn? Oh fuck yeah, I'm floating down the lazy river on that unicorn tomorrow. It's decided.

"There's something else," I say as we head back toward our room. "I keep thinking about what Brooklyn said—about not performing. I don't remember how to have sex without worrying about how I look."

Austin stops walking. "What do you mean?"

"Even with you, I'm always conscious of making sure I look good." The admission feels shameful. "It's been a very long time since I've completely lost control during sex."

"We talking years?"

"Probably. There's always part of my brain making sure my hair looks good or that I'm arching my back the right way instead of just feeling it."

Austin's quiet for a long moment. When he speaks, his voice is rough. "Tomorrow, you won't be able to direct anything."

The idea sends heat straight through me. "I know."

"The men will use you, and you'll have no control over who fucks you or where they decide to come."

"Austin..." My legs quiver.

"Is that what you want? To be a little slut that guys cover in cum?"

My pussy buzzes. Shit, what is he doing to me? "Yes."

We barely make it back to our room, hands everywhere, pulling and ripping at clothes until we're naked. But this time feels different—like we're both preparing for tomorrow's freeuse day.

Austin pushes me back against the sliding door to our balcony, his mouth slanting across mine.

"Tell me what you're thinking about," he demands, slipping his fingers between my legs to play with my clit.

"About a line of guys using all my holes."

"Fuck." His control cracks, and he spins me around. I press my palms to the glass door. "You want to be used without knowing who it is?"

"Yes." I moan as he enters me from behind. "I want to be completely ruined."

I can feel myself getting wetter with each thrust, my body welcoming him deeper. Austin fucks me with desperate intensity while I brace myself against the glass. My hair falls messily over my face, and I squeeze my eyes shut as the delight builds. I don't care if people can see us through the glass. I only care about the pleasure of his cock driving into me.

"Tomorrow," Austin growls, "you're going to discover who you really are."

"Who am I?" The question comes out broken by gasps.

"Someone who's gorgeous when she's completely destroyed."

He triggers something primal in me. My pussy ripples around his cock as I come with a cry, my body convulsing in waves of rapture. For those few seconds, I'm nothing but sensation and need.

Holy fuck. That's what I want tomorrow—to be nothing but a body experiencing pleasure.

Afterward, we lie in bed with the balcony door cracked, warm air blowing over our sweat-dampened skin. I should feel exposed lying here naked and messy with the curtains open, but instead I feel peaceful.

I yawn, and when I realize I'm going to fall asleep soon, I ask, "What if I chicken out?"

Austin rolls onto his side to face me. "You don't have to do anything you don't want to. But what if you go through with it and discover something amazing about yourself?"

I study his face in the moonlight. "You really want to watch other men use me?"

"Baby, I'm dying to watch you get fucked by strangers, but I don't want you to do it for me. You need to do it because you want it."

"Even if I like it more than I should?"

"Especially then."

I smile and curl into his side, my head on his chest, listening to his heartbeat. Tomorrow can't come fast enough.

The unknown terrifies me.

It also makes me wet all over again.

CHAPTER 4

I wake before Austin, staring at the ceiling while he sleeps beside me. The wristbands for the freeuse event sit on the nightstand like colorful temptations—pink, black, purple, and green. Four choices that will define my entire day. Excitement bubbles in my chest.

Austin stirs. "Morning, beautiful."

"I don't feel beautiful. I feel sick."

He props himself up on an elbow. "You don't have to do this. We can just have fun at the resort like a normal vacation."

The offer should be appealing, but instead, it makes me more certain of what I want.

"No." I sit up, reaching for the wristbands. "I want to do this and find out who I am when I can't control everything. I'm just nervous."

I pick up the pink band first. Vaginal access. "This one for sure." I stretch it over my hand to settle it on my wrist, and my skin tingles. "And this one." The black band—oral—goes on next since I've always enjoyed giving blowjobs.

Austin watches silently as I hold the purple and green bands. Anal and anything goes. I've done anal with him, but always carefully, with lots of preparation. Yeah, I'm probably not ready for that this weekend.

"I don't know about purple or green," I admit.

"You don't have to decide now. I could put them in my pocket and you could add them later if you want."

I set the green and purple bands on the nightstand. "That's a good idea. So two bands. Pink and black."

"How do you feel?"

"Other than like I might throw up? Horny." I laugh shakily. "But we're burning daylight, and I'm starving."

We shower quickly before getting dressed. I pull on the colorful bikini I selected for this trip—bright pink, blue, and purple that seems to shimmer. Following the resort's suggestion for easy-access clothing during the freeuse day, I slip a flowing white sundress over the bikini. My comfortable sandals slide on effortlessly. Austin keeps it simple with swim shorts and a blue T-shirt. I pull my hair up into a high ponytail and catch our reflection in the mirror—we make a striking couple.

Breakfast is served in the restaurant, but as we walk toward it, two men step into our path. They're both tall and muscular, wearing polo shirts with the resort logo and khaki shorts. They glance at my wrist and smirk as they block our way.

"Is your name Jenna?" the dark-haired man asks.

"Yes?" I respond, confused until I see they both have yellow wristbands. I swear my heart stops for a second. Are they here to–

"No, it's not," the other man says, his tone playful but firm. "Holes don't have names."

The dark-haired man steps closer, placing a hand on my shoulder and applying gentle pressure. "Kneel, slut."

My brain blips out as I stare up at the two men. Austin nods slightly in a silent affirmation that this is my choice, and steps back, giving me space. I take a shaky breath and slowly lower myself to my knees on the stone path. My sundress pools around me, and I'm suddenly aware of how vulnerable I am. I'm glad Austin is here with me, watching.

The dark-haired man unzips his shorts, freeing his cock. Knowing I'm about to suck on a cock that isn't my husband's for the first time in years makes my body tingle with delight. He holds my chin and tilts my face up as he guides his cock to my mouth, rubbing the head against my lips. I open for him, and his cock slides in. He's thick and smells different from Austin—there's musk mixed with a faint hint of chlorine, and I can tell he went swimming this morning.

I start to suck, tentatively at first, then with more confidence when I hear his groan of approval.

He thrusts into me slowly. "This hole is a good one."

"Let's see how good it is at taking two cocks," his blonde friend says, stepping forward. Suddenly, there's another cock tapping on my cheek.

I pull off the dark-haired man's cock and turn to take the second one. The blonde guy's shaft is slightly thicker, and I have to stretch my mouth to fit around him. I bob my head and suck on him for all I'm worth. He wraps my ponytail around his fist, guiding my movements.

"Fuck, you're good at this," he murmurs.

They take turns, their cocks sliding in and out of my mouth in a steady rhythm. I'm nothing but a receptacle for their pleasure, and the thought turns me into a puddle of neediness. Austin stands off to the side, and out of the corner of my eye, I can see the bulge in his shorts. Knowing he's turned on sends another wave of desire through me.

The blonde man pulls out suddenly. "I need another hole," he says, pushing me down onto all fours. My sundress rides up as he kneels behind me and pulls my bikini bottoms aside, exposing my wet pussy. He slides his cock in slowly while the dark-haired man sinks to his knees in front of me, feeding his cock back into my mouth.

I'm filled at both ends, stuffed and used, and it's everything I imagined. I can't think about anything but the growing ecstasy. The guy behind me picks up the pace, and the guy in my mouth speeds up in response. I can tell they don't care about my pleasure, and I love every second of it.

The man in my pussy grasps my hips tighter, his thrusts becoming urgent. "Fuck, I'm going to come," he groans, and I feel him swelling inside me. He grunts as he comes, his cock pulsing as he fills me with cum. He pulls out, and I feel a rush of wetness as his cum leaks out of me. The guy in my mouth speeds up until he explodes. I taste the bitterness as I try to swallow quickly. Saliva and cum drip down my chin as he pulls out.

"Good slut," he says, tucking his softening cock away. The two guys stand over me, smirking.

"By the way," the dark-haired man says. "We're part of the guest relations team. Just wanted to help you get warmed up for your freeuse day."

"Enjoy yourself," the blonde adds with a wink before they both laugh and head down the path.

As the cum drips out of my pussy, it hits me—they were doing what I wanted based on my preferences. The men were calling me a hole and using dirty talk, both things I indicated on the forms we filled out before check in. I didn't really expect the employees to know who I was or what I said I wanted. It's a nice bonus to the resort, adding an extra layer of excitement.

Austin is there instantly, sitting on the ground and pulling me into his arms. "You're amazing," he says, his voice filled with lust. "You're so fucking beautiful when you're being used like that."

The world is hazy and I'm so turned on I can barely focus. "I want more," I whisper.

"You'll get more, baby. You'll get all the cock you can handle. But first you need breakfast."

As he helps me to my feet and wipes my face off with the edge of his shirt, my pussy clenches with anticipation. This is just the beginning.

When we reach the dining area, the atmosphere is different today. There's an underlying excitement and sexual energy. Other women sport various combinations of colored wristbands.

I spot a redhead with a purple wristband who practically glows with confidence. My pussy throbs involuntarily as I imagine a train of men using her ass. The redhead catches me staring and smiles.

"First time?" she asks, approaching our table.

I laugh nervously. "Yeah."

"You have the look. I'm Sarah." She extends her hand, and I notice her manicure is chipped. Strange how that detail makes me feel better—she's not perfect.

"Jenna. And this is Austin."

Sarah nods to Austin, then focuses on me. "Two bands is perfect for starting. You can always add more later."

"That's what we thought. Do the guys get rough?" The question slips out before I can stop it.

"Sometimes. But in a good way. The kind that makes you feel alive." She glances at her purple band. "This is my third time. First time I wore black only. Second time I added pink. Today..." She grins. "Today I want to see how much I can take."

After she leaves, I eat half my eggs and push the rest around my plate. My stomach is too knotted for food.

"Second thoughts?" Austin asks.

"Nope, just processing. I didn't expect to be fucked on the way to breakfast."

He laughs. "Well, maybe you should have."

He pulls the resort's glossy brochure from his pocket. "So what should we do this morning? I know you want to try the lazy river, but is there anything else you want to do?"

"What're the options?"

"Here, you can read it and decide."

He passes me the brochure, and I scan the page of descriptions.

Welcome to Paradise:
Unforgettable Aquatic Experiences for Adults Grotto Glory Caves *Indulge in the sensual ambiance of our warm-water caverns, featuring waist-deep pools. Women select their preferred position at the holes in the wall, while men visit from the other side. Enhanced acoustics amplify the symphony of desire, and an upstairs viewing lounge offers a discreet vantage point.*

Water-Jet Enhanced Pleasure Pool *Experience the ultimate in aquatic ecstasy with our plunge pool, lined with benches and submerged vertical jets. Each bench features a variable-speed water jet and padded knee rests, allowing for the perfect position and ultimate enjoyment.*

Tidal Fuck Benches *Immerse yourself in our shallow tide pool, surrounded by elegantly curved acrylic benches designed to support your thighs comfortably. The strategic design allows for a variety of positions while passersby stroll mere inches away.*

Steam-Mist Labyrinth *Lose yourself in our enchanting maze of narrow, tiled corridors filled with a soothing 110°F mist. Low visibility heightens the sense of mystery and anticipation, as encounters unfold organically.*

Wet Bar Spanking Ledge *Swim up to our luxurious bar and indulge in a unique experience. Our marble shelf at waist height, complete with comfortable seats, invites you to kneel while ordering a drink. Complimentary impact-play paddles are available for those who wish to add a playful twist to their cocktail hour.*

__Temptation Float Lazy River Event__ A special evening event that starts at 6 pm on freeuse days. Drift away on our enchanting lazy river, where women can relax on whimsical animal floats. Join us for an unforgettable aquatic adventure, where indulgence and pleasure meet in perfect harmony.

Each one seems like a good time to me, but I have to choose.

"I want to do the Grotto Glory Caves first."

He smiles. "Okay, baby. Eat up and let's go."

The resort stretches out with bright hibiscus flowers and tall palm trees lining the stone pathways. Bird-of-paradise plants dot the walkways with their distinctive orange and blue blooms. The closer we get to the Grotto Glory Caves, the air becomes thick and humid, sticking to our skin. The sound of waterfalls grows louder as we walk, echoing off the rock formations somewhere ahead.

We follow the stone path past other couples. All of the women are completely naked, their colored wristbands noticeable on their wrists. Ugh, I'm the only one still dressed. Was I supposed to—? I glance down at my sundress, then at Austin, uncertainty prickling along my spine. Did I miss some unspoken rule? The sight of the other women's confidence sends a confusing mix of arousal and awkwardness through me. I have no idea what I'm supposed to be doing.

The entrance of the caves leads down to a series of waist-deep pools. The air is warm and damp, and the sound of water dripping echoes through the cavern. The lighting is soft, casting a gentle glow over the unique setup—a wall in the pool with discreet glory holes at perfect height, separating the women's side from the men's. There's a ledge in front of the wall to stand on with handles in various spots that people can hold on to.

Austin takes my hand and leads me to a secluded alcove that's set up as a changing area. "You ready for this?"

I nod, heart pounding. "Yes, I think so."

He gently removes my sundress, folding it and placing it on a nearby bench. I strip off my bikini top and bottoms and add it to the pile.

"I'll be in the viewing lounge," Austin says. "Remember, you're in control. You can stop if you need to.'"

"I know. I love you."

He gives me a reassuring kiss before climbing the stairs to the viewing lounge. I take a second to absorb the atmosphere. The water is crystal clear, and the air is filled with the scent of chlorine. Other women are already engaged with men on the other side of the wall, their moans echoing through the cavern. The sound makes my pussy clench with need.

There's steps leading down into the water, and I'm surprised at how warm it is. I approach the wall and choose a glory hole where, if I stand on the ledge and bend over, my pussy lines up perfectly. The handles on the wall are going to help me not fall face first into the water.

The stone is cool against my ass as I position myself, and within moments, a cock pokes through the hole. I grip the handles tighter as the man sinks into my pussy slowly. Holy fuck, this is so dirty and feels wonderful.

My breath comes in quick gasps as he thrusts into me. The anonymity of fucking a stranger makes this filthier. He's just a cock and I'm just a pussy for him to use. I close my eyes, focusing on the bliss as he fucks me roughly. Rapture swirls low in my stomach, but before I can come, he grunts and his cum splashes into me.

When he pulls out, I'm trembling from almost coming. When another cock pokes through the hole, I sigh with relief. This second guy doesn't waste time, pounding into me as my climax immediately builds again.

I hear someone chanting, "Fuck, fuck, fuck," and when I realize it's me, it tips me over the edge. I cry out and shudder as he fills me with more cum.

I let go of the handles and sink into the water, floating in a daze. Holy fuck, this is crazy. And I want more.

I choose another hole, this one is at mouth height if I kneel on the ledge. I take my position and press against the wall, and my nipples harden from the cool stone. A cock comes through the hole, and I open my mouth. His precum coats my tongue, and I start to suck.

The man groans as he fucks my mouth. I make a game of trying to suck harder each time he slides down my throat. When he finally explodes, it's more cum than I expect, and I can't swallow it all. Cum runs down my chin and onto my chest.

I pull back and take a deep breath. My body still buzzes with desire. I've never felt anything like this before—the thrill of being used, of being nothing but a set of holes for men's pleasure. And I love every second of it.

I'm greedy and I want another orgasm, so I select another hole at pussy height. I bend over and the cock that comes through this time is thick. I groan as he stretches me out. This time, he stays still and I grip the wall handles and pound against him. I go crazy as the ecstasy builds. I'm shuddering around his cock as he adds another load of cum to my soaked pussy.

When he's done with me, I float in the water for a few minutes, enjoying the aftershocks of joy before leaving. Austin is waiting for me in the alcove with my clothes when I head toward the exit.

"You're so fucking beautiful when you're being used like that."

He kisses me deeply, and my toes curl. If there weren't so many other attractions, I'd drag him back to our room right now.

"I want more," I moan.

"Then let's go get you all the cock you can handle."

He helps me into my bikini and sundress as I contemplate what to do next. I decide on the Water-Jet Enhanced Pleasure Pool since it doesn't sound like an experience I want to miss.

The area is impressive—a crystal clear pool lined with padded knee rests in the water. Underneath each one is a vertical acrylic tube that shoots jets of water on the person. Each seat has handlebars with a control panel on it to adjust the intensity of the jet. On the pool deck in front of each jet is a bench for someone to sit and watch.

The discreet billboard by the pool gives instructions on how to manipulate the jets to the preferred speed. Around me, other women are already positioned in the water and kneeling over jets, their cries of joy filling the air.

"Let's see how many times you can come from this," Austin jokes with me, and I laugh.

"I think I'm guaranteed at least one."

I slip off my sundress and bikini again, realizing why all the women walking around are naked—it's pointless to wear clothes. Austin takes my sundress and sits on a bench in front of one of the jets while I wade over in front of him and kneel on the chair, facing him.

When I turn the dial, the jets spring to life. The water hits my clit hard and my back arches from the intensity. I grip the handles tighter, trying to adjust to the overwhelming sensation coursing through me.

Austin's eyes burn with raw desire as he watches me, his breathing shallow, the obvious bulge in his shorts reveals how much my reactions are affecting him. I try to give him a smile, but end up crying out as I almost orgasm from the jet pulsating against my clit. I'm not going to be able to take much of this before I'm a writhing mess.

A group of naked men with yellow wristbands approaches and split off towards different women. I watch over my shoulder as a tall, muscular guy moves behind me. He doesn't say anything and immediately sinks his cock into my pussy. The combination of the jet and his cock is almost too much, and I moan as he fucks me. Each thrust sends waves of pleasure through my body, amplified by the jet's constant pressure.

"Fuck, you feel amazing," he groans as he fucks me steadily.

I can't form words, my mind wiped clean by the relentless jets and his thrusts. The dual sensations build into something unstoppable. When the orgasm hits, I scream and convulse, my body seizing as ecstasy tears through me.

He doesn't slow down as he pounds into me, and growls, "Such a good slut."

I climax again, and again. The pleasure turns me into a dirty plaything for whoever wants to use me. I want them all to do anything and everything to me.

The thought gives me another mini orgasm, while the guy inside me groans, his cock jerking as he fills me with cum. When he pulls out, I'm breathless.

Another man takes his place, his cock probing my entrance before I can fully recover. He grasps my hips tightly and slams into me, bottoming out with one thrust. My eyes roll back into my head from the pleasure.

"You're so fucking wet," he groans as he fucks me hard.

I almost say that we're in a pool of water so of course it's wet, but when I open my mouth a string of nonsense moans erupt instead. Ripples of delight run up and down my body and when I change hand positions, I accidentally adjust the jet pressure. Suddenly, the water is a staccato rhythm that almost blows my mind.

"Oh fuck, oh fuck, oh fuck," I'm crying out as the guy explodes inside me. He's immediately replaced with another guy, and suddenly it becomes a train of cocks on my ass.

I lose count of how many times I come. My body is a mass of sensation, every nerve ending alive and tingling.

Austin's eyes never leave mine, and I can see the lust shimmering in them. Knowing he's turned on makes this an amazing experience.

Suddenly, I come again and the pleasure is so intense, I slump forward and scream as a toe-curling orgasm leaves me shattered.

When the man pulls out, I'm trembling so hard I can barely see straight. Austin slips into the pool and pulls me into his arms.

"Hi." I cling to him and give him a dopey smile. His clothes are getting wet, and so is my sundress and bikini that he was holding, but neither of us seem to care.

"I love you," he murmurs. "That was so fucking hot."

I'm still reeling from the bliss and my mind is mush. "I think I need to regroup."

"And drink some water and eat," he adds.

"Yeah, let's go back to the room."

He carries me out of the water and toward our room. I snuggle him, letting him take care of me. His slut wife definitely needs a break.

CHAPTER 5

We order room service and I take a catnap until it arrives. By the time we're done eating, I'm refreshed and slip on a blue sundress–this time, without anything underneath.

Austin puts on dry swim trunks and a T-shirt. "Steam-Mist Labyrinth next?"

I stretch, feeling deliciously loose. "Actually, I was hoping for the Wet Bar Spanking Ledge."

His eyebrows shoot up. "Someone's getting specific about her desires."

"I want to feel the sting."

The old Jenna would've blushed at admitting that. This version just watches Austin's eyes glitter with hunger, and feels a deep satisfaction at letting her slutty side out.

"Fuck, I love seeing you like this." He pulls me close for a kiss. "But the labyrinth first, then you can get your spanking."

I giggle. "Okay, fine."

The afternoon sun beats down on us outside. My body still thrums from the morning's adventures, and the soreness between my legs feels like a badge of honor. Slut Jenna is definitely in all her glory today.

The walk to the labyrinth winds through dense tropical foliage, my skin dampening with sweat and anticipation. Other couples pass us—some heading back from attractions with that glazed, well-fucked look I'm starting to recognize. A woman with smeared makeup and cum glistening on her face and chest catches my eye and grins at me like we share a secret. I think all the people at this resort share the secret of how amazing this is.

The Steam-Mist Labyrinth entrance looks like something from a movie. Thick mist pours from narrow corridors, and the air shimmers with heat. My sundress clings to my skin before we even step inside.

There's another changing area with benches, along with instructions for the labyrinth. I strip off my dress without ceremony and leave it on a bench. I'm learning that clothes are just obstacles here.

"Ready?" Austin's voice sounds different—rougher, more primal, and it pulls at something deep in my core.

Anticipation coils tight in my belly. "More than ready."

The mist swallows us. It's so thick I can barely see Austin, even though our fingers are intertwined. The instructions recommended we keep our footwear on and I already know why. Every surface drips with condensation and the stone walls are slick.

My other senses sharpen in the limited visibility. Distant moans echo through the maze. The mist smells like eucalyptus, and I can't stop myself from joking. "This is the place to visit if you have sinus problems."

Austin laughs, and just when I'm about to crack another joke, a male figure materializes from the haze. This new guy is shirtless and wearing shorts, and from what I can see of him, he definitely works out.

Austin lets go of my hand, and I catch a glimpse of the new guy's yellow wristband as the man steps closer. He places one palm flat on the wall beside my head and uses his other hand to guide my hip back until I'm pinned between his body and the cool tile. His chest presses against mine as his fingers brush my cheek, and I lean into the touch without thinking. The gesture feels natural in this steamy otherworld where normal rules don't apply.

"Beautiful." He traces my jawline with his finger. "And ready to be used."

He kisses me—soft at first, then deeper when I part my lips. His tongue explores my mouth while he palms my breasts. My nipples harden and he pulls on them, making me gasp.

I'm not really sure what sort of freeuse moment this is, since he's being so tender, but after all the men this morning, I'm enjoying the softness.

The stranger slides his hands under my ass and lifts me easily. I wrap my legs around his waist as his cock slides between my wet folds. Oh hello, I didn't even notice his cock was out of his shorts.

He pushes in slowly, and holy fuck he's huge. The delight is overwhelming and my head tips back against the wall as he fucks me. His thrusts are controlled; each one sends ecstasy radiating through me while the mist turns this entire thing into a dreamlike scenario.

As he fucks me, the maze comes alive around us—breathless moans echoing from hidden alcoves, the slap of bodies meeting in the mist, desperate gasps that bounce off the stone corridors. My own cries join the symphony, and I know we're adding to the soundtrack of pleasure. Every sound reminds me that we're all here for the same reason, surrendering to pure desire.

"God, you feel so good," he groans, and I realize he has an accent, British maybe. "So fucking good."

I whimper in response, and my pussy buzzes with need as my orgasm builds slowly, like a tide gathering strength.

His pace increases, and he pulses inside me as he gets close. He reaches between us and rubs my clit in time with his thrusts. "Come with me," he demands. "Let your partner hear you coming for another man."

Thinking about Austin and what this experience must be like for him detonates me. Pleasure spirals from my core as the bliss crashes through me. The guy follows immediately, groaning as he empties himself inside me.

When he pulls out, I'm quivering and cum drips down my thighs, mixing with the condensation on my skin. He sets me down, then melts back into the mist like he was never there.

Another man emerges before I can catch my breath. This one is different—younger, more aggressive. He doesn't waste time with conversation, just turns me around and bends me forward. I brace myself with my palms on the wall as he slides his cock into my slick pussy. The angle is different, deeper.

"Fuck, you're already full of cum," he growls, his hips slapping against my ass. "Such a filthy little slut."

I love the dirty talk. "Yes," I gasp. "Need more cum."

Is this really me telling a man who isn't my husband that I want his cum? I've been hiding this filthy part of myself, and letting go of my filter and saying whatever I want is liberating.

He fucks me harder and my arms shake from trying to keep myself steady. He's pounding into me, and it's exactly what I need. I'm moaning with pleasure each time he bottoms out, and the sound echoes through the corridor. He's grunting with effort, and I feel like an animal operating on pure instinct.

He comes before I can, and he pulls out and shoots his load across my back. The warm cum slides down my sides as he slaps my ass and vanishes.

I lean against the wall, panting. My well-used pussy throbs, still raring for more. The steam makes everything feel surreal, like I'm floating in an erotic dream.

A third man appears. He turns me around and kisses me tenderly before lifting one leg so he can slide into me. This one is older, with silver at his temples.

I moan and my head spins from lust. I don't know if we're even going to explore much of the labyrinth at this rate.

"So wet," he murmurs, fucking me with a patient rhythm.

I'm still so close to coming from the last guy that I rock backwards, chasing another orgasm. He responds to my desperation, his thrusts becoming more forceful.

"That's it," he encourages. "Take what you need."

I finally come again, harder this time. My pussy flutters wildly as the orgasm tears through me. He follows with a low groan, adding more cum to the mess between my legs.

When he sets my leg down, my knees nearly buckle. Austin appears through the mist like a guardian angel, and takes me into his arms as the older guy leaves.

"How do you feel?" His voice is tight with arousal.

"Incredible. Like this is a dream, but I'm finally awake."

He kisses me softly. "You're fucking magnificent, but we need to save your strength."

We return the way we came and make our way out of the labyrinth slowly, my legs still unsteady. The cooler air is a shock, and I realize how overheated I became in there. Austin grabs a towel from a stack provided at the exit and wraps it around me. I don't bother putting my dress back on.

"We need a drink," he says, leading me towards the Wet Bar Spanking Ledge. "And another snack."

We stop at a lounge chair by the pool and leave our clothes. Austin keeps his shorts on, and we enter the warm water. The swim-up bar is built into the side of the pool and has a marble countertop. Under the water in front of it are stools where guests can sit comfortably or kneel while ordering drinks. On the wall behind the bartender, paddles hang on hooks—some leather, some wood, in different sizes. Guests who kneel can be spanked by other patrons while they drink. It's a straightforward combination of bar service and adult play.

Austin sits on a barstool while I kneel and rest my elbows on the counter. My ass is above the waterline.

"You're looking for a spanking in that position," the bartender observes as she sets glasses of water in front of us.

"What? I'm just thirsty," I joke as I sip the cold water gratefully, becoming more human with each swallow.

The bartender slides a plate of fresh fruit and a bowl of nuts toward me without being asked. Austin rubs my back as we nibble and drink. The simple touch reminds me that I'm safe, loved, and free to explore without judgement.

"The lazy river event starts in an hour," he says quietly. "Still interested?"

I meet his eyes and see my own eagerness reflected there. "Absolutely. But first–"

I don't finish my sentence because a man with a yellow wristband swims up beside me. He's built like a swimmer: broad shoulders, narrow waist, arms corded with muscle. His eyes rake over my exposed backside appreciatively.

He smiles at the bartender. "Hand me a paddle. There's an ass begging to be spanked."

I grip the edge of the bar as the bartender hands him a wooden paddle with airflow holes. He tests the weight in his palm before using it on me. The first strike is sharp and lands across both cheeks. I moan, my back arching involuntarily.

"Good?" he asks.

"Harder."

The second one is exactly what I need—enough force to make my skin pinken. The third makes me moan. By the fifth, I'm wiggling my ass to tempt him to keep spanking me.

"Such a good little pain slut," he says, running his palm over my reddened ass.

God, this feels good, and it's just what I needed. I try to take a drink, but the water sloshes over the side when he spanks me again. The experience is surreal. I'm actually being spanked by a stranger while my husband watches. The old Jenna would've been mortified. This version just jiggles her ass and hopes the spanking doesn't stop.

"More," I beg between strikes. "Please."

The bartender lays other paddle options on the counter and he switches to a leather paddle, the sensation different but equally intense. Each smack sends shockwaves through my pussy, a building pressure that's going to release.

"Touch yourself," he commands. "I want to see you come."

I slide my fingers between my legs and rub my swollen clit. It only takes a few strokes before I'm coming hard, my cries echoing across the water. The orgasm seems to last forever, my pussy spasming as pleasure crashes over me.

When it finally subsides, I'm boneless. The swimmer runs his palms over my marked skin one last time before setting the paddle down and swimming away.

Austin hauls me off the ledge with a quick "Thanks," to the bartender. He holds me close and we float in the water together.

I'm mentally fuzzy from the spanking, and his strong arms around me feel like heaven. He's my happy place.

After a few minutes of being in his arms, I realize his cock is hard. I reach down and rub him through his shorts. "Mmm, you sure you don't want to fuck me right now?"

"Oh, I can wait. I'm going to fuck you so hard later, baby, you're not going to know what hit you."

"Promises, promises," I tease as my body lights up with desire. It sounds like I'm in for a treat tonight. I stop torturing him with my hand. "I think I'm ready for the lazy river now."

He laughs, the sound rich with affection and desire. "My insatiable wife. Come on, let's go get you a float."

The lazy river awaits, and I'm ready for a little relaxation on a pink unicorn.

As he helps me out of the water and back into my sundress, I catch sight of my reflection in a mirrored sculpture. My hair is wild and my skin is flushed. I look thoroughly debauched. I look real.

This version of myself feels more authentic than any carefully curated photo I've ever posted. I'm finally becoming who I was always meant to be... which is apparently a slutty wife.

It's wonderful.

CHAPTER 6

My ass still burns from the spanking as we walk towards the lazy river. Each step is a reminder of how far I've come today. The soreness between my legs has become a constant throb—proof that I'm a little slut who has fucked so many men I've lost count.

I feel different. Raw. Like I've shed layers of bullshit and finally found myself.

The river is crystal clear and winds through lush tropical landscaping and fake rockery, but it's the men gathering along both sides that grab my attention. Some are sitting on the benches and chairs, some with drinks in their hands, while others stand along the edges. There are women too, some naked and some wearing bikinis. The entire thing has a party atmosphere. What could be this entertaining about a lazy river?

The river begins at a covered pavilion. Palm fronds create natural shade over the attendant station, and plants line the concrete deck. The water here is only knee-deep, crystal clear over smooth river stones. I can see where the current picks up about twenty feet ahead, pulling toward the first curve through the landscaping.

An attendant greets us from behind a thatched counter. "First time on the run?"

"Yeah."

She gestures toward the selection of floats on a rack behind her. "Any preference?"

I zero in on the pink unicorn. "That one."

Something about its ridiculous innocence appeals to me. Plus I can go home and tell Mandy and Brooklyn about the crazy time I floated naked on a pink unicorn.

She nods approvingly. "One of my favorites."

As she pulls it from the rack, I notice what I missed before—a thick dildo mounted in the center of the float. My stomach flips with anticipation.

"Oh fuck," I breathe.

Austin's eyes darken as he notices the detail. "Still want this?"

I strip off my sundress without answering.

"Guess so," he laughs.

The attendant explains how the float works. "This is a vibrator with three settings," she says casually, like she's describing pool temperature. "It activates automatically when you enter the current. If you need it to stop, use the red button on the unicorn's head. The white button changes the vibration speed."

"Got it," I nod, and she sets it in the water.

"Step right in here," the attendant says, pointing to a spot where the water is barely a foot deep. "Once you're ready, I'll give you a push into the current."

Austin helps me into the water. The unicorn is bright pink with a white horn and oversized cartoon eyes. The dildo is positioned in the center, protruding from the unicorn's back, angled perfectly for someone to straddle it. The float has padded rests on either side of the unicorn for my knees, allowing me to comfortably straddle the dildo without sliding off. I climb onto the float, naked, and position myself over the dildo. Austin and the attendant steady the unicorn as I slowly lower myself, feeling the dildo slide into me.

"Christ, you look incredible," Austin murmurs.

"Want a picture?" the attendant asks, and I look at Austin.

He grins. "Hell, yes."

She snaps a picture of me and takes our room number. "The front desk will send it to you when you check out."

The float rocks gently as I settle my weight and grip the unicorn's sides between my thighs. This is definitely going to be an experience.

"I love you," I tell Austin, meaning it more than I ever have.

"I love you too. And I'm going to go find a spot to watch. Have fun trying not to come."

I smile at him as he leaves. Yeah, he's crazy. Why would I try to stop myself from coming?

The attendant gives the unicorn a push. "Off you go."

The current catches the float, pulling me into the river. Within seconds, the dildo springs to life—a deep, thumping vibration. My fingers dig into the float's handles as delight radiates through my core. Oh fuck, there's no way I won't come multiple times before this is over.

I try to adjust my position as the pleasure makes me moan. Rounding the first bend, I see other women floating ahead of me. One of them is on a flamingo, her head thrown back in ecstasy as she rides a similar vibrating dildo. On the other side of the lazy river, a group of men stop her float. A guy pulls out his cock and she eagerly takes it into her mouth. The sight sends a fresh wave of desire through me.

Up ahead, there's more men waiting. A few of them stand close to the edge of the river. I bump up against the side, and one of them reaches out and stops my float.

"I caught a unicorn," he says with a smirk. He's tall and lean with an accent I can't place—maybe Australian. His companions laugh and one of the other men takes hold of the float.

"You caught her, so you get to use her first," one of them says.

I guess I now know why this is entertaining to watch. I glance around, looking for Austin, and see him sitting on one of the terraces built into the hill.

"Don't mind if I do," the guy who caught me growls, and pulls his cock out of his shorts.

He guides his cock to my lips, and I open eagerly, tasting chlorine and salt and something purely male. The vibrator pulses in my pussy as the guy's cock slides deeper into my throat. This is so fucking dirty and it sizzles my mind. I nearly come right then, but when the guy starts fucking my mouth, I get distracted.

"That's it," he groans, one hand tangling in my hair. "Such a good little cocksucker."

Another man stands beside him and strokes his cock, aiming it towards me. My orgasm slams into me without warning, tearing through me like lightning. I scream around the cock in my mouth, my pussy convulsing around the vibrator as my toes curl in bliss.

The guy in my mouth doesn't stop—if anything, he fucks my throat quicker. "She needs to come again. She tightened her throat when she screamed."

The guy stroking his cock over me groans and suddenly strings of cum coat my breasts. A second later, the guy in my mouth floods my throat with cum. I swallow desperately, but some escapes down my chin. When he pulls out, another guy steps up and feeds his cock into my mouth.

I suck on the new cock like it's a delicious treat, and when I come again, I squeal and rock against the unicorn. The men laugh, and two guys step up and start jerking their cocks over me.

I wanted to be covered in cum on this trip, but somehow I never imagined this is how it would happen. As the men come and coat me with their seed, more hands grab the float to keep it steady until all the men in this cluster have either come in my mouth or sprayed me with their cum.

When they let go of the float, I continue on down as my head spins. Jesus, how long did the brochure say this river was? I'd barely gotten out of the gate.

I float along for a few minutes, passing geysers and a mini waterfall. Another woman is right behind me and when I spin around, I realize it's Sarah from breakfast. She waves at me, and she's covered in cum as well. I don't have time to ask, but I hope she got all her holes filled like she wanted.

As I round another curve, more guys grab my float, spinning me around so I'm facing them. There are three men, and they eye me like I'm their personal feast.

"See you later!" Sarah calls out as she floats past, and all I can do is flash her a smile before one of the men grips my chin and turns my head towards his cock.

"Look at this mess," he says, running his finger through the cum on my chin. "You've been busy."

I moan in response. The vibrator hasn't stopped, and my pussy is swollen and sensitive from constant stimulation. When he taps his cock against my lips, I lick him and giggle before he slides it in.

Time becomes a blur as I bounce on the vibrator and the guys pass me between them like a toy. I come at least once while I'm sucking on a cock, and one of them comes on top of my head. He rubs the cum through the strands of my hair and steps back, pleased.

"There, she's a masterpiece."

A masterpiece of complete debauchery maybe. As I suck on another cock, somewhere in the haze, I realize I'm not performing. I didn't once think about taking scenery pictures for social media. I'm just existing in pure sensation, letting myself be exactly what I am in this moment—a vessel for pleasure, both mine and theirs.

The thought tips me over the edge again. This orgasm is different. It starts in my toes and rolls up through my entire body, leaving me shaking and gasping. The men cheer, their voices echoing off the water.

"That's what we like to see," a guy in the audience calls out.

The float continues its journey, carrying me to the next station. I'm covered in cum now—it drips from my chin, coats my breasts, runs down my thighs. My hair is a tangled mess, and I can feel more cum drying on my back.

I've never felt more beautiful.

I can see the end of the lazy river, but there's a final group of two guys waiting at the end. These men are different—quieter, more intense.

"Last stop," one of them says. He's older than the others, and my pussy clamps around the vibrator as another small orgasm hits.

They guys work together, and before I know it, I'm alternating between them, taking each of their cocks into my mouth in turn.

"Hey, lets see if she can swallow them both at the same time," one of them suggests and the older guy laughs as they both try to shove their cocks in my mouth together.

I stretch my jaw wide, and I'm laughing with them when we realize it's not going to work.

"Oh well, she can just suck on us one at a time then," the older one says, and presses on the back of my head to force his cock all the way down my throat. He holds me there and the muscles of my throat work around him until he explodes. When he pulls out, I'm coughing as cum and saliva mix and pour down my chest. Fuck, this is so damn filthy.

The other guy strokes his cock until he sprays my breasts with cum. I laugh in delight and rub the cum into my nipples and ride the vibrator. The complete freedom in this moment is beyond anything I expected to experience. I don't think this day could get any filthier.

When they let go of the float, I drift into a pool where Austin is waiting for me. He's in the water and he turns off the vibrator and pulls me off the float. He kisses me deeply, and I try to tell him not to do that because of how many guys I just blew, but then realize he's well aware of that fact.

I'm plastered to him, getting him filthy with me, and I can feel his cock surge against my stomach.

He pulls away slightly, tucking a stray lock behind my ear. "Hey, you back with me?"

I try to speak but only manage a whimper. My body feels like liquid, every muscle loose and satisfied. I'm covered in cum and river water, and I've never felt more myself.

"Need a drink," I finally croak.

He carries me out of the water, and an attendant comes to fetch the unicorn float. When he sits down on a nearby chair, he somehow magically has a bottle of water. The cool liquid soothes my raw throat, and gradually the world comes back into focus. We're in a shaded pavilion at the river's end, and other couples lounge nearby in various states of post-orgasmic bliss.

I'm in his lap, and as we snuggle, he pulls my wristbands off. I don't stop him.

"How do you feel?" Austin asks.

I consider the question seriously. How do I feel? Used. Transformed. Free.

"Like I finally know who I am," I say.

His smile could power the entire resort. "And who is that?"

I look down at my cum-covered body. When I meet his eyes, there's a satisfaction that mirrors my own reflected in them.

"Someone who doesn't need to pretend anymore."

He kisses me again, deep and claiming, and the entire resort fades around us. When we break apart, I'm breathless.

"Are you ready to be done?" he asks.

I giggle. "Can we sit here a bit and relax? I want to stay like this a little longer."

"Yes, baby."

He holds me and I melt into him, enjoying his strength. We watch other floats drift into the pool, and each woman looks wrecked and deliriously happy.

"Thank you," I tell him.

"For what?"

"For letting me experience this."

His arms tighten around me. "I just want you to be happy."

"I am. I really fucking am."

The breeze is still warm, despite the setting sun, and I make a decision. When we get home, I'm not going back to who I was.

That woman is gone, dissolved in the lazy river along with all her fears of being perfect. What remains is a person completely at ease. Someone real.

Eventually, I realize my husband's cock is hard under me, and when I wiggle against him he growls, "Behave, or I'll fuck you right here."

Mmm, should I tempt him to see if he would? Right when I go to wiggle again, he stands up with me in his arms.

"You little minx, we're going back to our room."

I slide my arms around his neck and rest my head on his shoulder. "Whatever you want."

Chapter 7

The door to our suite barely closes before Austin's mouth crashes into mine. He tangles his fingers through my hair with one hand while firmly holding my waist with the other. His hold is possessive, like he's trying to claim every inch of skin he can reach.

"Fuck, Jenna," he groans. "Watching you today...seeing you let go like that..."

The raw need in his voice sends heat pooling between my legs all over again.

"Austin—"

"I need you. Right fucking now." His voice turns commanding in a way I've never heard before.

He lifts me effortlessly, and I wrap my legs around his waist as he takes us to the bed. I'm still naked, and there's only his shorts between us as we tumble onto the mattress together.

"Tell me," he demands as he runs his hands over my cum-stained skin. "Tell me how it felt."

"Amazing," I arch into him. "God, it was everything I needed."

His mouth finds my neck, teeth grazing the sensitive skin. "More. I want to hear everything."

The desperation in his voice undoes me completely. This isn't just lust—it's something deeper, more urgent. Like he's reclaiming me, reminding us both that despite everything that happened today, I'm his.

"I loved being used," I admit. "I loved having no control, no choice but to take whatever they gave me."

He groans, and grinds his cock against my pussy through his shorts. "And now?"

"Now I want you." I reach up to cup his face, forcing him to meet my eyes. "I want my husband to fuck me like he owns me."

Something snaps in his expression. He pulls his cock out and enters me in one hard thrust. I cry out in pleasure. I'm sore from today, but his cock feels too good for me to want to stop.

"Mine," he growls, setting a punishing pace. "You're fucking mine."

"Yes," I moan, and dig my nails into his shoulders. "Yours. Always yours."

He twists my hair in his hand and pulls my head back so he can suck on my neck as he fucks me. I can tell he's going to leave a hickey, and his possessiveness sends electricity through my entire body.

"Tell me you love me," he demands. "Tell me this doesn't change us."

The vulnerability beneath his dominance breaks something open in my chest. Despite everything—all the cocks, all the cum, all the ways I've been used today—this is what matters. This connection between us.

"I love you," I gasp, meeting his thrusts. "I love you so much. This...to day...it made me love you more."

His rhythm falters. "How?"

"Because you gave me this." I pull on his head and meet his lips for a fierce kiss. "You let me find myself."

He kisses me back like he's trying to pour everything he can't say into it. When he pulls back, his eyes burn with emotion and lust.

"You were so fucking beautiful today." His thrusts becomes more erratic. "Watching you take all those cocks...."

"Did you like it? Really?"

"I fucking loved it." His confession comes out as a growl. "I loved watching you get fucked over and over."

He punctuates each word with a sharp thrust, and it pushes me closer to the edge. My orgasm builds like a tidal wave, threatening to consume everything in its path.

"Come for me," he commands and slips his hand between us to rub my clit. "Come one last time tonight for your husband."

The orgasm devours me. I scream, my body convulsing as pleasure tears through me. Every muscle contracts, every nerve fires, and for a moment I cease to exist as anything but pure sensation.

"Fuck, Jenna," he groans. "I'm going to—"

"Come in me," I beg, my voice hoarse. "I need your cum."

He explodes with a roar, his cock pulsing as he empties himself inside me. The warmth of his release mingles with the cum already coating my walls, and something about that feels right—like he's reclaiming what's his.

He collapses on top of me, and we're both breathing hard. When Austin rolls to the side, he holds me like he's afraid I might disappear.

"I love you," he whispers against my hair. "I love all of you. The polished version and this messy, real version."

Tears prick my eyes. "I didn't know I could feel this free."

"How do you feel now? Really?"

I consider the question. My body aches. I'm well-used and satisfied. I can tell my hair is sticking out in every direction, and my skin is covered in sweat and cum. I probably look like a complete disaster.

"Alive," I say finally. "For the first time in years, I feel completely alive."

"No regrets?"

"None." The certainty in my voice surprises me. "This is who I am. This messy, sexual person."

"Good." He smiles with pride. "Because this version of you is fucking incredible."

We lie in comfortable silence, skin cooling in the air conditioning. Through the balcony doors, I hear the distant sounds of the resort—laughter, splashing, the occasional moan. Other people discovering themselves, just like I did today.

"What happens when we go home?" I ask, softly.

Austin's arms tighten around me. "We live our life and be happy."

The words settle into my chest like a warm weight. "You know, I never put the purple or green wristbands on... would you ever consider doing this again?"

"The resort?"

"Or somewhere else. I want to explore this side of myself. With you."

Austin laughs. "Fuck yes. We'll find other places, other experiences. Whatever you want to try."

"Really?"

"Baby, watching you was the hottest thing I've ever experienced. I want to see how far we can take this."

I lift my head to study the man I married. The man who encouraged me to experience all the pleasure the resort had to offer. "I love you."

"I love you too."

His fingers trace hearts on my skin, and I close my eyes and sigh in contentment.

"Now rest," Austin whispers. "We have three more days here."

I smile, already imagining the possibilities. "Three more days to be a slut."

"My slut," he corrects, possessiveness edging back into his voice.

"Your slut," I agree, and warmth spreads through me.

As sleep begins to claim me, I realize I didn't spend the resort-allowed 30 minutes with my phone today.

And I don't miss it at all.

When we wake up in the morning, the freeuse day is over. With that chapter closed, we spend the rest of our vacation exploring the resort's other amenities—the ones that are safe for work. We snorkel in crystal-clear water without taking underwater selfies. We hike through rainforest trails without stopping for outfit photos. We have long conversations over wine without the urge to capture the lighting.

It's the most relaxed I've felt in years.

When we check out and we're in the shuttle heading to the airport, Austin pulls out his phone.

"I thought we were still staying offline," I protest.

"We are. But I wanted to show you something." He scrolls through his photos and hands me the device.

The image on screen makes my breath catch. It's me on the unicorn float. My hair is wild, my face is makeup-free, and I'm completely unguarded. I look blissed out.

"You're beautiful," he tells me, and I study the photo, expecting to find flaws to critique. Instead, I see a woman that no filter could improve—the happiness is too genuine, too radiant.

"Can you send this to me?"

"Of course. Though I'm surprised you want it. You're naked so it's not very social media friendly."

"That's exactly why I want it." I hand his phone back. "I want the reminder of who I am when I stop trying to be flawless."

Austin pulls me close, and we watch the scenery outside the car window.

The plane ride home feels like traveling between two different worlds. As we taxi toward the gate, I watch other passengers immediately reach for their phones, eager to reconnect with their digital lives.

My phone stays in my bag.

"Ready to go back to reality?" Austin asks.

I consider the question. The reality waiting for me includes a social media empire built on performance, brand partnerships that require constant content, and followers who expect a carefully curated version of my life.

But it also includes the possibility of something better.

"I'm ready to create a new reality," I say.

Austin squeezes my hand. "I can't wait to see what that looks like."

Neither can I. But for the first time in years, I'm excited to find out.

The woman who left for this trip was trapped in a prison of her own making, suffocating under the weight of the life she thought she wanted. The woman returning is free—messy, imperfect, and completely, authentically herself.

And she's never going back.

The End

Her Freeuse Holiday

First Time Watching His Wife Shared

Chapter 1

The front door clicks shut behind me. My briefcase thunks onto the entryway bench. Freedom, at last.

It's been a long day. Work was crazy, and I had a drink with a friend from college afterwards. The stories Jenna told me only highlighted how stale my marriage has become.

I catch my reflection in the hallway mirror—wavy brown hair past my shoulders slightly disheveled from running my fingers through it all day, big blue eyes tired but still bright. My yoga-toned body looks good in my tailored suit, the hourglass figure I maintain with regular workouts still turning heads. But what's the point? When was the last time Nolan and I did anything wild? Probably years. Our bedroom activities have become as scheduled as my court appearances—Sunday mornings at 9:30 with an optional mid-week romp if one of us is sick on Sunday.

Nolan's voice floats from the kitchen. "Welcome home, baby. Was the deposition rough?"

"Oh, yeah. The client lied about damages, and then the settlement meeting took longer than expected." I kick off my heels and sigh in relief. God, I've been dreaming about this moment since 2 p.m. "But wait until you hear what Jenna told me."

When I pad into the kitchen, Nolan's plating scallops like he's creating art, using tweezers to place each microgreen just so. My husband might be a head chef at some fancy restaurant, but honestly? I love that he spoils me with this kind of care at home too. If we livened up things in the bedroom again, life would be pretty damn sweet.

He doesn't glance up. "Do I want details?"

I pour a glass of water and slide onto a stool across the island from him. "Only if you want to hear about Jenna and Austin's freeuse resort trip."

My college girlfriends and their husbands have all gone on trips to a freeuse resort recently. Alyssa, Mandy, Brooklyn, Jenna—and each came back glowing. I'm the last holdout in our group. The only one still having predictable once-a-week sex. Meanwhile, my friends are out there getting ravished by strangers while their husbands watch. The thought sends an unexpected pulse between my legs.

Nolan sets the tweezers down. His throat moves as he swallows. "Jenna actually...participated?"

"Apparently. She said it revitalized their marriage. Turns out Austin's fantasized about watching her with other men for years and never said a word."

There's tension in his shoulders when he moves to the stove. "That's intense."

My cross-examination instinct kicks in. "Ever fantasize about watching me?"

The question hangs between us. Was I too direct? Fuck it—I'm too tired tonight to play games. Ten years of marriage, and we still dance around what we really want. I've spent hours today negotiating a settlement; I don't have the energy to negotiate my own desires.

He's quiet, focused on stirring the sauce. When he finally speaks, his voice is neutral. "Which part? The watching? Or the resort?"

"Either."

He turns off the burner and faces me. There's something in his expression I haven't seen in years—vulnerability mixed with desire. "Yes. I've imagined directing other men while they use you. Seeing you come apart completely."

Oh. His admission hits me like a physical force, and heat spreads through my body. Holy shit. My lovable, goofy husband has been harboring porn-director fantasies and wants to watch men taking turns with me? My panties are suddenly damp, and I'm not sure if it's from shock or arousal. Maybe both.

"How long have you been thinking about it?"

"Years." He unconsciously reaches toward the stove to adjust the flame that's already off. "But I never thought...you're so controlled, so analytical. I couldn't picture you wanting chaos."

"Maybe chaos is exactly what this lawyer needs."

The words surprise me as I say them, but they feel true. I spend my days controlling every variable, anticipating every outcome. The thought of surrendering that control—of being passed between men while my husband orchestrates the whole thing—makes my body tingle.

Nolan stares, then moves next to me and wraps his arms around my waist. "You want it?"

Holy fuck, I can't believe we're actually discussing this. My conservative mother would have a stroke. My law partners would die of shock. And here I am, getting wet at the thought of being used by multiple men. When did I become someone who thinks about this?

"Mmm, yes. I miss feeling like I might lose control. Does that make sense?"

There's a flash of pain in his eyes, and my stomach drops. I wish I could take the words back. This isn't how I planned on discussing our marital problems. Nice going, counselor. Way to hurt the man who just opened up to you.

"Rachel, I know things haven't been great lately." His voice roughens. "But if we did this, there's no taking it back. Once you've been with other men, that becomes part of our history."

I study him for a moment. He's flushed and his eyes glitter. Maybe my words initially hurt him, but he's also turned on. The realization hits me like a shot of tequila, warm and intoxicating. My husband wants to watch me with other men.

The knot in my stomach loosens, and I give him a saucy grin. "I'm aware of the ramifications. The question is, do you want to see your wife get fucked by strangers?"

The crude language feels foreign but thrilling. I never talk like this. In bed, I've always whispered politely—'A little to the left, please' and 'That feels nice'—like I'm asking someone to pass the salt. But "fucked by strangers"? Who is this woman taking over my mouth?

Nolan's eyes blaze with lust. "Christ, Rachel."

"Is that a yes?"

Instead of answering, he kisses me with more passion than we've shared in months. I can taste years of unspoken desires. Our tongues swirl together, and a tingle of pleasure runs up my spine. This is what I've been missing—this raw, unfiltered need.

When he breaks off the kiss and nibbles on my neck, I moan softly. "That seems like a yes."

He chuckles and murmurs against my skin, "I want to see you used by men who don't know your name. Who only care about your body." He cups my breast and brushes his thumb across my stiffening nipple. "I want to tell them how to fuck you while you squirm."

Um, wow. Liquid heat shoots straight to my core. Who replaced my husband with this dirty-talking sex god? And why didn't we have this conversation years ago? I reach down and squeeze his cock. "Then after dinner, let's research resorts."

Later, we're in bed, sitting up with our backs against the headboard while I search on my laptop. Jenna said it was easy to find the resorts. One deep dive into an online forum, and I have to agree with her. These places aren't exactly advertising on billboards, but they're not that hard to find either. Just like the best legal loopholes—hidden in plain sight.

"Here's the thing," I say, scrolling through various resort options. "All our friends went to tropical locations. Beaches, pools, that whole sun-and-sand fantasy."

Nolan kisses my neck. "And that doesn't appeal to you?"

"Ski season's here, and you know how we always do our annual trip?" I click through to a different resort. "If I'm going to step completely outside my comfort zone, I want to be a little different."

That's when I find it. "Shadowpine Ski Resort," I read aloud. "A couples retreat nestled in pristine mountain wilderness. Luxury accommodations, world-class skiing, and personalized intimate experiences on select weekends."

The photos show snow-capped peaks, cozy fireplaces, and hot springs steaming in mountain air. It looks like the kind of place we'd go for a normal vacation, which somehow makes it naughtier. My pulse quickens as I imagine being bent over a pristine snowbank while some stranger takes me from behind. The cold air on my skin, the warm cock inside me...I squeeze my thighs together at the thought.

Nolan reads, "Private shuttle access only. Sounds isolated."

"Exactly." I scroll through amenities and read about the intimate experiences it offers. "Look at this: 'Our wristband system during freeuse weekends ensures clear communication of boundaries while maintaining the fantasy element of your mountain retreat.'"

"So the same concept as the tropical resorts, but with skiing and fire-places instead of beaches and pools?"

"Apparently. And I like the idea of being...available...while surrounded by all that snow and mountain air."

Yep, I'm a slut who wants to be used at a ski resort.

He grins. "Maybe getting fucked on a secluded trail while I watch?"

"Yes. Or in front of a fireplace while snow falls outside."

His voice gets rougher. "I could watch you get fucked against floor-to-ceiling windows overlooking a valley. Is this really what you want?"

"Yes."

Nolan's eyes blaze with desire. "The thought of guys lining up to use you at a hot spring..."

I can't believe he's turned on by this idea, but he clearly is. I reach over and squeeze his cock through his pajama pants.

He slides a hand up my thigh and under my nightgown. I spread my legs slightly as he nibbles on my neck and growls, "Tell me what you're imagining."

"Being fucked by strangers whenever they want me." The words come out breathless as his hand brushes my panties.

He slips his fingers under the fabric. "You're so wet."

I am. I'm wetter than I've been in months. My body's screaming for things I've never dared to want.

When I close the laptop and set it on the nightstand, he's on top of me before I can gasp. He spreads my thighs apart and rubs against me through our clothes.

"Tell me," he growls, as his teeth scrape my neck. "Tell me how fucking bad you need my cock inside you."

My eyes widen. Nolan has never talked like this—ever. In ten years of marriage, our bedroom talk has been polite, almost clinical. This side of him thrills me.

"Say it." He pulls at a nipple through my nightgown. "Tell me what a greedy slut you are. How you've been dreaming about multiple men fucking you."

Shame burns my cheeks, but that just makes me wetter. The words 'greedy slut' from my husband's mouth should offend me—the feminist attorney who corrects opposing counsel for less. Instead, my pulse thunders in my ears.

"Yes...god, yes. I need your cock. Need to be used."

"Louder." His fingers hook into the waistband of my panties, dragging them off. He tosses them off the bed, and I spread my legs wider as he rubs my clit.

My husband, the thoughtful chef who plates microgreens with tweezers, has flipped the tables and become demanding. The contradiction makes my head spin.

I'm panting, arching into his touch as I gasp, "Please, fuck me."

"That's my good little fucktoy."

Fucktoy? The word sends a shock through my system. I've never been anyone's fucktoy. I'm a partner at a law firm. I negotiate billion-dollar mergers. And yet my pussy clenches at the degradation.

He pulls his pajama pants down and grinds the hard length of his cock against my pussy without sliding in. "How bad?"

"So bad. I need it, please," I moan, and he presses the head of his cock against my entrance.

"Need what?" He thrusts slightly, giving me just the tip. "Ask nicely."

Damn him, I did just ask nicely! His teasing is driving me crazy. I'm begging now and loving it. "I need your cock. Pretty please with sugar on top?"

He laughs and pushes another inch inside, making my inner muscles clench. "Admit how much of a slut you are for my cock."

The words trigger a pulse of wetness between my legs. My analytical mind is shutting down, replaced by pure sensation.

"I'm your slut," I pant, pushing back against him to try to get him to thrust in further. "Always yours—"

"Only mine?" He brings his hand between my legs and brushes circles around my clit. "You want more than this, don't you? More than just my cock."

Each filthy question pushes me further from the controlled attorney and closer to something primal I've kept buried. The dirtier he talks, the more I want to surrender.

"Yes!" I whimper, willing to say anything in this moment if it gets me fucked.

"Such a slut," he groans as he sinks in fully.

I wrap my arms and legs around him while he drives in deeper. "Tell me how badly you want other cocks stuffing every hole."

The image explodes behind my eyes—hands grabbing me, mouths on my skin, thick shafts pushing inside—and my pussy spasms around him. "I want it," I sob. "Want strangers fucking me while you watch."

"While I tell them how to use you," he corrects, hammering into me.

His filthy words are too much for me, and I cry out as my orgasm rips through me. I milk his cock as the pleasure ripples from my fingertips to my toes.

He fucks me through the convulsions. "Going to watch you suck cock after cock and swallow every drop," he groans. "You're going to beg for a stranger's cum."

Fuck, that's hot. I imagine him watching me on my knees as a train of guys fuck my mouth, and it tips me over the edge again. "I'll beg!" I writhe against him. "I'm just your dirty little slut!"

He roars as he explodes, pumping his load deep inside me. I feel each hot jet as I shudder from bliss.

When he's done, we both collapse into the mattress. My mind is fuzzy, and I'm not sure how long it is before I giggle, "So, when can we go?"

Chapter 2

The flight takes forever. I've read the resort's website three times, analyzing every detail like I'm prepping for a trial. Our health screenings are done, the privacy agreements signed, and we answered a very long questionnaire about our sexual preferences and desires. I'm not sure I ever blushed harder than when I wrote down that I wanted to be degraded and called a fucktoy and slut. My husband woke something inside me that I didn't even know was there.

We catch a shuttle at the airport, and my hands are shaking as our shuttle climbs the winding mountain road. I smooth down my cashmere sweater and adjust my fitted jeans, wondering if I should have worn something sexier for our arrival. The simple gold necklace at my throat feels too conservative now, too much like work-Rachel instead of about-to-get-fucked Rachel. God, I'm actually doing this. In less than an hour, I'll be at a resort where I might let complete strangers touch me—well, more than just touch me. The thought sends a delicious shiver down my spine. The driver mentioned we're the last pickup of the day—forty minutes from the nearest airport to complete isolation.

"Almost there," he calls back, taking a final curve.

Shadowpine Ski Resort comes into view, and I grip Nolan's thigh. My nails dig into the fabric of his pants.

"Holy shit," I breathe.

The place looks like a luxury travel ad. Modern alpine buildings blend into the mountainside—stone, cedar, copper accents gone green. Everything screams expensive elegance, not the debauchery I know happens here. If my colleagues could see me now—Ms. Perfect Planning about to surrender all control. They'd never believe it. Hell, I barely believe it.

"No one would think this place had freeuse weekends," Nolan says, mirroring my thoughts, as the shuttle parks in front of the resort.

I hum my agreement as we climb out and a valet greets us. Is he one of the men who might fuck me tomorrow? Is he imagining me naked already? The thought makes my cheeks flush and my core tighten.

"Welcome to Shadowpine Ski Resort. Checking in?"

"Yep," Nolan says. "We're here for the weekend."

"Excellent. I'll send your luggage up while you check in. The concierge will explain our amenities and tomorrow's special event."

Special event. The euphemism makes me want to giggle. I bite my lip to keep from laughing out loud. It's such a nice way to put it. Like we're here for a wine tasting instead of me getting railed by strangers.

The lobby continues the upscale theme. Soaring ceilings, a massive fireplace, leather seating. Classical music plays softly while couples snuggle on oversized couches. A woman laughs throatily, her hand possessive on her companion's thigh. Another couple shares a kiss that lasts too long for public, his hand tangled in her hair. I catch fragments of conversation about "boundaries," and "experiences," and "last time we were here."

A woman approaches with a smile that says she's seen everything. "Mr. and Mrs. Morgan? I'm Sarah, your guest relations coordinator. Follow me and I'll check you in privately."

She leads us to a discreet alcove, shielding us from the other guests. The sudden privacy makes this real. Tomorrow I might be on my knees sucking a bunch of cocks. The thought should terrify me, but instead, I'm wet just thinking about it.

"First time at Shadowpine Ski Resort?" she asks.

"Yes," I answer, proud that my voice sounds steady. Inside, I'm practically vibrating with anticipation.

"Wonderful. Let me explain how everything works." She opens a leather folder with our info, then produces a velvet display case full of colored wristbands. "You'll get wristbands like these that indicate your boundaries and availability. For women, pink means you consent to vaginal access, black is oral, green is anal access, and purple means you're available for everything. You can wear multiple bands and change them anytime."

I stare at the bands like evidence in a case. Simple objects for complex desires. Purple means everything. My pussy clenches at the thought. Could I really wear purple? Let complete strangers fuck me in every hole? The idea makes me dizzy with desire.

"What about men?" Nolan asks.

"This is the freeuse event for women, and the men wear yellow to identify themselves as staff facilitators or pre-screened guests authorized to participate. Only yellow bands can engage with consenting women."

"What colors do most women wear?" My legal training demands specifics. Though honestly, I'm just wondering how many women go full purple. Am I more depraved than average if I want that?

"It really varies, but there's usually a lot of pink and black. First-timers often start with one color and adjust."

"What exactly happens during the special events?"

"We have various activities throughout the resort. Hot springs for intimate encounters. Common areas for multiple partners. Private suites for exclusive experiences." She smiles brightly. "Everything's completely consensual and participant-driven. Everyone knows that 'red light' is the safe word. Don't hesitate to use it. You control your experience entirely."

Control. The irony isn't lost on me. I've spent my entire career maintaining perfect control, and now I'm paying thousands of dollars to surrender it. And I can't fucking wait.

Sarah slides a small velvet pouch across the desk. "This contains all the wristband colors. You can choose what feels right tomorrow morning—or change throughout the day as your comfort level evolves."

I take the pouch, feeling the weight of the bands inside. Each color represents a boundary I might cross. The purple one calls to me already. What would it feel like to be completely available? To be passed from man to man while Nolan watches? My thighs press together at the thought.

"Thank you," Nolan says, his fingers brushing mine as he touches the velvet.

Sarah makes a note in our file. "Now, Jason will show you to your cabin. He's one of our senior staff members and can answer any additional questions about tomorrow's activities."

A tall man in a tailored resort uniform approaches with a warm smile. "Mr. and Mrs. Morgan? I'd be happy to escort you to your accommodations."

As we follow Jason toward the exit, I clutch the velvet pouch in my palm. Tomorrow I'll choose which parts of myself I'm willing to surrender—and to whom. My body hums with anticipation.

Our suite exceeds expectations. Floor-to-ceiling windows, massive stone fireplace, king bed positioned for both views. Gourmet chocolates and spring water wait on the coffee table with a welcome note. I can already picture myself getting fucked on that bed.

"Amenities include full spa services, dining, recreation," Jason explains, handing us a pamphlet.

I can't help but notice the way his uniform fits across his broad shoulders. My gaze drops to his hands—massive, with thick fingers. A flush creeps up my neck as I imagine those hands gripping my hips as he plows into me. Jesus, I need to focus before I embarrass myself.

"Co-ed hot springs are clothing-optional tomorrow. The dining room is open tonight until ten; room service is twenty-four hours."

He opens the deck doors to reveal a cedar hot tub among pine trees. Steam rises invitingly. "Your suite has complete privacy, though the main springs offer more...social opportunities." His smile suggests he's seen some wild stuff.

Dammit, why can't it be tomorrow already? I'd love it if Jason bent me over the nearest flat surface, pushed my panties aside, and fucked me right now. I bet he knows exactly what to do with those massive hands.

After Jason leaves, I stand at the windows, staring at snow-capped peaks while Nolan explores the room. The thin air creates a natural high that already lowers my inhibitions. I twist the velvet pouch between my fingers. Purple. I want the purple one. I want it all.

"What are you thinking about?" Nolan asks, wrapping his arms around me from behind.

"Which wristband I'm going to wear," I admit. "I was imagining being fucked in all my holes."

Nolan's arms tighten around my waist. "Maybe tomorrow you can have exactly that. Unless you're having second thoughts."

"Second? Try third and fourth thoughts." I lean back against him. "But not about being here. About whether I'm brave enough to go through with it." About whether I'm brave enough to wear purple and let them have every part of me. About whether I'll lose myself completely in the pleasure of it.

"You don't have to do anything you're not comfortable with."

"I know, and I appreciate the sentiment, but I'm here to get fucked." The bluntness of my own words surprises me, but it feels good to be open about what I want.

Before he can respond, my stomach growls loudly. We both laugh.

"Dinner first," Nolan decides. "Then we explore the rest of the resort."

"Sounds like a plan."

The dining room shows rustic elegance—exposed beams, stone walls, mountain views. We're seated at a two-top near another couple, fortyish and attractive in that expensive gym-membership way. They're discussing tomorrow like people who've done this before. I lean slightly closer, pretending to adjust my napkin.

"Last time you loved the afternoon session by the hot springs," the woman says, cutting into duck breast.

"The guy from Denver was very attentive to your needs," her husband agrees.

I lean even closer as she continues. "I booked a massage tomorrow morning. After last time, I need to experience that again."

Her husband's smile suggests he likes the idea. Wait—what happens during these massages? My mind races with possibilities, each more explicit than the last.

"Eavesdropping, counselor?" Nolan asks quietly.

"Just doing my due diligence. There's a difference." I grin at him. "And it sounds like I should book a massage for tomorrow morning."

Dinner passes by, the food perfectly prepared and the conversation increasingly relaxed. By dessert, I'm feeling more adventurous than analytical. The wine has loosened my tongue and my inhibitions. I find myself staring at the server's ass as he walks away, wondering what he'd feel like inside me.

"Want to try the hot tub at our cabin?" Nolan suggests.

"That sounds lovely." And maybe I can convince him to give me a preview of tomorrow. My body is practically humming with need.

Back in our suite, I stand before the bathroom mirror, studying my naked reflection. I've always been confident about my body. But being here is different. Tomorrow I'm going to let strangers touch me—and see every inch of my body. Will they find me attractive? Will they want me? Will they fight over who gets to fuck me first? The thought makes me shiver with anticipation.

I slip into the resort robe, tying the belt with slightly shaky hands. The private deck offers complete seclusion among towering pines. The stars shine brilliantly, and the only sounds are gentle bubbling and wind rustling the trees.

"This is perfect," I breathe, untying my robe.

The cold mountain air hits my bare skin like a shock, but the heated water radiates compensating warmth.

Nolan groans. "You look good enough to eat."

I feel incredible. Even though it's just me and Nolan right now, just knowing that I'm here to fuck other guys makes my skin tingle. I wonder how many men I'll take tomorrow. Two? Three? More? The thought of being surrounded by hard cocks, all wanting me, makes me dizzy with desire.

The water's perfect—hot enough to relax every muscle without being uncomfortable. I settle onto the molded seat and enjoy the jets massaging me.

Nolan joins me, pulling me against his side. "How do you feel about tomorrow?"

"Overwhelmed. I keep thinking about that couple at dinner. How casual they were about sharing her."

"Does that excite you?"

Heat floods my cheeks. "God, yes."

His voice drops to that rough whisper that makes my core clench. I close my eyes, letting suppressed fantasies surface. "Tell me what you're imagining."

"I'm imagining being on my knees for strangers while you watch. Having their hands on me while you tell them exactly what to do." The words come out breathless. "I want to exist purely for pleasure—theirs and yours."

Nolan slides his hand between my legs and circles my clit with his fingers. "I want to watch you surrender control completely. I want to direct how they fuck your mouth. Tell them when to go deeper."

The crude language sends liquid heat straight to my core, and I gasp, "Yes. I want all of that."

"I want to watch you take it in every hole."

His words and skilled fingers push me over the edge. I come with a muffled cry, biting my lip to keep from being too loud. When I can breathe again, Nolan's watching me with an expression I've never seen—possessive and proud and hungry.

"What about you?" I reach for him, but he catches my hand.

"I want to wait. Tomorrow we both get what we want."

He's crazy, but if he wants to deny himself, so be it. I give him a cheeky grin. "Hey, so I'm thinking of booking a massage tomorrow. I want to see what that woman at dinner was talking about."

His smile is full of dark promise. "Do it."

I settle back into the hot water, feeling relaxed and happy. The analytical lawyer who arrived this afternoon would never have admitted to wanting to service strangers while her husband watched two months ago. But something tells me I'm going to beg a lot tomorrow. Beg to be filled, used, passed around like the slut I apparently am deep down.

I can't wait.

I wake before the alarm, my body humming with nerves. The massage is in two hours. Just two hours until I find out what was special enough for the woman at dinner to want to experience it again. My stomach does a little flip at the thought of a stranger's hands all over me, but I'm ready to step so far outside my comfort zone I might need a passport to get back.

My shower is a longer one so I can prepare for the day. When I'm done, I put my hair into a ponytail, hoping it won't be too miserable outside with wet hair. Nolan dresses in dark jeans and a green sweater that matches his hazel eyes. He looks good enough to eat, but there's no time for that. We have strangers waiting to put their cocks in me.

I pull on a simple outfit—soft, clingy black yoga pants with nothing underneath and an oversized sweater. The fabric of the pants skims my curves, making me feel sexy. Perfect for what's about to happen. I slip on a pair of boots to complete my casual outfit.

"How're you feeling?" he asks.

"Like I'm jumping out of a plane without knowing if my parachute works." I pull the purple wristband on, twisting it around my wrist.

He grins. "I'm your parachute, baby."

Normally, I'd groan at his cheesy joke, but today I blow him a kiss. I like having him with me as my parachute.

We grab breakfast at the lodge. Normal resort stuff—fancy fruit, pastries, coffee. But wearing the purple wristband while eating breakfast and knowing someone could fuck me at any moment makes everything more intense. The coffee tastes richer. The kiwi burst with flavor. Even the damn napkin feels sensual against my fingertips. Is this what happens when you finally admit what you want? The world becomes technicolor?

Suddenly, I'm distracted. At the adjacent table, a man sinks between a woman's thighs, his mouth working at her pussy while she arches against her chair, fingers tangled in his hair. My pulse races as I imagine those lips on mine, that tongue...wait, why is he eating her out if this is a freeuse weekend for women? Shouldn't she be the one sucking him? I know there are plenty of guys who enjoy going down on women, but for some reason I expected the resort to be full of men demanding to have their cock sucked.

Most of the guests are ignoring the woman's moans, but I'm fascinated and can't look away.

I murmur to Nolan. "Everyone seems so comfortable with this."

"Maybe they've discovered something you're just figuring out."

"Which is?"

"That surrender isn't weakness. It's power."

I blink at him. He's right, but I didn't realize he knew that. Has he been studying up on BDSM practices? Maybe this trip really will change everything.

We don't spend long eating, and after breakfast, we head to the changing room for my massage. I strip down fully and slip on a robe before we're led through a bamboo corridor to the massage table. The space radiates zen tranquility, but I can feel the charged undercurrent. My nipples harden, and my pussy throbs with each step. I've never been this turned on by anticipation alone.

Once we're in the massage room and the door closes, I don't have a chance to take a breath before hands are on me.

"I'm Joel," a low voice says against my ear, his breath hot on my neck. "Let's get this off."

Joel yanks my robe belt open. The cotton slides down my shoulders, pooling at my feet. Naked. Exposed. Nolan moves to sit in a chair perfectly positioned for watching.

A heavy palm suddenly slaps my ass, the sting radiating through me as I squeak in surprise.

"I'm David," another man announces from behind me. I hadn't even noticed him there. "Christ, look at these tits," he growls as he pinches my nipples between his thumb and forefinger. "Perfect to suck on."

I gasp. This is happening. Now. No pretense of professional massage.

"On the table, slut," Joel orders. "Face down, ass up."

My pulse hammers as I climb onto the table. God, I came here to be used, but I didn't expect this. It's fabulous. Before I'm fully settled, David's pouring oil between my ass cheeks, the warmth sliding down my crack.

"Look at her," Joel murmurs, spreading my cheeks apart. "This is an ass made for taking cock."

I shiver. Yes. Oh fuck yes. His thumb circles my asshole, and I push back against him. "Please..."

David's hands slide up my spine. "Please what?"

"Fuck my ass." The words spill out. Desperate. Shameless. Okay, so I didn't expect to be begging to take it in the ass right after breakfast, but a girl's got needs.

Joel laughs. "Too bad you don't get to decide what we do to you."

Ugh, what if no one fucks my ass today? It's not like I'm an anal slut or anything, but if I'm at a freeuse resort, I want to leave feeling thoroughly depraved.

Joel works oil into my ass crack and then presses his finger in. It burns, stretches—perfect. David's fingers dive into my pussy from behind. Two fingers, curling hard. Oh God. I moan and clutch the sides of the massage table.

"She's drenched," David grunts. "Always this wet for strangers?"

"You're her first," Nolan answers, and his voice sounds choked.

I turn my head, panting. "I've been fantasizing about being fucked by other men since we booked this trip."

Joel twists his finger deeper. "What does that make you?"

"A slut." I groan as he presses a second finger into my ass.

My head spins as they finger fuck me in both holes. This isn't anything like a massage, but at this point, I don't care. I just want to come.

They pull their fingers out, and Joel moves over to a sink to wash his hands while David says, "Turn over. I want to watch those tits bounce while you get stuffed."

I flip over so fast my ponytail smacks my face. David grabs my breasts, rolling my nipples as Joel spreads my legs wide.

"Look at that needy hole," Joel taunts. He slaps my pussy—sharp pain that zips straight to my clit. I cry out, hips jerking. "You want to be filled, don't you?"

"She'd take anything," Nolan says hoarsely. "Baby, tell them how many cocks you want right now."

I can feel myself sinking into the sluttiest version of myself as I gasp out, "Three." Joel slaps my pussy again. "Four—fuck—I'd take every cock in this resort!"

David unzips his pants, pulling out a thick, flushed cock. "Suck it, slut."

He shoves it toward my mouth. I open obediently, tongue out. I taste him—salt and skin. I hollow my cheeks, sucking hard while Joel brushes circles around my clit.

"Her pussy's clenching air," Joel laughs. "She wants cock that bad."

I moan around David's dick. I need to be fucked. David slides deeper, hitting the back of my throat, and I fight the urge to gag.

"Naughty girl loves choking on dick," David growls.

I can see Nolan out of the corner of my eye, and he's stroking his cock through his pants. Shit, that's hot.

Joel stops rubbing my clit and says, "I need her at the edge of the table. I need to fuck this greedy cunt."

David pulls out of my mouth, and the two men tug me to the end of the table so my ass is at the edge. Joel's cock is already out, and he spreads my legs, holding onto my thighs. His cock is long and angry red. He slaps it against my pussy lips, making me twitch.

"Please," I whine. "Put it in. Fuck me raw."

"You'll take it like a good slut?" Joel rubs his head through my wetness.

"Hard," I gasp. "I want to feel you splitting me open."

Joel grins. "I fucking love greedy sluts." He slams into me with one brutal thrust. My back arches and I moan as he bottoms out. Oh god, this is exactly what I needed.

David wraps his fist around my ponytail and stuffs his cock back into my mouth.

"Choke on it, fucktoy," David orders. I suck, slobbering.

Joel fucks me with deep, sharp strokes. "Tell your husband whose cock feels best."

"Yours!" I cry when David pulls out to let me breathe. Spit drips down my chin. "God, yours!"

"Louder," Nolan demands. "Tell the whole fucking resort you're a cock-slut."

"I'm a cockslut!" I shriek as Joel grinds his cock inside me. "I want strangers hammering my pussy all day!"

Joel groans as he fucks me furiously. David pinches my nipples hard. "Gonna come for us?" David groans. "Such an easy slut."

I try to beg for it, but the cock in my mouth muffles me.

Joel grinds deep and circles my clit with his thumb. "Come for us, filthy girl. Squirt all over my cock."

The orgasm detonates. My pussy spasms. Clamping, fluttering. I scream around David's cock. Pleasure whips through me.

Joel keeps pounding. "Again," he grunts. "Give us another."

He slams against a pleasure point repeatedly. Oh fuck. Another wave crashes over me, and my thighs shake from pleasure. I writhe, impaled and sobbing.

When David explodes in my mouth, I can barely swallow his massive load. His cum is bitter and tastes different from Nolan's. Taking my first load of jizz from another guy makes me feel even more like a slut.

Once David comes, Joel isn't far behind. He shivers and groans as he slams into me and unloads shot after shot of warm, sticky cum.

"Perfect," Nolan murmurs as the guys pull out.

I'm a trembling mess while Joel wipes his cock on my stomach. "You should check out the hot springs. You'd like it."

Nolan helps me sit up. My pussy aches deliciously. "Thanks, guys," he says, and I almost laugh at my husband thanking two men for fucking me.

"Want to try the hot springs?" he asks me.

I grin. "Sure. Let's see how many strangers can fill this needy pussy today."

Ten minutes later, I'm walking through the resort, still wearing just the robe and my boots. Nolan is carrying my clothes. We decided there was no point in my putting them back on just for the walk. The mountain air is invigorating, and I feel eyes tracking my movement as we head to the terraced hot springs. I feel like I'm in a movie—the prim attorney transformed into a wanton exhibitionist. The thought makes me want to laugh and moan at the same time.

The natural stone pools are carved into different levels, steam rising from mineral-rich water heated underground. The main pool fits about twelve people, while smaller, intimate pools seat four to six. Several couples are already enjoying the waters. I wonder how many of them are here for the same reason we are. How many women have been fingered to orgasm in these pools?

I pause at the edge, feeling like a completely different version of myself. I'm a woman available to any man with a yellow wristband. Available to be touched, used, pleasured by strangers while my husband watches. The power in that availability is intoxicating. Professionally, I'm the ice queen attorney who never loses control. Now I want to lose it completely.

I take my robe off and hand it to Nolan before slipping off my boots. I don't waste any time getting into the water. Conversations pause as a few guys watch me with interest. I feel their desire like a physical force, and instead of making me self-conscious, it makes me feel powerful. Their eyes on my body are like hands, touching me from a distance. I want them closer. I want them on me, in me.

The warm water envelopes me as I take a seat on an underwater ledge. The water is just below my breasts. My nipples peek above the surface, hard from the contrast between the hot water and cool air. I wonder how many men are looking at them right now. I hope all of them are.

Nolan positions himself across from me, leaning against a stone wall where he can see everything. The message is clear—I'm available, but I still belong to him. The thought warms me more than the hot spring. He's giving me freedom while keeping me safe. He really is my parachute.

It doesn't take long for a man to join us.

"First time here?" he asks, sliding beside me. He's attractive, in his forties, with a confident presence that suggests experience. His yellow wristband is clearly visible. I wonder how many women he's touched in these pools. I wonder what he'll do to me.

"Yeah," I manage, voice breathier than usual. I sound like a woman in a porno, but I can't help it. My body is already responding to his proximity.

"I'm James," he says as his hand finds my thigh under water. The touch is electric, made more intense by knowing Nolan's watching. I spread my legs slightly, an invitation I never thought I'd extend to a stranger. But here, in this place, with these rules, I want his hands on me. I want everyone's hands on me.

"You're beautiful," James murmurs, hand sliding higher. "Your husband's a lucky man."

"He knows," I breathe, not adding that it's really me who's the lucky one. Nolan is letting me explore this need I didn't even know I had. Sure, we're doing this together, but not many men would want to watch their wife get reamed in every hole at a freeuse resort. I truly am amazingly lucky.

James slips his hand between my legs, and I gasp. The mineral water makes everything feel slippery. His fingers find my clit unhesitatingly, confirming my suspicion that he's done this before. Knowing he's touched other women in this same pool makes me impossibly wetter.

"She likes that," another man says as he joins us. Younger, early thirties, dark hair and intense eyes. Two men touching me at once. Again. Is this my life now? If so, I never want to go back to the old one.

I rock my hips against James's exploring hand. I need his fingers inside me like I need air.

"I think we should use this hole," James says, and the second man murmurs his agreement.

Ohhh, yes. I said in the paperwork that I wanted to be treated like just a hole to be used, so their words ping a part of my brain that's been dormant. I immediately feel like a filthy little slut for letting the men use me however they want. Who knew that being reduced to a "hole" could feel so liberating?

Four hands are on my body—James working between my legs while the younger guy massages my breasts and pulls at my nipples. Their touch and the heated water create a dreamlike state where nothing exists except sensation. I'm floating in pleasure, anchored only by their hands on my body.

"Her husband's enjoying the show," James observes, and I glance over to see Nolan stroking himself through his jeans.

Well, that's nice and filthy. I really didn't expect him to touch himself, but knowing he's letting himself go in front of other people gives me a thrill. We've both changed in the best possible way.

The two men work me with increasing intensity. James finger fucks me while the other guy continues to pinch my nipples. I'm dimly aware that other guests have stopped to watch, but instead of embarrassing me, the audience turns me on even more. Look at me. Look at what these men are doing to me. Look at how much I love it.

Their skilled touch makes me orgasm quickly. I come with a cry that echoes off the surrounding stone. My body convulses against their hands as waves of delight crash through me. I don't care who hears. I don't care who sees. I want them all to know exactly what these men are doing to me.

They don't stop. The younger guy continues working my breasts while James adds a third finger to my pussy, stretching me while his thumb maintains pressure. The overstimulation borders on painful, but in the most delicious way.

"Again," Nolan says. "Make her come again. Show my wife what a perfect little slut she can be."

My husband just called me a slut in front of strangers. The old Rachel would have been furious This new Rachel wants it tattooed on her skin.

"Please," I gasp, not sure if I'm begging them to stop or continue. Both. Neither. I just need more of whatever they're giving me.

"She likes that," James observes, adding a fourth finger that stretches me deliciously. "She likes being called a slut while strangers finger fuck her pussy."

He's right. I do like it. I like being reduced to nothing but nerve endings and need.

"Tell us what you are," the younger man demands, hands working my nipples. "Say it so everyone can hear."

I look around and realize we have a full audience. There are three guys fucking a woman in the other pool, but at least eight people have stopped to watch me being pleasured. What if all these men touched me? What if they all took turns? The thought makes me clench around James's fingers.

"I'm a slut," I gasp as James's thumb circles my clit. "I'm your fucktoy." The words feel foreign on my tongue but right in my soul. For these moments, that's exactly what I want to be.

"Whose fucktoy?" the man at my breasts asks, pinching harder.

"Everyone's. Anyone who wants to use me." The admission rushes out, and I realize I mean every word. "I want to be used by whoever wants me." In this place, in this moment, it's the absolute truth. I want to be passed around like a party favor. I want to be filled and used until I can't remember my own name.

"Good girl," Nolan says approvingly, and being called a good girl shocks me. Okay, yeah, he's totally been reading up on BDSM stuff. My husband has hidden depths I never suspected.

My next orgasm is even more intense, my back arching as I cry out. The men work me through every aftershock until I'm shaking and gasping. I've never come this hard in my life. Not even close.

"Enjoy your day," James murmurs, finally withdrawing his fingers.

"She's just getting started," Nolan says, moving closer. "Aren't you, Rachel?"

I nod, not trusting my voice. My body hums with satisfaction, but underneath is a growing hunger for more.

The guys move away as Nolan comes over and kneels next to me. "Want to go skiing, baby? The conditions are perfect."

I almost pout that I didn't come here to ski, but I hold it in. I'll do a couple of runs and then we'll be able to tell people at work the skiing was great without having to lie if anyone asks. Besides, who knows what might happen on those secluded trails? The possibilities are endless, and we've only just begun.

<h1 style="text-align:center">CHAPTER 4</h1>

Thirty minutes later, we're on the slopes, breathing in the crisp mountain air. I'm wearing form-fitting black thermal ski pants that show off my ass and a puffy blue jacket that amplifies the heat radiating from my core. Underneath, I've got on a tight-fitting moisture-wicking thermal top that hugs my curves, and I opted for no bra today. My hair is pulled back in another high ponytail, exposing my neck to the occasional brush of cold air. My body still hums from the hot springs, a pleasant vibration that hasn't faded.

As we wait for the chairlift, I notice a guy in a bright red ski jacket standing a few people ahead in line. He turns, scanning the queue, and our eyes meet briefly. He's handsome—strong jaw, mirrored goggles pushed up on his forehead, revealing intense blue eyes. My stomach does a little flip. Damn. That's the kind of man you notice even when you're not looking. I bring my arm up to casually play with my ponytail, hoping he notices the purple band I made sure was visible. His gaze drops to my wrist, lingering for a moment before he smiles and turns back around.

Oh. So he knows exactly what I'm here for. The thought sends an unexpected thrill through me—being recognized as someone open to experiences.

"How're you feeling?" Nolan asks as we finally board the chairlift.

"Like I'm flying," I admit, making him smile. And I am—floating above my normal life, where every minute is accounted for and every action has a purpose. Here, the purpose is simply pleasure.

"We're only getting to the appetizer course," he murmurs against my ear.

God, I love when he talks in food metaphors. It means he's in his element, confident and in control. This new Nolan—the one who orchestrates encounters rather than just preparing meals—is a revelation.

I spot the red jacket again, three chairs ahead of us, his head turning occasionally to glance back our way. The weight of his attention sends a surprising thrill through my already sensitized body. Is he watching me specifically? The idea that a stranger finds me interesting enough to keep looking makes me sit up straighter, arch my back just slightly.

Nolan and I ski a couple of runs, my performance suffering as arousal continues to course through my body, making concentration nearly impossible. I've always prided myself on precision, but now I'm sloppy, distracted by the memory of hands on my body and the promise of more to come.

On our third trip up, we're joined by another skier. The guy is in his thirties with an athletic build that suggests serious gym time. Not as immediately striking as Red Jacket Guy, but definitely appealing in that outdoorsy, confident way.

"Great conditions today," he says conversationally. "I'm Derek."

"It's beautiful here," I answer, and his eyes immediately drop to my wrist, as if he's checking what color of band I'm wearing. The purple band feels like a VIP pass to a club I never knew existed.

"We were discussing the Pine Trail," Nolan says to Derek, his voice carrying that subtle note I'm beginning to recognize as his dominant tone. "More private than the main runs."

We were? I raise my eyebrows at my husband, silently questioning this alleged prior discussion. I'm charmed by his new boldness. This is the man who's been hiding behind careful meal preparations all these years?

"Perfect choice." Derek smiles. "Very secluded. Great for...appreciating nature."

Nolan draws my attention to a spectacular view of the valley below, pointing out the way the light catches the snow-covered peak. I find myself mesmerized by the scenery and tune the guys out for a moment. This resort really is beautiful.

By the time we reach the top, the unspoken agreement is clear: Derek's joining us for whatever happens next. My inner thighs clench in anticipation.

The Pine Trail branches off the main run, winding through dense forest that provides natural screening from prying eyes—though not complete privacy, I note with a strange thrill.

We ski single file, Derek leading, me in the middle, Nolan bringing up the rear like he's herding me toward some predetermined destination. I wonder briefly if they discussed this formation too, positioning me between them like the filling in a very adult sandwich.

Halfway down, Derek stops at a small clearing where a massive old-growth pine sits on a slight rise. The location is partially hidden from the main trail while still visible to anyone who knows to look. Someone's done this before. The thought that we're following in the footsteps of other adventurous couples makes me wonder what other resort traditions we might discover.

We click out of our bindings, the release mechanisms snapping with finality. I plant my skis upright in the snow beside me, poles crossed through the bindings, a ritual that feels oddly formal given what might happen next. Derek and Nolan do the same, creating a small forest of equipment at the edge of our clearing.

"This is one of my favorite spots," Derek says, eyes fixed on me with predatory focus.

I can hear other skiers on the main trail below, voices carrying through thin mountain air. The risk of discovery makes my pulse race with an exhilaration I've never permitted myself to feel before.

"Rachel," Nolan says, voice carrying that commanding tone I'm learning to crave. "Take off your jacket."

"Here?" I ask, though my hands are already reaching for the zipper, my body responding to his direction before my mind can file an objection. Who is this woman who strips in the woods at a man's command? Certainly not the Rachel Morgan who triple-checks contract language before allowing it to leave her desk.

"Here. Now."

I unzip and let my jacket fall to the packed snow. Cold air hits my skin through my thermal top, making my nipples immediately visible through the fabric. Two men are staring at me like I'm the most fascinating thing they've ever seen, and it's intoxicating.

"Fuck, those tits..." Derek murmurs, eyes glued to my chest. "Your husband wasn't exaggerating about how gorgeous you are."

"When did you two..." I glance between them, trying to identify when this negotiation occurred. My husband, the chef, has apparently been cooking up more than meals.

Nolan grins. "We had a conversation while you were admiring the view."

So that's why he encouraged me to look at the mountains. Sneaky, sneaky husband.

Derek moves closer, his movements deliberate like he's stalking me. "Turn around and put your hands on the tree."

I look at the massive pine, then at the main trail visible through the trees where other skiers pass frequently. Some have already noticed our group and are slowing for a better look—our audience assembling for the performance. My heart hammers against my ribs. I'm about to have sex outdoors where people can see.

Through a gap in the trees, I catch a flash of red—the guy from the lift. He's stopped on the main trail, goggles lifted, eyes fixed directly on us. My breath catches as our gazes lock for a moment before I place my gloved palms against the bark. The intensity of his stare makes my knees weak, like he's touching me from twenty yards away.

Derek moves behind me, pulls my hips back so I'm bending over, and slips his hands into my ski pants' waistband.

"Everyone on the main trail's going to see you get fucked," he murmurs. "They're going to watch you take my cock."

"Yes, please." The thought bubbles up before I can censor it. I want to be seen.

My breath catches as Derek tugs my ski pants and panties down to my knees in one fluid motion. The freezing mountain air hits my bare ass, sending goosebumps racing across my skin like electrical currents.

"I bet your pussy is going to be the perfect cockwarmer on a cold mountain day."

The contrast between the biting cold on my exposed lower half and the heat building between my legs makes my head spin like I've had too much wine. I'm drunk on sensation, on newness, on the sheer audacity of what we're doing.

"I told you she was eager," Nolan says from somewhere behind us, and that new edge of command in his voice makes my inner muscles clench in Pavlovian response. He's talking about me like I'm not here, like I'm a treat he's sharing with a friend.

Derek runs his gloved hand over my ass, and I gasp at the strange texture. "Take the gloves off," I demand, then bite my lip—who am I to be giving orders in this situation? Old habits die hard, even when you're bent over in the snow with your pants around your knees.

"You hear that?" Derek asks Nolan. "Your wife's trying to run the show."

"She does that," Nolan replies with amusement. "But she's learning to let go."

Am I? Yes, I suppose I am. One cock at a time.

Derek leans close, his breath hot against my ear. "I don't take orders from sluts who present their asses to strangers on ski slopes."

The degradation shoots straight to my core. This is how I wanted to be treated. I press my forehead against the tree bark in surrender.

I hear the sound of a zipper behind me. Derek's cold, bare fingers spread my ass cheeks apart. "Look how wet she is already," he announces, like he's presenting evidence to a jury. "Your wife's pussy is dripping for my cock."

I feel a perverse pride. Yes, look at how much I want this. Look at what you do to me. Look at what I've become.

"Show me," Nolan says, moving closer.

Derek slides two fingers inside me, and I moan at the sudden intrusion. My inner walls grip him greedily as he pumps in and out, collecting physical evidence of my arousal. "See? She's soaked."

Through half-lidded eyes, I spot the red jacket again. He's moved closer, partially hidden behind a cluster of pines. His intensity is palpable even from this distance. I wonder what he's thinking. Is he imagining it's his fingers inside me? Is he wishing he'd approached us at the lift? I hope he's still watching when I come.

"Fuck her," Nolan orders, his voice husky with lust. "I want to watch her take your cock right here where anyone can see."

My husband, the voyeur. Who knew? If I'd known sooner. We could have been having so much more fun.

I glance toward the main trail, my vision slightly blurred by desire. Two skiers have stopped, pretending to adjust their equipment while clearly watching us. And there he is again—red jacket guy, now leaning against a tree, making no pretense about why he's stopped. The knowledge that I'm on display sends a fresh flood of wetness between my thighs. I'm performing now, and I want to make it good for my audience. For him.

Derek positions himself behind me. The head of his cock nudges my entrance, and I push back instinctively, seeking the fullness.

"Eager little slut," he mutters, gripping my hip with one hand to steady me. He slams into me with one hard thrust that steals my breath. He groans, "Christ, she's tight," before pulling back and driving in again, making me cry out in pleasure.

"How does she feel?" Nolan asks, his voice husky with arousal.

"Fucking incredible," Derek answers, establishing a punishing rhythm that makes my knees weak. "Her pussy's gripping my cock like it never wants to let go."

I moan as he pounds into me. I'm vaguely aware of more people stopping on the main trail, but my attention keeps returning to the man in the red jacket. He hasn't moved, and his stillness is hypnotic.

"Look at them watching you," Nolan says, noticing my glance toward the growing audience. "They're seeing what a perfect little fucktoy I married."

Fucktoy. The word echoes in my mind. Not counsel. Not Ms. Morgan. Not even wife. Just a toy for pleasure.

Derek's thrusting speeds up, the sound of skin slapping against skin echoing through the trees. "You like that, don't you? You like being watched while you get fucked by a stranger."

I push back to meet his thrusts. "God, yes."

Who is this woman speaking with my voice? This creature of pure desire who doesn't care about her dignity. I like her. I want to be her more often.

My orgasm builds with startling speed, pressure coiling tightly at my core like a spring wound to breaking point. Derek reaches around and finds my clit, rubbing circles that match his relentless pace.

"She's close," he tells Nolan. "Want to see your wife come on my cock?"

Yes, Nolan, say yes. Let me come for our audience. Let me come for the man in the red jacket. Let me come for every stranger watching from the trail.

"Make her scream," Nolan commands. "I want everyone on this mountain to hear what a slut she is."

Derek pinches my clit as he slams into me, and I shatter completely. Colored lights sparkle along the corners of my vision as pleasure tears through me, radiating from my core to my fingertips like an electrical surge. I scream—a primal sound I barely recognize as my own—as my inner walls clamp down on Derek's cock with vise-like intensity.

I'm coming on a stranger's cock in public while my husband watches. The Rachel from three days ago would faint at the thought. This Rachel wants to do it again. And again. With different men. In different positions. Maybe two at once next time?

As waves of pleasure crash through me, my eyes lock once more with the man in the red jacket. His hand is pressed against the front of his ski pants. The knowledge that my pleasure is creating his adds another dimension to my orgasm. I'm not just feeling good, I'm making others feel good too.

"Fuck," Derek groans, his rhythm faltering as my body squeezes him. "I'm gonna come."

"Pull out," Nolan commands with perfect timing. "Come on her ass. I want everyone to see my wife marked."

Derek withdraws, and I whimper at the sudden emptiness, my body protesting the interruption. Three quick strokes and he's groaning, hot spurts landing on my exposed skin while I shudder through the aftershocks of my orgasm.

I stay there, bent over with my pants around my knees, trying to catch my breath as reality slowly filters back through the haze of pleasure. I've just been fucked against a tree in public by a man whose last name I don't even know.

And I loved every second of it. More than winning cases. More than closing deals. More than any achievement that's ever graced my resume.

Derek tucks himself away while Nolan approaches with tissues from his pocket. He gently cleans me up, his touch possessive yet tender—reclaiming what's his while caring for me.

"You're incredible," he murmurs, pulling my pants back up. "How do you feel?"

My legs are shaking, and I giggle. "Like I want more." More men. More positions. More of this freedom I never knew I needed.

Derek laughs. "The main lodge has a lounge with a great fireplace. Very comfortable seating arrangements for meeting new people."

If that's where all the action is happening, I want to be there.

"Sounds perfect," Nolan says, helping me stand upright and adjust my clothes. "We'll head there after we finish this run."

As we ski down the remainder of the trail, my body hums with satisfaction and anticipation. It's only midday, and I've already crossed boundaries I never imagined possible.

I can't wait to see what happens next. Or who happens next. Maybe the man in the red jacket. Maybe someone else entirely. For the first time in my life, I'm not planning ahead—and it feels magnificent.

CHAPTER 5

I push through the lodge doors, my ass still sticky from Derek's cum. Three men materialize next to me. Strangers with hungry eyes and rough hands. Wow, talk about a welcoming committee. Not even time to order a hot toddy first.

They don't speak as they lead me over to the nearest sofa and bend me over the arm. One of them yanks my ski pants and panties down. The lodge's ambient noise—glasses clinking, logs splitting in the massive stone fireplace, murmured conversations—continues uninterrupted around us. Just another Saturday at Shadowpine Ski Resort. Nothing to see here, folks—except, you know, me getting railed in the middle of happy hour.

A thick cock is shoved into me from behind. I'm still soaked from my skiing encounter, so he slides in easily. I'm practically providing a slip-n-slide service at this point. The man pins me down, and I glance over my shoulder. Pleasure ripples down my spine when I recognize the red jacket. Of course it's him—apparently, voyeurs make the best encores.

I catch a glimpse of Nolan leaning against the wall, his eyes fixed on me. There he is—my husband, the chef, offering me up like his favorite dish for everyone to sample.

Someone unzips my jacket and pulls my top up, exposing my tits. My nipples immediately stiffen into hard peaks, and he slides his hands between me and the sofa to twist and pinch them.

I moan against the leather as Red Jacket Guy increases his pace, his pelvis connecting with my ass rhythmically. Each thrust sends jolts of pleasure through my core.

Movement registers in my peripheral vision. A bearded man in a green sweater drops to his knees in front of me on the sofa. Hello, cock number four—or is it five? Neither my pussy nor my brain is keeping score. I giggle at myself. I'm clearly cockdrunk.

He tips my head up. "Open."

I part my lips and his cock slaps against my tongue—salty, thick, with velvety skin. Another day, another dick. This one's got girth. My throat works on instinct, muscles contracting around his shaft.

The conversations in the room flow uninterrupted, as though my public use constitutes normal background activity. Which, let's be honest, it does today. I've become part of the amenities—somewhere between the complimentary breakfast and the hot tub.

"...heard they're expecting fresh powder tomorrow..."

"...let's visit the hot springs before dinner..."

They're discussing the weather while I'm getting spit-roasted. This place is surreal—and I'm absolutely here for it.

Red Jacket Guy grunts behind me, his rhythm faltering. His hips stutter against my ass, driving deeper. His cum floods me with heat. That's another load today—at this rate, I'll need extra hydration. He withdraws with a wet sound.

The emptiness lasts all of two seconds before another cock—thicker, curved—rams into my used hole. Tag team efficiency—no waiting required.

I don't see the owner. I just feel the stretch, the pressure, the delight as my pussy molds around him. That curve is hitting places Derek and Red

Jacket missed entirely. I whimper around the cock in my mouth, and the guy groans as the vibration travels through his shaft.

Nolan hasn't moved, but his stance has shifted subtly. His arms are crossed, and his jaw tightens. His gaze remains steady—heavy, approving, possessive. Even as strangers use me, I'm always his.

The guy in my mouth pulls out suddenly and strokes his shaft over me. Hot streaks paint my face—across my eyelids, lips, chin. Facial moisturizer, Alpine style. I lick what hits my mouth.

The guy fucking me groans as he watches me get painted with cum, and he unloads deep inside me. I can feel him flooding me, and I moan with him as he whacks against my ass several times before pulling out.

Nolan finally pushes off the wall. He crosses to me, taking my arm with gentle pressure. He doesn't wipe the mess from my skin. Doesn't acknowledge the cum dripping down my thighs or decorating my face. He just pulls up my pants and leads me through the crowd.

I stumble beside him, legs trembling. My body catalogs each sensation: the slide of fluid down my inner thighs, the cooling tracks on my face, the stretched emptiness between my legs. I've been thoroughly fucked by—what, four men so far? Five? Six? God, I don't even know. But Nolan has watched it all.

My mind attempts to categorize the experience, to file it under appropriate headings, but fails to find adequate terminology. No spreadsheet could capture this. No contract could define it.

The only word that surfaces is: Amazing.

"Let's clean up and get some dinner," Nolan murmurs, and when my stomach growls, I realize he's right. I need to fuel up.

I give him a dopey grin. "Okay, love."

I'm going to need to up my game tonight. I'm determined to get a cock in my ass before I pass out from too much pleasure. This resort is, hands down, the best ski resort ever.

CHAPTER 6

After dinner, Nolan's palm is warm on my spine as he guides me to the game room. I'm wearing a sexy sweater dress that hugs every curve, the material clinging to my hips and thighs. The deep burgundy color makes my skin look creamy in contrast, and I've paired it with thigh-high boots that disappear beneath the hem. I'm flying high because I just serviced four men under the table at the restaurant. Luckily, Nolan made sure I got actual food in me, too. A diet of cum might not sustain me for long.

We push through the heavy wooden doors into the game room, and the scent hits me first: cigar smoke layered over leather and whiskey. Masculine energy radiates from the dark wood paneling, the green felt pool tables, the cluster of men laughing near the stone fireplace.

Their conversation dies mid-roar when we enter. Eight pairs of eyes lock onto my wrist, then flick to Nolan's hand at my lower back. Permission granted. Prey identified. Look at them. They've gone from laughing to hunting in three seconds flat. And I'm the gazelle who wandered into the lion's den—except this gazelle came deliberately.

"Mind if we join?" Nolan asks, steering me toward them. His palm presses firmly between my shoulder blades—go on. He's practically gift-wrapping me. Husband of the year, delivering his wife to a pack of strangers.

The tallest one stands. "Hey, boys. Looks like the birthday party entertainment has arrived."

Oh, what's this? Suddenly, I imagine I'm a party favor being passed around. My body buzzes with pleasure. Yeah, I'm good with this idea.

Four men surround me. Hands grab my elbows, steering me toward the nearest table. Someone removes my boots while another person unzips my dress and peels it off me. The fabric pools at my feet before I can blink. These men don't have time for seduction—and honestly, neither do I.

"Hands on the surface," the tall one orders, pointing at the green felt of the pool table.

He presses my shoulders down, and I catch myself, my palms flattening on the table before I get a face full of felt. Behind me, zippers rasp open. It's the sound of men freeing their cocks, all for me. My panties disintegrate beneath multiple hands, and I don't even have time to protest the loss before a cockhead presses against my entrance—no warning, no prep. Just a thick invasion as he sinks inside.

I gasp, back arching, as I peek over my shoulder. It's the tall guy. He fucks me hard, fingers digging into my hips. A tattooed guy appears next to me and pulls the front half of my body off the pool table, forcing us to pivot, and presses his cock against my lips.

"Suck."

I open my mouth, and he slides between my lips. The tall guy behind me thrusts deep, jolting me forward and forcing the cock deeper down my throat.

Nolan sits at the end of a long couch, watching. "She likes being called filthy names," he tells the room. "Don't hold back."

A redhead grabs my hair, yanking me off the tattooed guy's cock. "My turn."

He slaps his cock across my cheek before shoving in. My gag reflex triggers briefly, but it's the perfect amount of roughness. This is exactly what I need—to be used so thoroughly I can't even think about anything but cock.

The man behind me drills in steadily. "She's got the purple band. I think she needs someone in her ass."

As if they choreographed it, the guys pull out at the same time and haul me over to the couch Nolan is sitting on. The tall guy sits at the opposite end from Nolan and pulls me down to straddle him. I'm facing him as I sink down onto his cock.

I roll my hips, and the pleasure makes me moan. The redhead moves behind me, and suddenly I hear the pop-top of a lube bottle. Oh, thank god. I didn't think to bring my own lube.

The redhead pushes me forward, and I hold onto the tall guy's shoulders and look over at my husband while cool lube is poured on my ass.

Nolan has a glazed look, and I give him a cheeky grin. "Hi, love."

That makes him smile. He mouths, "I love you."

I blow him a kiss and then whimper as a cock presses against my asshole. The pressure builds, and there's a stretching, burning sensation while I try to breathe deeply.

"Relax and let me in, slut. It's my birthday after all." The guy's voice is gruff, and I focus on the pleasure of the cock in my pussy.

I force my muscles loose, and the cock slides past the tight ring.

The redhead bottoms out, and I'm completely filled—stretched between two strangers while my husband watches. The fullness is overwhelming, that delicious pressure where pleasure borders on pain.

"Fuck, she's tight," the redhead grunts, his fingers digging into my hips. "The perfect birthday fuck."

The tall guy beneath me grins up at me. "Let's see how well you take it, princess."

They start moving—not in tandem but in opposition. One pushes in as the other pulls out, creating a relentless rhythm that leaves me no moment to catch my breath. My body becomes a vessel for their pleasure, and the thought sends a sharp spike of arousal through me.

"Look at her face," someone says. "She fucking loves it."

I glance at Nolan through half-lidded eyes. His jaw is tight, pupils blown wide, as he watches his wife being used by strangers. His hand rests on his thigh, inches from his obvious erection, but he doesn't touch himself. Just watches. Records every moan, every thrust.

"Tell them," Nolan says, his voice low and controlled. "Tell them what you are."

The redhead yanks my hair, arching my neck back. "Yeah, tell us what you are while we fill both your holes."

"I'm—" The words catch as they hit a perfect rhythm, sending sparks of delight through my nervous system. "I'm a fucktoy slut who wants all her holes filled."

"Louder," the tall guy demands, thrusting up hard enough to make me gasp. "So everyone can hear."

"I'm a slut!" The admission tears from my throat. "I'm a fucking slut who needs more cock."

The tattooed guy appears next to the arm of the couch, stroking himself. "Prove it. Open up."

I part my lips without hesitation and have to lean over slightly to take him into my mouth. Three cocks fill me now—airtight. Evidence of my complete surrender to base desires.

Someone in the crowd murmurs, "Fuck, this is better than any strip club."

I'm vaguely aware of two more guys moving to each side of me. The couch dips, and suddenly, there's a cock in my hand. Oooh, hell yeah. The other new guy stands next to the dude I'm sucking on, and he's just in reach for me to stroke him.

Suddenly, a sense of power washes over me. I'm a fucking sexual goddess. I'm pleasuring five men at once.

The rhythm becomes primal—five cocks, one me. I'm solving an equation with my body, finding the perfect balance between the thrusts in my pussy and ass while maintaining suction on the cock in my mouth and keeping my hands moving in steady strokes on the others.

My thighs burn. Sweat gathers between my breasts. And I've never felt more alive. The pleasure builds in layers as I'm stretched beyond what should be comfortable, yet my body accommodates, adapts, and welcomes.

The tattooed guy grips my hair, controlling my movements on his cock. "Look at this greedy little slut. Taking dick everywhere she can get it." His thrusts become erratic. "I'm gonna come down this slut's throat."

I moan my approval around his cock. When his first spurt hits the back of my throat, I swallow instinctively, working my tongue against the underside of his shaft. The men in my ass and pussy pick up their pace, their rhythm faltering as they chase their own release.

"Fuck, she's milking my cock," the redhead grunts behind me, his fingers digging deeper into my hips. Each thrust pushes me forward onto the tall guy beneath me, creating a chain reaction of pleasure that ripples through my body.

The guy in my left hand comes next, painting my shoulder and breast with hot streaks. The sensation—warm fluid cooling rapidly on my skin—sends a shiver through me. I'm going to be one filthy slut when they're done with me.

"Look at your wife," someone says to Nolan. "Taking dick like she was born for it."

The guy on my left moves away after coming, and I catch my husband's gaze. His eyes are dark with desire, jaw clenched tight. He's memorizing every detail of his wife's debasement.

"Tell everyone who you belong to," Nolan commands, his voice tight with restraint.

The tall guy beneath me grabs my chin, forcing me to look at him. "Yeah, whose fucktoy are you?"

"My husband's," I gasp as the redhead slams particularly deep into my ass. "I'm his fucktoy, but he—he shares me."

"And what does that make you?" the guy in my right hand demands as he holds onto my wrist and jackhammers against my palm.

"A slut," I moan. "His perfect little slut who loves cock."

The tall guy beneath me growls, his hips bucking up sharply. "Gonna fill this pussy up."

"Do it," I urge, grinding down to meet his thrusts.

He comes with a shout, pulsing inside me as his fingers dig into my thighs, hard enough to leave marks. The sensation of his release triggers the redhead, who slams in deep and holds, his cock throbbing in my ass as he adds his load.

The fullness is exquisite—stretched and filled and dripping. The last guy in my hand groans as he finishes, adding to the mess on my skin. I'm covered, filled, used thoroughly, and still craving more.

My orgasm builds at the edge of my consciousness, a gathering storm of sensation. The tall guy reaches between us, his thumb finding my clit.

"Let's see this slut come," he says, circling the sensitive bundle of nerves. "Show your husband how much you love being used."

The redhead is still buried in my ass, grinding slightly as he comes down from his climax. The dual sensation—cock still throbbing in my ass, skilled fingers on my clit—pushes me over the edge.

My orgasm crashes through me, muscles clenching around both cocks still inside me. I cry out, back arching, thighs trembling. Wave after wave of pleasure radiates outward, leaving me gasping and shaking.

"That's it," the tall guy murmurs, continuing to work my clit through the aftershocks. "Squeeze every drop out of us."

When the last tremor subsides, the redhead carefully withdraws from my ass. The sensation makes me whimper—empty now where I was so thoroughly filled moments before. The tall guy helps me lift off his softening cock, and I feel the evidence of our activities leaking down my thighs.

Suddenly, someone lifts me off the tall guy's lap. "She needs more cock."

My head spins as I look up at a massive guy I haven't seen before. He truly looks like a mountain man, beard and all.

He carries me over to the pool table and lays me on it. My ass is on the edge as he pushes my knees towards my chest. I barely have time to moan before his massive cock is sinking into me.

I cry out as he stretches me further than anyone else has tonight. My body should be protesting after everything it's just endured, but instead it welcomes this new invasion.

"Fuck, she's still tight even after all that," Mountain Man grunts. His massive hands pin my knees against my chest, folding me nearly in half against the green felt.

I catch glimpses of other men circling the table—some stroking themselves back to hardness, others just watching with hungry eyes. The air reeks of sex and sweat. My body is a canvas of their use—streaks of cum drying on my skin.

"Look at her take it," someone says. "Greedy little cunt."

The words send a fresh wave of arousal through me. I've spent my entire professional life being respected. Feared, even. Now I'm spread on a pool table with cum leaking from two holes while a stranger rams into me. I never imagined how amazing this would be.

Mountain Man establishes a brutal pace, each thrust jolting me against the felt. The table creaks beneath us, balls clicking together with each impact. I'm vaguely aware I'm making sounds I've never heard from my own throat—animal, desperate, pleading.

"You like being our entertainment tonight?" he growls. "You like getting fucked while your husband watches?"

I manage to turn my head toward Nolan. He's moved closer now, standing just feet away. His eyes haven't left me once. This is his fantasy too—seeing me completely surrendered to pleasure, my carefully constructed walls demolished by pure sensation.

"Answer him," Nolan commands.

"Yes," I gasp as Mountain Man hits a spot that makes my vision blur. "God, yes—I love it."

Mountain Man shifts his angle, driving even deeper. "Fuck, I'm gonna come in this tight pussy."

"Do it," I urge, my voice raspy from use. "Fill me up."

He slams in deep, holding himself there as he pulses inside me. The sensation of his release—hot and thick—triggers my orgasm. It rips through me, more intense than the last. My body convulses, clenching around him, milking every drop as stars explode behind my eyelids.

Before I can catch my breath, Mountain Man withdraws and another man takes his place. They're tag-teaming me now, a relay race of cock with my body as the finish line. The new arrival doesn't give me time to adjust—just drives in hard, making me gasp.

I lose track of time. Faces blur together as cocks fill me; voices call me filthy names. Some come on me, others in me. I climax so many times the night blurs into a never-ending pleasure where I can't tell where one orgasm ends and the next one begins.

Through it all, Nolan watches. His presence anchors me—reminds me that this debauchery is safe, sanctioned, desired. Each time our eyes meet, I see his approval, his arousal, his love. This is his gift to me—freedom from my own constraints, permission to be the slut I never knew I wanted to be.

When the last man finishes, painting my stomach with warm streaks, I lie boneless on the pool table. Every muscle aches. I'm cover in cum and my pussy and ass feel deliciously used.

Nolan finally approaches, his expression a mixture of pride and raw desire. He runs his fingers through the mess on my stomach, tracing patterns in the combined release of multiple men.

"Mine," he says simply, claiming me even in this state—especially in this state.

I smile up at him, drunk on endorphins and satisfaction. "Always yours," I whisper, my voice wrecked from use. "Even when you share me."

He helps me sit up, then stand on shaky legs. My dress is somewhere on the floor, but I make no move to find it. Let them look. Let them remember what they had—what Nolan allowed them to have.

"Thank you, gentlemen," Nolan says to the room, his arm around my waist, supporting me. "My wife needed that."

Pride swells in my chest at his words. I did need that—needed to be used beyond reason, beyond thought. Needed to surrender the control I cling to everywhere else.

Nolan helps me into my dress and boots. When he slides the purple wristband off my wrist, I grin at him. Yeah, I've had enough.

He leads me from the room—leaking, thoroughly used. I catch sight of myself in a mirror on the wall. I barely recognize the woman reflected there. My hair's wild, skin flushed, eyes bright with satisfaction. She looks nothing like a controlled attorney.

She looks free.

And as Nolan's hand presses possessively against my lower back, guiding me toward our cabin and whatever he has planned next, I realize that's exactly what I am.

And I never want to be anyone else ever again.

CHAPTER 7

I can barely walk back to our suite. My legs shake with each step, my body still processing what just happened—so many men using me. I would have taken on the entire resort if they had lined up.

Nolan's arm around my waist steadies me. Other guests nod as we pass. I'm giddy and punch-drunk, and when I spot a woman being fucked against a tree, I giggle. It's going to be a long night for some people.

Our cabin is the same as we left it, but I feel different. Something has shifted in my brain, and I know I'm not the same woman I was earlier. I'm the new and improved Rachel.

The door clicks shut behind us, and the silence feels enormous after hours of voices, hands, cocks, constant attention. My body's still humming, still expecting the next set of hands, the next cock sliding inside me.

I stand in the middle of our room, swaying slightly as I remove my boots. My dress clings to my body, the thin fabric damp with sweat and other fluids. I feel deliciously sore and weirdly proud. Like I just discovered a superpower I never knew I had.

"Look at you," Nolan says, his eyes tracking every detail of my disheveled appearance.

Suddenly, I realize this isn't the gentle chef who creates perfect dishes with careful attention. He's not the supportive husband who let me control everything for years. This is the man who's been hiding behind that gentle smile. The man who knew exactly what I needed before I did.

"I can barely think," I whisper. "I can barely remember who I was before today." My brain feels wonderfully empty.

"Good." He moves closer, fingers brushing my hair back from my face. "Because this version of you is beautiful."

His words give me a jolt of pleasure, and when I glance down at the bulge in his pants, I'm desperate for him to get the pleasure he's denied himself all day.

"What do you need?" I ask.

His smile transforms into something predatory. "Get on your knees and beg for my cock. Tell me how it felt being used by strangers while I watched. Plead for your husband to reclaim what's his."

My knees buckle instantly. I sink to the carpet, the position feeling right—kneeling, looking up at him, waiting for commands instead of issuing them.

"Please," I breathe, reaching for his belt with trembling fingers. "Please let me have your cock. I need you to reclaim me."

"Tell me what you are first." His voice roughens with satisfaction. "Tell me what you became tonight."

"I'm your slut," I say without hesitation. "I'm your fucktoy who needed strangers' cocks to discover what she really is."

His fingers tangle in my hair, tightening just enough to make me gasp. "What else?"

"I'm holes to be filled. I exist purely for your satisfaction and whoever you choose to share me with." I claw at his belt, becoming more desperate.

He helps me free his cock. I moan at the sight—harder than I've ever seen him. Has he always been this big? Or does he just seem massive because I'm seeing him through new eyes?

"Look how hard I am from watching you surrender," he says, hand firmly gripping my hair. "Look how much I loved seeing strangers use my wife."

I wrap my lips around him, taking him into my mouth. He tastes like salt and desire—and I want to show him how grateful I am for this trip.

"That's it," he groans as I take him deeper. "Worship your husband's cock with the same mouth that serviced strangers."

The reminder sends heat straight to my core. I moan around him, the vibration making him thrust deeper into my throat.

"Tell me how it felt," he commands, pulling my head back. "Every detail."

"Like never-ending pleasure," I gasp. "Like finally discovering what I was made for. When they filled all my holes at once, it was pure pleasure."

He pulls me up, and his mouth crashes against mine in a kiss that claims rather than asks. When he breaks away, his eyes blaze with intensity.

"Get on the bed. Hands and knees. I'm gonna fuck you while you tell me what you want to try next time."

I move to the bed and pull my dress up to my waist before positioning myself exactly as ordered. I catch our reflection in the windows—me on my hands and knees, him standing behind me like he owns every inch of my body.

"You're so wet," he observes, fingers sliding through my folds. "Still dripping from being used but desperate for your husband's cock."

"Please," I whimper, pushing back against his touch. "Please fuck me. I need you."

He slides inside slowly, and I gasp at the sensation. After hours of being stretched by multiple cocks, he feels different—familiar but new, like experiencing him for the first time again.

"Fuck, you're perfect," he groans as he drills into me.

Each thrust sends aftershocks through my oversensitized system. I'm still tender from earlier, but my body responds immediately, welcoming him home.

"Mine," he growls, his fingers digging into my hips as he thrusts deeper. "You let all those men use you, but you're still mine."

"Yes," I gasp, dropping my head between my shoulders. "Yours. Always yours."

He reaches around to grip my breast through my dress, pinching my nipple until I cry out. "Tell me your dirtiest fantasy."

My mind spins with possibilities—things I never would have admitted to wanting before today. "I want—I want to be blindfolded," I pant between thrusts. "Tied up somewhere public. Not knowing who's touching me or how many people are watching."

His rhythm falters for a moment. "Fuck, Rachel." He slaps my ass, the sting sending another wave of pleasure through me. "What else?"

"I want you to auction me off," I confess, the words tumbling out before I can analyze them. "Set rules for how they can use me, but let them bid for time with your slut."

He groans, his pace increasing. "My fucktoy. Look how far you've come—from scheduling sex to begging strangers to use you."

His words should humiliate me; instead, they fill me with pride. I've shed the constraints I placed on myself. I've discovered what truly satisfies me.

"I need you to come on my cock," he demands, reaching around to circle my clit. "Show me you're still mine after all those men."

The orgasm builds quickly, different from the others—deeper, more intimate.

"That's it," he encourages as I tighten around him. "Let go for me. One more time."

The pleasure crashes through me, and I collapse onto my elbows, face pressed against the mattress. I'm crying out words I can't even understand, begging and thanking him simultaneously.

He follows me over the edge, his body tensing as he empties himself inside me. His final claim—marking me from the inside after I've been used by so many others.

We slump onto the bed, his body covering mine, both of us breathing heavily. After a moment, he rolls to his side, pulling me against his chest.

"You're incredible," he murmurs against my hair.

I turn to face him, searching his eyes. "I can't believe we wasted so many years. All those days I scheduled sex on my calendar when what I really needed was—"

"This," he finishes for me. His fingers trace my cheek. "The freedom to be exactly who you are without judgment."

"Who knew that what I really needed was to surrender control?" I laugh softly. "All those years of managing every detail, when what I truly craved was letting go."

He kisses me gently. "We've found our recipe now. The perfect balance of ingredients."

I smile at his chef metaphor. "Is that what this is? A recipe?"

"The best ones take time to perfect," he says, pulling me closer. "We just needed to adjust the proportions. More surrender, less control. More trust, less planning."

His hand strokes down my spine, soothing my well-used body. "You're really okay?"

"Hell yeah," I giggle and nestle against his chest, listening to his heartbeat. "Thank you for knowing what I needed before I did."

"Thank you for trusting me enough to try," he counters.

We lie together in comfortable silence, and for the first time in years, my mind isn't racing with tomorrow's to-do list. I'm simply present.

"I love you," I murmur, sleep beginning to claim me.

"And I love you," he whispers back.

As I drift toward sleep in my husband's arms, I realize we've negotiated the most important contract of all—one without terms and conditions, without clauses and stipulations. Just trust, desire, and the freedom to be exactly who we are.

The End

ABOUT LACEY CROSS

Lacey Cross is a wife sharing erotica writer with over 100 short stories published since she started in 2021. Her stories emphasize the pleasure found from the wife living her best slut life and embracing the hotwife lifestyle. She explores themes of free use, submissive wives with dominant bulls, BDSM...and oh-so-many men.

www.ingramcontent.com/pod-product-compliance
Lightning Source LLC
Chambersburg PA
CBHW021147310726
48971CB00002B/519